Before the Flood

JOHN HOULIHAN

John Houlihan has been a writer, journalist and broadcaster for over twenty years, working in news, sport and especially videogames. He has been employed by *The Times*, *Sunday Times* and *Cricinfo* and is the former Editor-in-Chief of *Computer and Video Games.com*. He currently works for Modiphiüs Entertainment as a narrative designer and for Wizards of the Coast as Editor-in-Chief of *Dragon+* magazine.

His first novel was *Tom or The Peepers' and Voyeurs' Handbook* and more recently he has written *The Trellborg Monstrosities, The Crystal Void* and *Tomb of the Aeons* in the *Tales of the White Witchman* series. The Trellborg Monstrosities has also been converted into a game scenario for Call of Cthulhu and Savage Worlds which is published by Modiphiüs.

He has recently published *The Cricket Dictionary*, a modern guide to the words, phrases and sayings of the greatest of all games and has also edited a collection of short stories called *Dark Tales from the Secret War* which is published by Modiphiüs set in the Achtung! Cthulhu universe. Forthcoming work includes a sci-fi novel *A Late Flowering Deity.*

Away from the written word he has an unnatural fondness for cricket, football, snowboarding, cycling, music, playing guitar and all forms of sci-fi, fantasy and horror. He has an unnatural dread about writing about himself in the third person and currently lives in his home town of Watford in the UK, because, well frankly, someone has to.

For latest news and information see http://www.John-Houlihan.net or follow @johnh259 on Twitter

Cover Illustration is by **Borja Pindado** who is a freelance illustrator living in Madrid with his wife and his daughter. He spends most of his time drawing on his computer fantasy art and comics, drinking coca-cola, listening to music and, from time to time, collaborating with other artists. You can see his portfolio at borjapindado.com.

Cover design and typography by **Thomas Shook** a graphic designer based Westerm Australia, with his wife and two kids. Cover is based on the original work of Mark Mitchell.

ALSO BY JOHN HOULIHAN

The Seraph Chronicles
The Trellborg Monstrosities
The Crystal Void
The Crystal Void Illustrated Edition
Tomb of the Aeons
Before The Flood

The Seraph Chronicles Volume One: Tales of the White Witchman

Tom or the Peepers' and Voyeurs' Handbook
The Cricket Dictionary
Dark Tales from the Secret War (as editor)

THANKS

Special thanks to Martin Korda for his eagle eye, solid
advice and enduring friendship
Thanks to my panel of readers, especially
Paul Barker and Adam Selby-Martin

Before the Flood

Contents

CHAPTER ONE

The Island

'Pip ... pip ... piiiiiip. It is 7 o'clock and this is the voice of the Free BBC, today, October 9th, 2034. Minor incursions continue, but no major engagements with the creatures have been reported in the last 48 hours.'

'Unconfirmed reports of a newly surfaced island structure off the coast of Anglesey have been dismissed by Ruth Miller. The Internal Security Minister for the Provisional Government said 'All kinds of wild rumours and gossip are swirling during the current conflict. I urge our brave defence forces to remain calm and treat such wild speculation with the healthy pinch of salt it deserves. The creatures...'

'Turn that *fucking* thing off.' I growled at Adams and, with surly reticence, he obeyed. 'You can switch off the attitude too,' I said. 'I'm in command here and I don't give two fucks whether you like it or not. Now, make yourself useful, raise HQ and get me an activity report for this sector. Something doesn't feel right here, and I want to know why.'

Adams slapped his headphones on with a grunt and fiddled with the buttons on the ancient set. He was probably cursing under his breath, mouthing silent obscenities while he thought I couldn't see him. Well fuck him. Fuck them all. I didn't volunteer for this. Who in their right mind would?

I regarded my militia unit as it huddled dolefully in the ruins of a booth in the abandoned fun fair, where they were doing their best to shelter from the sheets of rain, which came down like stair rods. It was a bitter cold night, harsh and unforgiving as it gets on the Welsh coast in late autumn and the rags and tags which these 'soldiers', had scrounged together, provided scant protection against that kind of weather.

They weren't much to look at at the best of times but now they resembled drowned rats rather than any kind of proper fighting force, the ragged Union Jack armbands, their only common insignia, made them look even more pathetic. What an ongoing joy it is to serve in the militia, such a privilege to command such people.

And I was supposed to lead them into battle? Some fucking hope, they'd fold like a paper house at the first Devil patrol we met. They were beaten, we all were, though some of us weren't quite ready to admit it just yet.

I'm rambling, sir? Do you want me to tell the story or not? Okay, so let me get to it in my own way and then you can judge for yourself. We've got a little time now haven't we? Time is not quite so much of an issue any more, that at least you'll have to admit?

My name? Stokes, recent promotion notwithstanding … Sergeant Emma Stokes, 43rd Wessex Army Reserve or the TA in old money. Call me Stokesy if you must call me anything, sir.

Thanks, I will take a smoke.

How did we happen to be there at that particular place, at that particular time and meet that particular man? I've no idea, it wasn't a conscious decision. Fate, circumstance, kismet, call it what you will.

What I can tell is my men weren't keen. I'd had to kick, haul and bully them practically every step of the way. You can't blame them I suppose, conscripts don't make the best soldiers and besides, who's ever keen to march towards their own death? Not that they had much choice. Everyone's got to do their duty nowadays haven't they, sir? Otherwise they're just a walking waste of rations. It's either march, starve or be hanged and sometimes you could toss a coin for which of the three is the worst.

Anyway, we'd been out for a couple of days by that stage and the Devils were busy, much busier than normal. They were out in force and we'd slipped past several patrols, before finally going to ground in an abandoned holiday home. I'd spotted another chain of them, lurking down by the shore, which meant they weren't going to be so easy to evade, so, making sure my men were hunkered down, I crept closer for a shufti.

At my side was Challis, my corporal and second in command, the only other real soldier in the patrol. Him, at least, I knew I could count on. Together we watched the Devils pass from the shelter of a dilapidated old seaside fun fair, its peeling posters and rotting rides providing us with decent cover as they sauntered by. Ten braves and one shaman, hopping and flopping in that disgusting way they have on land. I shouldered my weapon and led them a little through the red dot sight, imagining squeezing the trigger and opening up with a three — round burst that would have split that shaman's fishy skull. A little bit of payback for London and everything we've suffered since — I was owed — we all were.

Engage them? Really? Are you taking the piss ... sir? My orders were to recon the island, take as many photos as I could grab and report back, period. Nothing mentioned about engaging Devil patrols, or in fact, about signing my own death warrant.

Besides Challis and I had the only functioning weapons and they were old SA-80s, Civil Servants (you can't make 'em work and you can't fire 'em), practically obsolete to all intents and purposes. The rest? Well they had the odd shotgun, a pistol or two and some improvised clubs and pitchforks, whatever the hell they'd managed to rustle up. We might as well have engaged them with sticks and stones for all the good they'd have done, small arms like that would have just bounced off most Devils' hides, never mind the payback from that shaman's battle magic. Taking them on would have been like writing the shortest suicide note in modern military history.

I passed my weathered rifle to Challis, so he could take a look through its scope, pretty much the only decent optic we had. Challis was my corporal and best shot, a tough, weathered Antiguan, hard as nails with short dreads like an early period Bob Marley; a vet of Iraq and the 'Stan, and a dozen of those other dirty, pointless oil wars we managed to drag ourselves into before the Flood.

'What do you think?' I asked.

'Shit, well they're all heading somewhere with a purpose and it don't take too much working out.' He inclined his locks toward the island. 'Let these fuckers pass, it'll be dusk soon and then we can have a stab at it.' He handed me back the weapon and spat, the spittle hanging like foam off a nearby sideshow counter. Overhead a seagull shrieked.

'Agreed.' I said and watched the Devil patrol recede along the shoreline until it was out of sight.

How did I come to be commanding that patrol? By default, of course sir, how else? Anyone with even the vaguest hint of combat experience is at a premium nowadays, hell I heard they even gazetted the Royals' goat up to major for surviving that siege at Swindon. Oh yes even NCOs from the Reserve are considered prime leadership material nowadays for that sort of mission, sir, though most of them would have trouble leading a latrine detail.

I sound bitter? Yeah well I'm glad that's coming through. Anyway they don't spare proper officers for that kind of recon work, I'm valuable enough, but not too valuable, expendable in an 'acceptable risk' kind of way. Put it this way, no-one would have been organising a state funeral with full military honours, if I hadn't come back.

My motivation? I have my reasons sir, same as everyone else. Survival mainly, revenge partly. We really are all in it together now aren't we, in this people's war, or whatever the fuck you want to call it?

Before? I don't really remember too much detail from before, this is all I seem to have known for ever and a day: futility, evasion, retreat.

But that's changed hasn't it now, after the outcome of this particular mission? I doubt the spooks from Military Intelligence (the shortest two-word paradox in the language) expected things to take quite the turn they have.

Before the Flood? Of course I remember … some of it at least, though it seems like a different world, one I haven't lived in for a long, long time. Oh I remember the reports, remember as we watched the waves slowly rise, year on year, letting our stupid desire for cheap energy and stupider fripperies subsume everything else.

And for what? To watch some bullshit reality show on a giant flat screen TV, argue on Twitter about banalities or allow a succession of liars to sell us endless shit we didn't want, and didn't really need.

Oh in our pride, our arrogance, we thought we could hold the seas back, but when the waves slowly claimed most of East Anglia, we didn't worry too much about it, just retreated to higher ground, told ourselves we still had plenty left and besides, the defences would hold. Year by year, yard by yard, the waves crept higher, slowly swallowing this septic isle inch by inch. And still we did nothing, or at least nothing meaningful. Ever heard of King Cnut? Swap a couple of letters, add an 's' and put 'blind' in front of it — that was us — down to a tee.

So should we really have been surprised when it all finally came to pass? Oh, it was a shock alright: a mix of our complacency and their monstrous ambition no doubt. But with all our satellites and all our science and all our state surveillance schemes, how come we didn't spot an entire alien civilisation lurking on the ocean floor?

Oh I forgot, we were too busy, fighting petty wars amongst ourselves, fucking each other for a cheap quid or a cheaper gallon, or maybe we were just looking in all the wrong places. We were so worried about the terror within, we completely missed the terror from the deep.

Some say the Devils have been at it for years, centuries maybe: plotting, scheming, making their unfathomable alien plans and just waiting for the moment to strike. The worst thing is, we actually helped them, *actually* helped them invade us, with our own blind, short term stupidity. When the waters crept high enough, they finally saw their chance and they struck and it's us, the survivors, who've been drowning by inches ever since.

CHAPTER TWO

The Things in the Marsh

W E WAITED THE DAY OUT until darkness began to bleed into the miserable slate-grey sky and then we were ready to make our move. The Devils don't see too well in twilight, that's the story anyway and I wanted to wring out any small advantage I could, so we could just get the job done and come the fuck home, without contact or casualties. Well, we all know how that turned out...

We slunk through the broken houses and deserted landscape like foxes, Challis on point, me at the rear and the rest of our ragged little band stretched out between us. We rounded the headland and that's when I caught my first proper sight of it, the thing which had spontaneously surfaced off the coast, wreathed in enshrouding mists and burning with a strange malevolent light. It was an ominous sight, squatting there about four or five miles off shore and it seemed to hum and vibrate with some kind of primitive energy, as if it were singing some unholy song, calling to the Devils in its own strange language.

When it first appeared, a week previously, there was all kinds of talk and rumours about what it might be and what it might mean. No one believed the propaganda or the Provisional Government's fervent denials: some said it was a new threat, others, a temple to the creatures' dark god. There were even a few that thought it was some new kind of surface home for them, meaning they might retreat there and leave us alone.

Wishful thinking, those fish-eyed bastards want us enslaved or extinguished, nothing more, nothing less — anyone who believes anything different is a fool. I couldn't even begin to guess what the island was then, didn't want to, that's way beyond what any grunt needs to know, but you could tell it was important, it mattered. There were enough of them swarming around it at any rate. My best guess back then? Some kind of spawning ground maybe, or a focal point for the dark magic their shamans employ.

Still, that was irrelevant now, I had a mission and a purpose and the sooner it was completed, the sooner we could get the fuck out of there and come back home.

In front of us was a small trawler, which would make an ideal observation post, but further up the shoreline lay the beached, rotting hulk of the *Prince George*, the last of our great aircraft carriers, which had been lost during the Royal Navy's final stand off the Isle of Man. Crippled and crewless, she had finally drifted down to this forlorn shore, where her prow had ploughed into the shallow shingle, before coming to rest with a great crunching sigh. She now lay over on her side, great rents still visible in her hull and superstructure, where they had been blown open by the Devils' magic. Listing and listless she sat there like the carcass of some great forgotten leviathan that had come here to die, giving up its body to rot and corruption, cloaked in a burial shroud of rust, seaweed and barnacles.

I whistled up Haines, a scrawny looking red-headed kid, perhaps fifteen or sixteen, difficult to tell these days but she was thin as a scarecrow and about as much use in a fire fight. I don't why, but ever since she'd been assigned to our happy little band a few days earlier, as a replacement for another dead nameless kid, she'd looked at me like I was a combination of Wellington and Churchill or something. Maybe it was the gun, maybe the stripes…

I nodded at the island. 'You're the shutterbug right? Time to do your thing.' I handed her the battered digital camera which had been entrusted to me. 'Listen up Haines, you're going to sneak over to that fishing boat, take as many pictures as you can of that thing and then get back here pronto, understand? So try to keep them in focus and of course, remember the most important thing … try to stay alive.'

She gulped, nodded and looked nervously towards the deck of the beached trawler. 'Don't worry,' I said, winking, trying to put some courage into her. 'I'm coming too, keep you company, okay?' Her answering grin was as earnest as it was pitiful and I had to half turn away, pretending to check my weapon, as I bit my lip.

I left the rest of them hidden in the ruins of an abandoned cottage with Challis detailed to keep them in line and after a last hasty scan of the coastline, Haines and I broke cover and sprinted, sliding into the lee of the rusted hull. We waited but the only sound was the gentle lap of the waves nibbling the shore, so I heaved myself up onto the listing deck and then helped Haines shin up after me. Keeping low, we sneaked onto the corroded bridge.

I peeped over the broken helm, glancing at the island's craggy, misshapen rocks, its shifting skirts of mist and spume, which momentarily parted to reveal hints of the stark, alien geometry underneath. It didn't pay to stare directly at that place for too long, it unsettled the mind and sapped the will, but a brief glance satisfied me that nothing had changed, so I let my eyes slide off that fearful unnatural architecture and ducked back down.

Anywhere close to the shoreline is guaranteed to put you on edge, you never know when the Devils might emerge from the depths, but as I listened, all remained quiet. I nodded to Haines who took out the camera, holding it with the reverence you might afford a religious object. She was just about to bob up to take the first reel, when I put a hand on her arm.

'Is the flash off?' I whispered. 'Don't want to give away our position now, do we?'

'Shit, sorry sir.' She look mortified but then nodded, fiddling earnestly with the settings.

'All set? Frame it through the viewfinder, use the auto-focus and then fire away. Don't look at it directly, understood? '

'Yes sir,' she said emphatically and then began to snap away. I kept my eyes peeled on the placid waters rolling against the shore, but they remained undisturbed. After a couple of moments, Haines ducked down and turned her urchin's eyes on me.

'All done.'

'Good. Okay…'

'It looks really spooky Sergeant, like something from a fairy tale or a nightmare. What do you think it is really? Is it true what they say about it?'

'Don't know, don't know what they say about it. Above my pay grade, which means it's way way above yours. I doubt it means anything good for us though, it never does. You done?'

'I think so, I've got plenty of pics, standard and IR, some good detail I think.'

'Good, we'll call that a day then. Let's get the fuck out of here.' We eased ourselves out from the wheelhouse silently and I could almost feel the relief emanate from her. Could feel it start to emanate from me too.

Instinct makes you cautious out there beyond the frontier and as I cast a last glance back I was glad I had, for there, beginning to emerge from the waves not a hundred yards away, was the long frog-like chain of another Devil patrol. They were mob handed too, two dozen or so braves, a couple of shamans and a brutal looking chieftain.

'Let's go!' I hissed and I dragged Haines towards the rusting stern. We both went over the side and as my boots bit into the sand, cushioning the landing, I was already flipping off my safety. Long, tense moments passed as we nestled there behind the shattered rudder, listening to the crunch of sand beneath their flippers. If they decided to come this way, we'd be fish food.

Over in the cottage, I could see Challis covertly making the clenched fist signal; hold position. I readied my weapon, resting my index finger on the trigger guard and gripping the handle so tight my palm started to cramp. Time beat itself against the drumming of my pulse, but were the Devils' sounds diminishing, or was that just wishful thinking?

Then the air split, a great terrible croaking roar, like the tearing of a shroud, and my index finger slipped onto the trigger proper. Behind me I thought I heard Haines whimper as the shaman's cry echoed across the bay, indicating our certain discovery and imminent death.

Challis was still signalling, 'hold', 'hold' and while I trusted my corporal with my life, I could see the snout of his weapon peep over the lip, being readied too. 'Hold', 'hold', his signal didn't change and the tension became almost unbearable. I readied myself to spring around the corner and unleash a burst into the heart of them. With a little luck, maybe we could take down enough to…

Then his gesture changed and now Challis was beckoning us back toward him and the cover of the cottage. I exhaled, letting go a breath that seemed to be have been held forever and chanced a look around the hull. The Devils were moving away from us, heading north, their scaly backs and angular fins turned toward us. Go left … go right, on such small margins do the fortunes of war — and so much else — turn.

I grabbed Haines and we flew back at the double, vaulting over the ruined stones of the cottage and panting, sank down, backs against the wall. I don't think I've ever been so relieved in my life and my grin was half exhilaration, half rictus. Challis smiled, but the rest of the patrol stared at us with a mixture of incredulity and indifference.

'Nice to see you fuckers too,' I spat, then while Challis and I covered the beach and the retreating Devils, I ordered the rest of the patrol back through the abandoned culvert which had masked our approach. Silent as rats, they scurried off. Challis and I followed, keeping our weapons trained in the creatures' direction, until finally we were out of sight and clear.

The further away from the beach we got, the more I liked it and after that, we put as much distance as we could between us and the sea. Unless they're feeling bold or after something specific, the Devils don't like to venture too far inland as you know sir, and so we found an old gutted pub and went to ground there. I set a watch, but stayed awake anyway, still buzzing on the adrenaline and preparing for the vigil to wait out the long hours of the night. I was relieved, we'd accomplished our mission without being detected *and* without any casualties and nowadays, I call that a major win. Now all we had to do was bide our time and filter back inland once dawn broke. Even the wretched pile of bones and bleached skulls piled up in the corner didn't unnerve me. They were ancient and didn't count anymore. Only the living counted now. I was feeling good about things, or about as good as you can get nowadays.

࿐

I set a watch and everyone else bedded down. Hours passed. I don't sleep much, if at all these days and virtually never out on patrol, so I stayed awake and listened to the sounds of the night for a while. Perhaps I was half dozing, perhaps lost in contemplation, but I must have felt something before I heard it, for suddenly I was fully awake, eyes wide and senses alert.

The unit slumbered on oblivious, but I went and roused Challis, who instantly came round.

'Something's up, wake them, but quietly. I'm going to take a look.'

'Want me to come with?'

'No, stay here, sit tight and dig in. If I'm not back in half an hour, you're in command. Don't come looking … and that's an order. Get these photos back to HQ,' I said handing over the camera, 'and the rest of them if you can. The photos take priority.'

'Understood.'

'Haines.' I whispered to the teenager who happened to be on watch. 'Come on, you're with me.'

We stalked out into the darkness in the wee small hours when your mind and body are at their lowest ebb. You could just about see your hand in front of your face, but my instincts aren't often wrong and I've learned to trust them. Oh, I'm the first to shoot down any of that supernatural bullshit, but intuition? Out there in the wilderness, well let's just say you get a feel for certain things and I'd trust my instincts over a thousand intelligence reports.

An unnecessary risk? Maybe sir and it's true normally on a mission of that kind, I'd have dug in, stayed put and ignored any distant drums from the deep. But something about this felt different, like my presence was … required. I needed to take a look and that's about all I can tell you, sir.

So we padded along, taking a circuitous route to cover the ground, the darkness populating the night landscape with indistinct menacing shapes.

Haines gave a gasp and my rifle snapped up. It was a pyramid of human skulls and assorted bones, perhaps six foot high and gleaming palely in the wan light. One of the Devils' sign posts or perhaps an indication of their sick sense of humour. Do Devils even have a sense of humour? For answer the empty eye sockets seemed to bore right through us, but the bones had long ago been picked clean. It was a grim sight, both a reminder and a warning that were now beyond the pale and about to enter the badlands — or the very worst of the badlands. What remained of our ailing isle was pretty much all badlands nowadays.

'What are we looking for, sir?' Haines voice wavered as we pushed on, still half freaked by that macabre landmark.

'I don't know exactly,' I admitted. 'But something's not right out there and whatever it is, it's not far away. And call me Sarge, not sir, that's for officers.'

'Yes si … Sarge. Do you think it's Devils?' Haines asked wide eyed. The creatures were nicknamed after some old Doctor Who episode or something. I never watched that kind of crap before the Flood, never had time for it. But the creatures apparently resemble some of those old cardboard and plastic TV monsters pretty closely. Devils? Dagons? Deep Ones? What did it matter what they were called in the end?

'Maybe, but there's something else…' I didn't have time to finish my sentence for about five hundred yards away small pinpoints of light suddenly flashed, fiery interruptions in the dark. Faintly, I could hear the retort of weapons, human weapons, though much quieter than anything I had ever heard before.

'What's that Sarge?' asked Haines nervously.

'Not sure, but we'd better take a look. Stick close by me and silent as the grave, or that's where you'll be heading.'

'Yes sir,' she said, forgetting again. Fear made her voice waver.

We picked our way cautiously across the boggy marshland, the filthy water squelching and sucking at our boots as if it was trying to pull us in. Tall grasses and reeds rasped against my face but I scarcely noticed them as the sounds grew louder, muffled retorts, a regular *thud thud thud* and the pinpricks of light grew more intense. We came to within fifty yards and I pulled at Haines' arm, dropping us both low. There was little light to see by, the night was black and unforgiving. I could only make out the presence of vague amorphous shapes as I sighted along the barrel of my rifle. Of course we didn't have anything useful like low-light or IR scopes, they don't give those out to the militia.

One by one the lights began to be extinguished and the sounds diminished too, until there was just a single one left. There was a last stifled sequence of recoils and then it faded away, leaving only darkness and silence.

I put a finger to my lips but even in the darkness the whites of Haines' eyes were wide, staring, like she was on the point of totally freaking out. I didn't blame her, I wasn't far away myself, but the training took over and I signalled Haines to keep her shotgun low (and pointed away from me) and we proceeded. We circled cautiously toward the cover of some scrubby trees where we could observe, without stumbling smack bang into the middle of whatever the hell it was that was happening out there.

Nerves taut, we slipped across the marshy ground, flitting from cover to cover, but I kept my weapon raised, ready to open up at so much as the slightest provocation. Have you ever been in a situation like that, when you know every next step could be your last, sir? Focuses the mind somewhat, it's not easy, but experience helps and although my heart pounded like a rave bass line, we made it into the copse without further incident. Again we waited, made ready for whatever was out there to reveal itself but the silence remained unbroken and after a couple of minutes, the moon decided to peep out from behind covering cloud, providing us with the first half decent bit of illumination.

It shone onto a small clearing in the marshland, a raised gap in the surrounding sea of tall grasses and there, amidst the mud and brackish water was a scene of utter carnage. Bodies, human and Devil lay locked together, stretched out or half submerged around the fringes of a small, scrubby island slightly raised above the surrounding waters.

It didn't take me long to read the lie of the land: this is where those humans had made their last stand; they had died in a ring around its perimeter, singly or in pairs, back to back in some cases. There were only about a dozen of them from my rough count, but they must have taken down four warbands worth of Devils, on their own, at the very least. *Their* bodies were everywhere, piled high one upon the other, maybe seventy braves in total, slaughtered as they charged in for a headlong hand-to-hand assault.

That was unusual, the Devils had some ranged weapons, harpoons, spears and the like plus that infernal battle magic and they weren't usually so reckless as to engage a defensive position in a headlong charge like that. I could only think they wanted to take these people alive and had expended many lives in trying to achieve that aim.

The humans weren't exactly standard issue either. These didn't look much like ordinary grunts, they were big, strapping, physically impressive men and women, nothing like the desperate, malnourished odds and sods I led. They were kitted out in some serious military gear too, state-of-the -art hardware and then some: masks, body armour, night scopes and rifles the like of which I'd never seen before. They seemed to have barrels that were more than half silencer, which probably explained those ultra quiet *thud thud thuds*.

Still nothing moved and now I began to smell the blood and muck of the brutal aftermath. Flies were already beginning to swarm and surely it wouldn't be long before that would draw more Devils to investigate?

Who were these people and what the hell were they doing here, miles from any-where? I hadn't a clue, but there was no saving them now, they were just so much fish bait. HQ would probably want to know of course, you don't just lose an outfit like that and not want to know the reason why, but frankly, sir, duty didn't much come into it.

What I saw was opportunity, a golden opportunity to kit my people out with that advanced gear and I simply ached to take it. Whoever this unit were, they had no use for it now and it would mean our chances of survival, of actually making it back home, just went up by several notches. I listened again, but it was still quiet, so I sketched my plan to Haines and while she covered me from the copse, I stalked forward, intent on helping myself to those tempting goodies.

18

I waded through the floating Devil bodies and the smell was as rotten as a barrel of mouldering fish guts. They had died in their dozens, their soulless eyes glinting vacantly, eerily in the moonlight. The only good Devil is a dead Devil and there's nothing much to add to that, but my finger hovered on my trigger, just in case any of them lingered.

Closer to that islet, the corpses were piled high and I was forced to shoulder arms and physically turf a couple aside so I could reach solid ground. I was glad I was wearing gloves, for I really didn't want to have to touch that flabby fishy flesh. Nose wrinkling with disgust, I rolled a couple of braves over until they went belly up then heaved them with the toe of my boot, so that they floated off into the stagnant waters.

But this was no time to linger and quickly, I went from body to body, stripping them of those unusual weapons, night vision goggles, spare ammo, masks and anything else I deemed useful and readily portable. Their uniforms were black, almost featureless, some kind of light absorbing semi-adaptive camo I guessed, with integrated body armour, but they bore no insignia or markings I could readily identify.

No dog tags either, were these boys and girls even ours? Their kit was like something from a sci-fi movie, but hurry, I told myself, there's no time to ponder and I worked quickly and methodically, stripping the bodies as respectfully as I could, making neat piles of their gear,

Towards the centre of the isle, knee deep in Devil dead I found their CO. She must have been the last to fall, for she was surrounded by Devil corpses, a silenced pistol gripped in one hand and an F-S knife still locked in the fist of the other. She'd plunged it right between the eyes of the nearest brave in her death throes. A trident had taken her through the throat, half ripping off her mask and cutting the armour clean through to her chest. She was a captain, there were three pips adorning one tattered shoulder and there, on the other, that distinctive badge, etched into the armour so subtly I hadn't seen it at first: a wreathed world, topped with coronet and tailed with anchor and the words *Per Mare, Per Terram* — 'By sea, by Land'. This officer — and presumably her men too — were Royal Marine Commandos.

Shit, these were serious soldiers, hard fighters, the kind of elite unit that rolls up and routinely fucks the enemy without even breaking stride, or passes through them like a sea of ghosts so that you wouldn't ever know they'd even been there. I didn't think we even had any of these guys left. What the hell were they doing out here in this godforsaken hole? Why had they engaged these warbands? They were all set up for stealth by the looks of it, those suits and silencers were a dead giveaway, so why had they become involved in a stand-up fire fight?

Perhaps they'd had no choice? Spotted or possibly tracked here, surrounded, forced to make a final stand, they'd died to a man and taken the best part of four warbands with them, before measuring out their lengths in this hellish marsh. What was the story here?

Not my business, I told myself, just recover the gear, remember what you need for the report and be thankful it's not you. I knelt and slipped the captain's pistol and spare magazines into my belt and closed her sightless eyes for the last time, whispering 'rest in peace' for want of anything better to say. I half turned, ready to lever myself up when Haines' voice shrieked 'Sarge!'

Where it came from I had no idea, perhaps it had been wounded and my words had roused it or maybe it was just lying there, waiting for the unwary. Either way suddenly looming over me was the massive steaming bulk of a Devil chieftain, spiked mace raised as it chittered its filthy war cry. As I brought up my rifle I can remember thinking, 'boy trust me to draw a huge bastard' and I even had time to notice the dancing necklace of human ears which it wore as a macabre trophy. I tried to fire the SA-80 on the rise, but it was way too late and the chieftain's mace shattered its barrel, sending the remains spinning off into the darkness with a distant splash.

The force knocked me back clean off my feet and I landed hard on my back, air forcefully expelled from my lungs. My fingers clawed for a weapon, scrabbling desperately for anything to use, but they came up empty and the creature hopped forward and planted a webbed foot on either side of me, raising its club for the killing blow. I heard two clicks as Haines' shotgun misfired and I almost laughed at the absurdity of it all. I wanted to shout, 'forget me, run! run!' but found my mouth as dry as if I were breathing sand. I looked up into those soulless saucer-fish eyes and in that instant almost felt glad, glad that my struggle was over, the pain, the loss, all swept away with one quick swish of its mace. A moment of agony and then sweet nothingness and finally, peace…

But of course it didn't quite happen that way, otherwise I wouldn't be sitting here making this report, would I? I'm not ashamed to say that I cringed, eyes screwed tight, teeth clenched for the cruel impact which would crush my skull and end it all. Yet the long moment played out and somehow it didn't arrive. I was still alive. Why?

I unscrewed one eye and looked up, still wincing at the anticipated blow, but the chieftain's eyes suddenly seemed to bulge even wider, if that were possible. The mace raised above its head slipped from between webbed forepaws and it staggered, tottering and bleeding, falling to its knees. There was a flash like quicksilver, so bright it seemed like liquid moonlight and where seconds before the chieftain's face had blazed with fierce malice, now, there was simply an empty void and no head at all. Something bounced wetly across the turf and then the creature's body sagged, as if all the air had been let out of it. I watched it crumple, black ichor pumping from its neck, a black waterfall staining my fatigues.

'My apologies … Sergeant is it? I seem to have bloodied your battle dress.'

A figure emerged from behind the chieftain's corpse.

'What the holy living fuck?'

'Oh, nothing quite so blasphemous. Please, allow me.' A gloved hand reached out and helped me to my feet.

'Thank … you.' I mumbled.

'My pleasure, naturally.'

'Who the hell *are* you?' I asked.

'Hands where I can see them! *Now*, or I will shoot you down!' Haines came thrashing through the waters, brandishing the shotgun and now had both barrels levelled at this newcomer, who was nonchalantly wiping clean the heavy, leaf-bladed knife with which he'd performed the dreadful execution. He sheathed the *Khukri* and adjusted the helmet and respirator which cloaked his face. Long pale hair spilled over his collar and he wore the same dark uniform as the fallen soldiers, but with a single OF-3 crown on each shoulder.

'Yes, I do believe you would young lady. I would say your threat would carry slightly more conviction if you had reloaded after your misfire, though.'

'Stand down Haines,' I said, 'He's on our side. You are on our side right, Major?' I added with slightly less certainty but he nodded graciously.

'Oh, absolutely. Nice to make your acquaintance, Sergeant?'

'Stokes, call me Stokesy, this is Haines.'

'Well good to meet you both, though I wish it were in happier circumstances. What's brought you to this forlorn place, if you don't mind me asking?'

'Curiosity sir. I saw the muzzle flashes and decided to investigate. The rest of my unit is holed up in a ruined pub about half a mile away.'

'Curiosity hm? A dangerous trait that and not just for cats. Well, I see you've made a start on salvaging the marines' gear.'

'I, well…'

'Don't apologise Sergeant, Poor Captain Priestman and her brave lads won't be needing it any more. I should not have left them here, but other, more pressing matters seemed to demand my attention, an apparently wild goose chase that…' His rich rather plummy voice dwindled mid sentence. 'I should never have allowed myself to be separated from them, but the prize seemed worth the risk. I'm only glad I was able to return to lend you a hand.'

'As am I sir, and that you're so handy with that blade.'

'A most dependable little pocket knife,' he said as he slid the *Khukri* into a leather sheath on his belt. 'I'm only sorry I wasn't back in time to help these brave marines. Still, spilled milk and all that. Now, let me lend you a hand, then we can repair back to your hidey hole and plot our next move.' He had such an air of calm, the quiet authority of a natural leader, that I didn't even think to question his orders and simply moved to obey.

A short while later and piled high with commando gear, we had made our way back to the ruined boozer, still on the alert for more Devil patrols. Our mysterious masked major said little, but led the way as if he already knew where we were going.

I was secretly more than a little pleased with Challis' whispered challenge and the row of pointed weapons which halted us at the perimeter. I made the counter sign and Challis emerged and quickly hustled us inside, where we stacked the marines' gear up in neat piles. The remainder of the unit roused themselves and looked at it and us with a mixture of avarice, curiosity and indifference. The major strode into the centre of the room and said quietly.

'Please, do help yourselves, it may look a little daunting, but it's good quality kit and easy enough to get the hang of. Here, let me show you.' The major began distributing advanced weaponry and equipment like he was Santa and the unit suddenly transformed into a set of wide-eyed kids on Christmas morning. I ushered Challis to one side and handed him the battle suit and rifle closest to his size.

'Nice haul,' he said, understated as ever, giving the body armour a solid punch and then checking over the silenced rifle with an approving eye.

'Thanks. Question: it's been over forty minutes since we left. Why are you all still here?'

'Thought you'd earned yourself a small extension. Five minutes more mind and we'd have been out that door and heading for the hills … as ordered.'

'I see, well I'm glad you decided to cut me a little slack.'

'No problem. So who's the Rodney?'

'Not sure. I found him or I should say he found us amongst a bunch of dead Bootnecks and the remains of four warbands about half a mile east.' Challis emitted a low whistle.

'Marines? Forceful guys. What they hell are they doing out here?'

'No idea, though he doesn't look like any marine I've ever encountered,' I said. 'Chieftain had me cold, but he carved him up single-handed, beheaded the scaly bastard using one of those Ghurkha knives.'

'Sounds like he's eminently qualified then. A *Khukri*, hm? That rings a bell, though I can't quite place…'

'Yeah, there's something unusual about him, something I can't quite put my finger on.'

'Well, gift horses and all that…' said Challis, examining his new weapon with evident relish, while I continued to keep an eye on the major.

Soon the unit had divvied up the marines' gear between them, levered themselves into it with only passing comic effect and in a low light or at a distance you might even have mistaken them for real soldiers. Truth to tell, the rations and field packs were as welcome as any of the weapons and these were soon broken out and torn into with gusto. Quiet smiles and nods lit up their dirty faces as they consumed this unexpected windfall and for the first time in a long time, they grinned and murmured contentedly, as they stuffed themselves stupid.

I watched Haines almost inhale a k-ration whole and gently chided her to slow down in case she choked. The major who had removed his mask but not his visor, leant back against the bar and watched them with a half-amused smile playing about his lower features. He seemed genuinely happy to let them revel in their sudden good fortune and I took the opportunity to offer my gratitude.

'Thank you, sir. This means a great deal.'

'It is the small victories, hey, Sergeant? Though there have been few enough of those in recent times.'

'True enough, sir.'

'Well, let's get down to business. Tell me, what's dragged you out to these god-for-saken shores?'

'That island, sir. We were one of several militia patrols dispatched from the forward base at Chester. Three days out and the place has been buzzing with Devils, I'm not sure if any of the other patrols made it. Guess they thought if they threw enough of us at the wall, one was bound to stick. The rest? Expendable. But HQ wanted pictures of that island desperately if we could lay our hands on them. Turns out we could.'

'I see and what did you make of what you saw?'

'Difficult to say, sir, the place was wrapped in fog and mist, but we saw lights, some weird structures, unusual geometry. They're up to something out there and I doubt it means anything good for us. With those bastards, it never does.'

'Most perceptive of you Sergeant, but I now believe the threat is somewhat graver than even your local HQ might suspect. With your permission, I'd like to address your men.'

'You don't need my permission sir and they're barely...'

'I know, but I'm asking it nevertheless.'

'Floor's yours.'

The major ambled into the centre of the room and while he didn't say so much as a word, the focus immediately shifted and in a few moments, the unit's attention was fixed wholly on him.

'Good evening. I'm glad you're enjoying the food, please don't stop on my account, continue to eat while I talk. As you know, these are desperate times, the recent appear-ance of this island artefact has signalled a grave new development in our ongoing conflict with the Devils.

'For a while now I've been seeking a way to change the balance, something that might swing the odds back our way, something that might change the course of this war completely.'

The men digested this information silently, though not a one paused chewing.

'I thought I'd come close to finding it, instead, all I've found is betrayal and death. Now I fear things may begin to run very badly for us...'

'Worse than they already are?' someone muttered.

'Much worse,' said the major, 'What that island represents could alter the balance decisively in the creatures' favour. So to be frank, I need...'

'Oh I can see where this is going,' piped up Adams.

'And where's that?' answered the major placidly.

'Volunteers isn't it? You want volunteers to lay down their lives for king and country?'

'Adams!' growled Challis.

'No it's fine, let him speak,' said the major.

'With respect ... sir,' said Adams, 'that's not us, we're not regular soldiers Major, we're militia, scum of the earth, or might as well be. We were sent out to get photos and we've managed to do it, more by luck than judgement. The other patrols are dead or worse, captured. So you can see, we kind of feel we've done our bit, risked enough...'

'I understand completely,' said the major, 'you're the brave ladies and gentlemen of the militia, the people's army, the last line of defence against threats foreign, domestic and now alien. You're conscripts, civilians, you fight for food, shelter, survival, you're not even real soldiers are you? My apologies if I mistook you for such, it can be a bit difficult to tell who's rank nowadays and who's file.'

Adams and several of the others nodded and muttered, some vigorously.

'That I can understand, respect even, but there's something you should also understand. This war is going badly for us, perhaps far worse than you suspect and not just here. The American coasts are overrun, the continent is in chaos and if Britain falls, then Europe follows. We've become a stepping stone and if we go under, the Devils will chase anything that remains all the way back to the Alps.

'This is no longer a war in the conventional sense. There'll be no ceasefire, armistice or surrender on honourable terms come the end of it. Make no mistake, it is survival as a species that we are fighting for. If we don't stop them, we will be enslaved or extinguished in short order and that'll be the end of it — and us.'

The major's gaze swept around the room, some like Adams glared defiantly back at him, some bowed their heads and looked away, some even had the decency to look shame faced.

'My original mission is now over. I intend to change tack, alter my frame of reference and go seek guidance from someone I know I can trust. The cost of realising my

24

mistake? One marine unit, twelve brave men and women, the ones whose clothes you now wear and whose food you're now eating.

'But it's more than that. If I succeed, I believe I can offer a way to strike back.' The major turned his eyes on me.

'Let me be frank Sergeant, you look tired and your men look beaten. What I'm offering is a chance to change that, a chance to earn a measure of revenge for all the suffering the Devils have inflicted on you, on all of us.

'In fact I can promise you here and now, that if I succeed in what I have in mind, I intend to teach these amphibian bastards a lesson they'll never forget for all their bulbous-eyed, live long days. I'm going to make them sorry they ever crawled out from under the waves and showed their ugly mugs on land — our land, our island.'

'Stirring words sir, but how many of us will it cost?' Unedited, the words slipped from my mouth.

'Some, all, none, it's difficult to say. I can't tell you exactly, but whatever it costs, it will be worth it. I can promise you that.'

'So how can we help, when even a whole squad of marines couldn't?' asked Challis.

'A reasonable question,' said the major. 'What I've come to realise is: I don't need soldiers, I need survivors, people adept at scavenging, blending into the landscape, blagging their way unnoticed behind enemy lines. Unless I'm very much mistaken, that's your forte. It was an error to bring marines along, one that was forced on me, against my better judgement.

'From here on in, I don't intend to confront the enemy head on, but to slip by them unnoticed and deliver a knock-out blow once we've reached our ultimate goal.'

'And that goal is?' I asked.

'Classified, I'm afraid and must remain so, until we're past the point of no return. But I can tell you this, it will involve a journey up the coast, with a very specific objective in mind.'

'Further up the coast? A coast that's already positively swarming with Devils?' said Adams. 'We've made it this far by the skin of our teeth and now you want us to go even further into the Devils' heartland, like we were strolling out for a day at the beach?'

'Well you can pack your bucket and spade if you like, but I wouldn't advise it,' said the major. 'Listen, all of you. You know I could make this an order and I could have any dissenters shot for treason.' There was a collective murmur at this pronouncement.

'But I'm not going to,' he continued. 'I want volunteers on this mission, people who actually want to make a difference, people who will stand up and be counted.'

'And that's us?' I said, almost to myself.

'I spoke just now in disparaging terms about 'the militia'. Deliberately so and totally for effect. You should never forget what this country's 'people's army' has achieved: it deposed a tyrant king, ushering in centuries' worth of democracy; it stood alone against the might and madness of the Third Reich and now it — you — are pretty much all that remains in our ongoing struggle for survival. When it's backs against the wall time, it is the people you can ultimately depend on. That's exactly the kind of men and women I want for this mission.'

The major removed his visor and helmet and his long, almost unnaturally white hair flowed down onto his shoulders, throwing his rather equine features into sharp relief. There were more murmurs, disbelief, disquiet, maybe even a little awe.

'Shit,' Challis whispered, I thought he seemed familiar. You know who that is right?'

'Should I?'

'It's Seraph, the White Witchman, one of the chief spooks from section E. They say he's killed over a thousand Devils with his own fell hand and can wield magic more powerful that their strongest shaman.'

'No kidding. I've heard the stories, I thought it was all just propaganda.'

'Well he looks real enough to me…'

'Know this,' said the major, his eyes piercing the circle around him, so that he seemed to see into each individual's soul. 'I want to start the fight back, right here, right now. I intend to forge a victory and a victory is a powerful thing in these dark times.

'Anyone who wants to make a difference, come with me. The rest of you can eat your fill and then take yourselves back to HQ for all the good that will do you.

'You have five minutes to make up your minds. Use them wisely.'

CHAPTER THREE

Strait Talking

FIVE MINUTES LATER, the room had divided. Challis, Haines and I stood with the major, Adams and the rest of the unit regarded us from the other side of the ruined bar.

'Four of us, sir? Will it be enough?' I whispered. 'There's still time, I can order them to...'

'I'd rather have four willing volunteers, than an entire battalion pressed into service.'

'But it's practically desertion, they could be sho...'

'It's not desertion. I offered them a choice and they've made it. Let them go Sergeant, you three will do more than admirably.'

'I wish I shared your confidence.'

'You will Sergeant, you will,' he said quietly and then addressed the others. 'But now we must say our fond farewells.' The major strode over to Adams who had assumed the role of ringleader of the disgruntled faction. To my surprise, he offered him his hand.

'Now, Adams is it? No hard feelings, make sure you get the rest of them back safely. Good luck and god speed.' Adams looked uncertainly at his hand for a moment, then took it. A brief perfunctory shake and then he led the rest of them out of the pub with scarcely a backward glance.

We were alone.

'Poor beggars,' muttered the major.

'Sir?'

'Well, they're practically dead men walking, they'd have actually been much safer coming with us, though more of a burden. I wonder if they'll even make it a mile?' He shook his head sadly and then continued.

'Well, we'd best be going, we've a long way to travel before dawn, shall we?'

We headed out into the darkness in single file, the moon ducking in and out of the clouds above. The marines' gear felt strange at first, the reinforced body armour was strong and supple, strangely flexible and light as a feather — although all enclosing and extremely figure hugging, it bordered on the downright pervy frankly.

Still, that was a small price to pay. We were accustomed to trudging along in the cold and wet and it was welcome to be dry and warm for a change. Haines gave me a grin from underneath a helmet that was at least a couple of sizes too big for her.

'Do you remember superheroes Sergeant?'

'Batman? Spider-Man, that kind of thing?'

'Exactly, this suit kind of makes me feel like I could be one of them, si … Sarge,' she said grinning and wriggling inside the armour which fitted her slightly better than the oversized battle bowler. I returned her smile, almost in spite of myself.

'We could probably do with a few superheroes on our side.' I said.

'Nonsense,' whispered the major, 'we'll do just fine all on our own. Now, why don't you familiarise yourselves with the suit's vision enhancer? You'll find it comes in very handy.' I flipped the integral helmet visor down.

'Wow.' I said, despite myself, as the marshland lit up like a summer's day, the outline and contours of the water-sodden landscape leaping out at me. I could see the residual signatures of the fallen marines perhaps a mile off and much further away, small exclamation icons signifying more potential threats, perhaps outlying Devil patrols?

'Grade A tech,' Challis whistled softly, 'no expense spared.'

'Impressive, no?' said the major. 'Best preserve them though, the batteries won't last forever.' I flipped my visor up and returned, blinking, to the shadows of the night time landscape.

'You don't use them, sir?' I asked.

'Technology is all well and good, but I prefer more, shall we say, old-fashioned methods,' said the major and as if to demonstrate, he loped off briskly into the gloom.

Soon we were deep into the marshland again, wading through brackish water and reeds and testing our footing on the odd piece of solid ground. Switching the visor on to scope out the lay of the land was a constant temptation, but the major seemed to know where he was going instinctively and led us with surefootedness and purpose.

When we came to the marines' final resting place, Challis drank in the scene with a scowl and a muttered expletive and Major Seraph inclined his head in a slight bow to his fallen former comrades. But we were soon past that dreadful scene of execution and with some determined yomping, the major led us to a position about half a mile or so north of the marines' graveyard.

'Are you feeling strong, Haines?' enquired the major, to which awed, the girl nodded vigorously.

'Of course you are. Come on then, lend me a hand,' said Major Seraph and with Haines assisting, the pair began peeling away undergrowth and branches at the spot which he had designated. Gradually, several shapes revealed themselves, three dinghy-like boats, with rounded prows and low hulls, painted with dark camo and definitely configured for stealth. Haines and the major carried one out between them and slid it silently into the salty marsh waters.

'A last gift, courtesy of the marines, we stashed them here while I went on to … recce ahead,' said the major. We looked on suitably intrigued.

'Well you don't imagine I proposed to walk the entire way did you?' said the major. 'Come on, hop in.'

We clambered aboard, a little unsteadily it must be said, for few people nowadays have what you might call sea legs. The major started the small, sleek-looking outboard, the dinghy glided silently across the surface, scarcely leaving a ripple in its wake. Taking the tiller, the major guided us unerringly through the stagnant waters, while above, a sickle moon darted in and out of banked cloud, cloaking and uncloaking the marsh in pale, otherworldly light.

The waters may have been still, but its denizens were not. I slid my visor down again and almost recoiled as it came alive with threat indicators, outlining the locations of at least a dozen Devil warbands. I strained and could hear their low frequency chittering, each calling to each across the waters, a riot of disgusting alien undertones. We were caught in the mesh of a giant Devil net spread over the contours of the marsh. I uttered a low curse.

'That many?' said Challis softly.

'That many … and a few more besides,' I replied.

'Utter silence now,' said the major from the stern. 'Raise your visors too, it's best you don't see this next part.'

But I ignored his advice. Horribly fascinated, I knelt in the prow, letting the weight of my new weapon bite reassuringly into shoulder. If we were discovered, then those Devil bastards were going to pay for it, and I would exact the heaviest possible price I could.

Then we were amongst them, but the major manoeuvred the small craft so skilfully, so deftly, that it seemed to merely kiss the water's surface, swirling and drifting silently past the monstrous hordes.

Seconds became minutes, my nerves were as tight as a tripwire and sometimes we passed so close to the patrolling bands, that I swear I could have almost reached out and touched them.

Time seemed to take on a whole new meaning there in the foetid rankness of the marsh and in between each encounter, I began to study the major with a new found respect and not a little awe. He was as good as his word too, always sure, never hesitating, as if he always seemed to know exactly where to go, where to turn, when to stop and when to wait, with senses that bordered on the uncanny. Perhaps the things they said about this White Witchman and his sorcerous abilities were true?

What exactly did they say about him? I'd have to interrogate Challis more closely once — if — we made it through.

There was just one moment when I came close to doubting him.

We had drifted so close to a hideously repulsive chieftain that I thought we must surely be discovered and I readied myself to deliver the burst that would have blown its vile head clean off. I was biting down on my back teeth so hard I could feel my gums cramp. But just as it seemed it must turn and discover us, the beast merely sniffed at the night air, then waved its hideous forepaw and gave an echoing croak which set its braves off in another direction.

I looked back at the major who sat there like a pale echo of the ferryman. He wore no visor, indeed seemingly eschewed the technology which we carried, but a faint star light seemed to play around his eyes and he had an indefinable air of certainty about him. My back teeth ached with tension, but we never came quite so close again and before long, we had slipped through their net, like minnows threading their way through a trawler's rough mesh.

Then, finally, we had left the main bulk of the Devil patrols behind, their threat icons receding into tiny afterglows in my visor and a timeless space passed, as we moved stealthily through that flooded landscape.

It might have been an hour, it might have been several, but after a while the marsh-land began to give way to a ragged mix of coast and mountains. Here we proceeded, if anything, even more cautiously, for the rising wind brought with it an unmistakably saltier tang, meaning we had strayed dangerously close to the sea.

By my rough reckoning we can't have been too far away from what remained of Anglesey, the Welsh island which had now been almost totally claimed by the waves. This seemed to be confirmed by the sighting of three long slivers of land which interrupted the expanse of dark green water over to our left.

Major Seraph's keen eyes shone, reflections of silver moonlight, piercing the dark and the fog, seeking out the way. But which way, where was he taking us now? Surely not out onto the open ocean, into the very domain of the Devils themselves?

Yet that seemed to be exactly his intention, for he pointed the prow of our craft towards an open stretch of water which connected the two distant shorelines. In the harsh glare of the moonlight, the dark, foam-capped water was punctuated by the wreathes and curls of sinister looking fog banks.

The comparative safety of the far shore looked a long way off now as we bobbed out into the gentle embrace of the tide and to add to my sense of foreboding, far away, the Devils' island was in sight again, casting its long, baleful gaze across the intervening waters.

In response to my unspoken question, the major whispered, 'Yes Sergeant, I do intend to cross this particular bar. This was once the old Menai Strait, the thin vein of water which divided that ancient and holy isle from the mainland.'

Major Seraph regarded the three slivers of land to port with a look, that was at once both pained and wistful.

'Something wrong, sir?'

'Not exactly, it's just that the last time I was here … a long time ago … it was covered in trees and you could still see lights in the sacred groves.'

'Holiday was it?' enquired Challis dryly.

'Not exactly,' said the major, coming fully back to the present. 'But that's for another time. Now, visors on and safeties off if you please. But no — and I mean absolutely no — firing unless I give an explicit order. Understood?'

'Sir.' We answered as one.

'Good, now I know the open water will seem daunting, but I'm confident we'll make it across. You'll just have to trust in your pilot and remain completely quiet … as silent as the grave.'

'Not exactly how I'd have phrased it, sir.'

'Quite so,' His mouth configured into something that might have been construed as a crooked smile. 'Well, let's just see if we can avoid swimming with the fishes, at any rate.' He throttled the outboard and quietly, we got underway.

Heading into the open waters, the major steered us adeptly, insinuating us between fog bank and fog bank, darting swiftly and silently across the open passages of the strait, then losing us in the enshrouding mists once again.

Challis, stoic, was in the prow, Haines had starboard and I, port, while the major steered from the stern, but the gentle lapping of the waves against our hull felt like gunshots and the low, almost imperceptible hum of the engine seemed like a siren. I could feel tension in the air and my senses were alive and as fully alert as they had ever been.

All the while, that evil island hummed and buzzed with a strange low frequency tone, which travelled across the water assailing the ears. Unearthly lights flashed and a smouldering malevolence seemed to emanate from its misty shrouds.

But we passed the opening couple of miles uneventfully, giving us less than half a mile to go. I was counting down the distance with every passing breath, when the major hissed.

'Contacts to port. Keep your nerve, hold your fire.'

'Where?' I found myself scanning the surface, searching for a target, but there was nothing, nothing, had the major..?

There was a tremendous surge of white water and then, not twenty yards from where our boat ghosted on the edge of a fog bank, three massive shapes broke the surface in a welter of spray and salt. Long leathery necks stretched up into the night air, bulky misshapen bodies trailing spray and spume in their wakes, gnarled fins beating the water.

It was as if the Loch Ness monster had got jiggy with some of the nastier dinosaurs from Jurassic Park, spawning a horribly misbegotten litter and there, riding at the base of the neck of these three monsters from a forgotten age, were a coven of Devil shamans. The red dot of my scope flickered on the neck of the middle one, ready to blow it away before it could begin an incantation.

Steady Stokes, no need, they haven't seen us. They're moving away..

I relaxed a fraction and the dot faded. One of those monstrous steeds craned its neck and emitted a horrible squawking cry at the pale moon and then, flukes beating the water in tremendous strokes, the creatures set off at speed, making toward that cursed island.

The major steered us back into an enfolding fog bank and soon we were lost from their sight. Haines had eyes like saucers, but Challis merely offered, 'Didn't fancy yours much,' and then all of us were grinning as the adrenalin drained away. The major nodded indulgently.

'Well played, well played. Those unholy steeds were Stronsay beasts no less. I've never seen them this far south before, they're usually only found up around what remains of the Orkneys. My, the creatures are growing bold. Well, let's take a fresh guard and not let up now. We're almost at the other side and safety.'

'What next then, sir?' I enquired.

'Before we head any deeper into their spawning grounds, I need to check in with someone, an old friend, good woman to know in a tight spot ... if she's still alive that is. We'll head her way after we've taken a little breather.'

We settled ourselves back, still alert, but a little more relaxed and as we crossed the final stretch of the sound, I saw a strange artefact poking out of the waters to port. It was the skeletal remains of one end of a huge road bridge, its rusted metal struts and sagging concrete supports thrusting upward like a titan's fingers. A broken tarmac thread dropped away, disappearing into the waters: a literal road to nowhere. On the mainland side, long rows of decaying cars and lorries sat inert, abandoned long before they could reach higher ground — the safety of the rocky spines of the Peak, Dales and Lake districts.

Haines watched solemnly as we drifted past these broken fragments from another time.

It was only then that I realised: out there, during the most dangerous point of our crossing, the major's warning, it had seemed to come from inside my head rather than being actually spoken out loud. Was that possible or had I just imagined it? We drifted on in silence, but mine was the rather more uneasy disquiet.

CHAPTER FOUR

Saucy Sally

The last embers of the false dawn were dying and now the first streaks of true day were beginning to thread through the retreating darkness. The major turned the tiller decisively and pointed our craft towards the shore.

'Daybreak is not far away, time to hole up I'd say. Let's see if we can find somewhere suitable.'

We were soon cruising quietly through the remains of a small town, its broken streetlights and forgotten telegraph poles poking up from the waters, while the tiled roofs of submerged houses peeped through on higher ground.

This had probably once been a thriving town, but it was now totally deserted and had long since been claimed by the Flood, flotsam and detritus clinging like filthy skirts around its fallen walls. To the north, a line of pylons lay fallen like a cascade of dominos, hundred of tons of metal and girders, twisted and bent, in abject ruin. The electrical nervous system which had once sustained us, carrying power and light to millions of homes now lay tumbled down, like the picked clean skeletons of those mythical titans which were said to have founded the ancient isle of Albion.

The major nudged our boat towards the outskirts, where a rise in the land had created a series of islets and smaller patches of solid ground. A faded, peeling billboard advertising some long forgotten movie proclaimed 'The ride of your life', a somewhat prescient pronouncement, given what was to come.

True daylight began to bleed into another granite grey day and as if on cue, the rain started to come down like stair rods, as the major steered the boat into a bank of reeds. Cutting the engine, he slid into the water and tied her up, before carefully arranging the reeds behind us to camouflage it from prying eyes.

'There should be somewhere suitable just over there, if memory serves. Eyes open though, you never know what might be lurking over the horizon and I've a feeling we may not be alone.'

It was just about bright enough now to distinguish between the myriad blocks of grey which made up the eerie pre-dawn and the major took point and led us up and over the small ridge beyond the shore. As he reached the top, he suddenly flattened and signalled us to keep low, then with a small wave, beckoned us forward. Dropping onto our bellies, we crawled up to join him.

An ancient stone-built cottage perched above the swollen banks and shattered lock gates of a waterway that had once been a canal. Despite its age and weatherworn appearance, the cottage's roof and doors were intact, although its shutters were split and falling away from the windows. Dry, secluded and far enough off the beaten track, it would have made an ideal place to rest up. Ideal that is, apart from the two braves and a chieftain which lolled by its banks, attempting to spear themselves some breakfast.

'Hm, awkward, but I'm beggared if I'm going to let them stand in our way,' the major whispered. Closing his eyes for a moment, his brows furrowed, then he said.

'Good, none of their brethren are nearby. A decent chance to field test your new weapons I would have thought? Would you care to do the honours, Sergeant?'

'With pleasure, sir,' I whispered back.

We unslung our rifles and slid into position. I had no doubts about Challis, he could have taken down all three without blinking, but Haines? I wasn't so sure. I whispered to her.

'You up for this?'

'Yes Sarge,' she said bravely, but her eyes told a different story.

'Challis, you take the chieftain on the left, I've got the one on the right, Haines you take the one dead centre. All set?'

If she missed or panicked, I knew either one of us would easily be able to cover her target. Quietly, we spaced ourselves out and lined up to take the shot. The major wriggled in next to Haines and whispered.

'Press gently until the red dot appears, then pause. Let the air empty out of your lungs. Squeeze, don't pull the trigger, try and do it all in the one same easy motion. Got it?'

'Yes sir,' she said and seemed to take heart from his instruction.

'Corporal, if you could take out that chieftain with a body shot, I'd be most obliged. I'd like its head intact,' said the major. Challis nodded assent. 'Excellent, in your own time then, Sergeant.'

'3' I whispered and gently pressed the trigger.

'2' Beams of light lit out to paint our targets.

'1' My red dot settled between its bulbous eyes. The sight was so powerful I could see its hideous gill flaps pulse.

'Fire.' The rifle whispered with barely a sound and hardly any recoil. My brave's head erupted in a welter of brains and gore, but I was already moving to cover Haines' target. I needn't have bothered, all three Devils were already stiffening in the mud.

'Did you see that, Sarge? I blew its head clean off!' said Haines exultantly. 'Clean off!' She leapt up and did a little dance on the spot.

'I saw,' I said, 'well done, the first of many I hope, but you can calm down now.' Yet Haines' enthusiasm was infectious. Challis patted her on the head with a gruff 'shot', which was about as high a compliment as you'd ever get from him. The major winked and said, 'Remind me to arrange a little visit to sniper school when we get back.' Haines' face shone.

Buoyed, all four of us made our way down to the lock keeper's cottage and I thought perhaps this mysterious White Witchman was right. It was the small victories which count most of all.

The cottage was long abandoned, but dry and warm enough. Two of the Devils were consigned to the waters and we heaved their pallid, scaly bodies into the flood without comment. But the major had retained the chieftain's corpse and while I watched from inside, he cradled its revolting head in his hands and produced a strange looking totem made of intertwined hawthorns from inside his jacket. Eyes closed, his lips moved inaudibly and a strange light seemed to play underneath his furrowed brows. He stayed like that for a while, then abruptly broke off and rolled its body into the swirling waters which carried it away.

Haines had curled herself up into a ball like a cat and Challis' snores were already echoing from the rafters by the time the major pushed aside the door.

'I'll take first watch Sergeant. Get some rest. I don't mind, I don't sleep much when I'm in the field anyway.'

'Perhaps in a little while sir, I like to see the lie of the land, before I bed down.'

'Hm, sensible.' He said and settled himself into a seat by the empty fireplace. The silence lasted unbroken for a little while, then I said.

'Can I ask sir, what were you doing just now?'

'Attempting to gather intelligence.'

'From a dead Devil?'

'Yes Stokes, the mind's patterns — especially an amphibian's — linger a little while after death … if one knows how to look.'

'Freaky-weird.'

'Yes, well I'm sure my reputation proceeds me. Just be grateful I found what I was looking for quickly and didn't have to open up its head and consume the entire brain to learn more.' My jaw dropped, but the major smiled.

'And don't believe everything you hear Stokes, especially about me.'

'Fair enough. So what did you learn, sir?'

'It seemed mainly occupied with its breakfast, though there were a couple of items of interest. That accursed island featured heavily and there was something else, something it — they seem to fear. Their thoughts are very difficult to translate, but it came through as apprehension, a dread of something. Something that patrolled the surface but hunted in the deeps. Not theirs, not natural, but something of ours ... Mean anything to you?'

'No sir, not a thing.'

'Understandable, but it sounds like we're starting to head in the right direction. At any rate, I'm sure my friend will be able to shed some further light.' He looked oddly elated at the prospect, a certain mischievous light playing about his sharp features.

'If you say so, sir.' I decided to seize the opportunity. 'Do you mind if I ask you something?'

'Please ... ask away.'

'It is true, you're able to use magic? Like the Devils' shamans?'

'Not like their magic exactly, but I do command certain gifts, certain abilities, that are perhaps not entirely ... usual. Oh, and I've also been doing this for a very long time, one can't but help pick up the odd useful tip here and there.'

There was a silence while I digested this.

'So, one more thing, do you know what we did to deserve this, sir?'

'*This?*'

'This conflict, this war. Why did they attack us?'

'Hm, now we're heading into deep waters indeed. Perhaps it was our greed, our pathetic stewardship of the planet which altered the balance, or maybe they just saw their opportunity as the waters rose. There's all manner of theories, but I still don't know for certain what provoked them into mounting all-out war. Their minds are very different from our own, truly *outré*. Perhaps our own follies drove them to it, or maybe it was just a whim of their great, dark slumbering god? Their motives seem unknowable from our perspective, perhaps our motives seem the same to them?'

'I only wish it hadn't fallen on our shoulders, sir.'

'You're not alone in that. Yet perhaps it won't always.'

'I'm sorry sir?'

'It's an idle thought perhaps, but if you subscribe to the idea that all things are possible in an infinite universe — and in an infinite number of universes, then here, now, is just one possible future, one of many.'

'A strange idea … sir. Do you mean that somewhere, somewhen else, I, another me could be reclining on a beach, enjoying the sun, sipping a cocktail and deciding which waiter to cop off with?'

He smiled. 'Quite possibly, Sergeant.'

'Well that's some small comfort at least. I hope other me is making the most of it.'

'So, now, a question for a question, why did you decide to join me Stokes? Why did they?' He indicated the recumbent bodies. 'You could have easily walked away with all the others.'

'Well Challis is a pro, one of the last, Haines is just an impressionable kid, I guess they're used to following me. '

'And you?'

'Me? Oh that's easy, revenge, pure and simple. You offered a chance to extract some and I liked what I heard.'

'A rather … dark motive.'

'Maybe, but I was there you know, the day that London fell. I saw that thirty metre wave sweep up the tidal line like a tsunami, thousands of them riding in on it, smashing through the old Thames barrier, engulfing the entire city. It was biblical, apocalyptic, the beginning of the end of days.'

'I see,' the major said quietly.

'Perhaps you do, but not entirely sir. That was the same day I lost my little boy. We'd come up to London to see the sights, instead, we saw the end of the world.

'We ran for higher ground, but I can remember staring up at that towering wall of water, which stretched from horizon to horizon and still not quite believing my own eyes. I heard my boy cry out and we tried to run but there was nowhere to run to. I had enough time to snatch him up and then the fringes of the wave took us both. He was wrenched from my arms, swept away. I never saw him again.

'How I survived I don't know, but there's not a day goes by, that I wish I hadn't drowned with all those millions of others. It would have been easier than living through this.

'You ask me why I joined you? It's simple. I'm tired of the emptiness, I'm tired of running, I'm tired of defeat, if there's even the slightest chance of paying back those Devil scum for what they did, then I'm in … all the way … up to the hilt … balls deep.' Tears had welled unbidden, but I fought them back.

'Good,' said the major quietly. 'A chance for that at least, I can promise you … and in spades.'

Eventually I must have nodded off for the next thing I knew, Challis was nudging me awake and the greyness of dusk was seeping in through the cottage windows. My sleep had been troubled … fingers grasping, unwinding, lost, pulled away, but the images were insubstantial and slipped away as consciousness returned, leaving just a vague sense of unease. Challis had heated up one of the marines' k-rations for me and I picked at it, watching Haines lick the inside of hers clean. It had been a while since we'd regularly had hot food in our bellies and I suppose I should have been grateful, but my mind was clouded, anxious, as I chewed mechanically, only waking from my reverie when the major strode in.

'Ah, I trust everyone's breakfasted well? Ready to move out?'

'Yes sir, where are we heading?'

'Back to the boat first, then onto pastures — or rather waters — new. I mentioned an old friend and colleague? I've a mind to see if she's taking callers.' He pointed an arm in the general direction of a range of snow capped mountains which rose inland. Away from the coast, I thought, well at least that's something. We packed our gear quickly, made a hasty latrine stop and then found our way back to the boat. The three of us clambered aboard immediately, but Haines stood amongst the reeds for a moment, looking solemn before she said.

'Sir?'

'What it Haines?' said the major as the outboard whispered into life.

'I was wondering, our boat sir — does she have a name?'

'A name?'

'Yes sir, my brother, he was a fisherman. He told me every boat should have a name, it's unlucky not to.'

'I see, well the marines called her SB-03, but it was more of a designation than a name.'

'Could we give her one then, sir? Call her something?' I don't think Haines had ever looked more serious.

'Haines I don't think this is quite the time…' I tried to interrupt but the major waved my objections away.

'Seems reasonable. Did you have anything in mind?'

'What about … the *Saucy Sally*? That was the name of my brother's boat.'

The major appeared to give this his deepest consideration.

'Hm, well I don't see why not. The *Saucy Sally* it is then,' he said. 'And god help all who sail in her.'

Haines beamed and clambered aboard as if she had just won the food lottery. Even

Challis' rugged features parted in a craggy smile. With that, the major cast off and we headed out into unknown waters.

The moon peered inquisitively from behind banked cloud, as we traversed further inland, into the interior. Here, the flood waters washed up against the impermeable masses of mountain and hill, creating a series of fjords and we navigated them cautiously, although there seemed no trace of Devil or indeed any other activity. It was a blank, sterile landscape, rimed by tinges of frost and snow, like sailing across a featureless lunar surface. The only noticeable landmark was an ancient downed Apache attack chopper, two of its rotor blades had been sheered clean off as it had fallen out of sky and the remaining two were mangled and twisted. Its heavily armoured body had been crushed and its forward gun bent and buckled by the impact. The under-wing missile pods were empty and spent, so at least it had gone down fighting. But now grasses and weeds threaded their way through the rusted wreck, a once mighty fighting machine reclaimed by a resurgent nature.

Branching off from the main artery of one of these fjords was a swollen river which seemed to gush between the surrounding mountain giants' toes and the major turned the newly-christened *Sally* towards the mouth of its rushing waters.

Now we passed through long abandoned hamlets and I lowered my visor briefly and watched their tenantless windows and tumbledown walls drift by. They had been either abandoned or picked clean by raiders. Human or Devil, it was difficult to tell, for feral humans posed every bit as much of a threat as the creatures themselves. I'm not spooked easily, but it was eerily quiet, not a sound punctuated the landscape unless you counted the low, long distance monotone of the island which was now mercifully far behind us. We ran silent and slow and after a while, the gentle murmur of the waters lulled the senses, so that the landscape took on a haunted, dream-like quality.

Signs of habitation grew ever sparser and soon, only the occasional remote house or ruined shepherd's hut marked our progress. We were gaining altitude too and now we exhaled frosty cones of moisture and any sliver of exposed flesh was frozen and deadened, as the air grew stubbornly chill. I pulled the suit's collar up around my neck for warmth.

The major said nothing but watched the banks with predator's eyes, his fey, rather saturnine features constantly weighing and evaluating beneath those arched brows. Eventually he turned us into a narrower tributary which forked off from the main watercourse and began climbing steeply towards the heart of the mountain range. The engine note changed, growing slightly deeper as it strained against the oncoming current.

I raised a quizzical eyebrow, but the major's finger at his lips stalled my unspoken question and I had to be content with keeping a vigilant watch. The banks of this rivulet were overgrown with dense, scrubby trees and thickets of sharp, twisted vegetation and even though I continually checked with the visor's targeting system, it revealed nothing. It was not difficult to imagine being spied upon by rows and rows of unseen eyes. Don't let yourself get spooked, I told myself, tightening the grip on my weapon and quickly checked the others. Challis seemed completely unfazed as usual, but Haines peered uncertainly out into the darkness like the lost child she mostly still was. Fortunately, the major was completely imperturbable and retained his firm hand on the tiller and calm sense of purpose. He, at least, seemed certain of what he was doing.

Before long, a new sound began to establish itself above the natural noise of the current. Low at first, it swelled the further we travelled and as we rounded a final bend, the source was revealed as a great torrent of green water, cascading from high above and emptying into a deep, dark pool below.

The waterfall must have been a hundred yards high and it churned up the waters and made the air saturated with vapour, but the major steered us towards one of the banks without further comment and we beached the boat, camouflaged it quickly and then waded ashore. Safely hidden in a small clearing in the midst of the foliage, the major gathered us close and said.

'We'll be on foot from here on in and our objective lies up there.' He indicated above and beyond the waterfall. 'It's a decent enough climb, but not too taxing, thirty minutes to an hour at most, depending on what we encounter.'

'What's our objective, sir?'

'An observatory, a deep skies observatory. Before the Flood, this whole area was a national dark sky park. Remote, very little light pollution and of course, way off the beaten track. A perfect place to observe the heavens.'

'And now? What are we looking for up there?'

'As I said, an old acquaintance of mine. I do hope she's still up there — and still alive. I haven't heard from her in a little while, though whether that's by choice or circumstance, it's difficult to say. She can be a bit eccentric and as you'll appreciate, coming from me, that's saying something.'

'I see. Any intel on what we're likely to find up there?'

'Last I heard, this area had been overrun and was choked with Devil patrols.'

'Hm, unusual,' said Challis in what for him, practically qualified as an outburst. 'An old observatory doesn't strike me as a very high value strategic target.'

'Very astute Corporal, this is no ordinary observatory and our rendezvous, if we can make it, is with no ordinary astronomer. Once we reach our goal, I'll be able to let you know more, but for now, please concentrate on the task at hand, as this is likely to prove a somewhat tricky infiltration. Let's move fast and silent, but above all silent. Questions?'

41

We regarded each other for a long moment, but there didn't seem anything further to add.

'Good. Well fortunately I know a short cut that means we won't have to expose ourselves out in the open. This way, follow me.'

We edged our way round the foaming pool and into the shadows at the base of the waterfall. Here the sound was tremendous, as the cascade pummelled the waters below and the air was sodden with spray. We worked our way back behind the tumult and there, carved into the rock itself was a set of crude steps, which had been hacked up into a rough-hewn, funnel-like chimney. It was too loud to speak, but the major indicated the first step and shouldering his weapon, leapt up and began to half-climb, half swarm up the rocky stairway with surprising agility. I made Haines go next, then followed with Challis bringing up the rear.

The steps were smooth, caked with algae and lichen and slippery through long exposure to the flowing waters and damp atmosphere. Idly, I wondered how the major had known about this route and who had made it originally, but he was a man of many secrets and I had no chance to ask. Soon I had enough to focus on, what with making sure I didn't slip and causally plummet to my death. Up we went, ever upward, more climbing than walking now, using both hand and footholds to progress up the vertiginous ascent.

I'm not the best with heights and kept telling myself not to look down, to just keep transferring my weight, put one foot, one hand, after the other. After we had ascended what felt like a mile or more, I looked up to see the darkness of the sky and the first stars outlined in the open expanse above. I gave a shudder, glad that our climb was nearing its end.

We had risen above the overwhelming sound of rushing water now and were perhaps thirty feet from the top of the shaft when the major suddenly stopped and signalled us to halt. He cupped a hand to his ear and pointed and we froze, instinctively flattening against the walls, as the distinctive chittering sound of Devil speech drifted down.

Long moments passed in the darkness as we held there, suspended like rats in a drain pipe, but the sounds weren't particularly high or fast as they are when the Devils become agitated. For all we knew, they might be discussing the weather, or perhaps even more likely, the price of fish.

The minutes stretched out and finally, when I thought we must surely be discovered, the high-pitched clicks and whistles began to drift away as the creatures moved off in search of … well, whatever it is they go in search of.

Moments later, the major had swarmed his way to the top, poked his head over the lip and then signalled the all-clear. Haines hopped up and then I gratefully heaved myself over the ledge and saw why our stairway had remained undiscovered. We had emerged in the midst of a dense clump of bracken and thorns, perfectly hidden away from the Devils' prying eyes. At this altitude, the rain had turned to sleet and a bleak, snow-covered landscape of mixed rock and ice stretched before us. There, close to the summit, was our objective, the dark skies observatory, its solid walls and domed telescope framed against a background of stars.

Just one problem, the intervening half a mile's march was swarming with Devils, several warbands at the very least, a fact rapidly confirmed by a quick visor scan, which lit up with a Christmas tree's worth of threat icons.

'Fucksticks,' I swore.

'How are we going to get through that lot?' whispered Haines.

'Interesting, I wasn't counting on running into so many,' said the major. 'I wonder what can have drawn them here?'

'Can't say, but the ground's way too open, we'll never make it across undetected,' opined Challis.

'Major?' I enquired, already not looking forward to what seemed like an inevitable retreat down that rocky chimney.

'We'll be fine,' said the major. 'A quick stroll, then we'll jog on up that track and across the bridge.'

'Sir?' I said struggling to keep the hesitancy out of my voice, 'are you insane?' Before I had time to check them, the words came tumbling out.

'Hardly Sergeant. This can be done. Trust me. You do trust me don't you?'

'Trust's one thing … I'

'They say suicide's a form of insanity,' whispered Challis. 'And that's what we'd be committing if we stepped out there in full view.'

'But what if we were invisible?' said the major.

'Oh yeah, well if we were *invisible*, then we could wander across easy as you like. Perhaps we could even stop for a picnic on the way?' I said.

'Excellent, well that's settled then,' said the major to our increasingly confounded faces. 'And by the way Sergeant, you can drop the sarcasm, it really doesn't suit you.

'Now, while it may very well *sound* insane, becoming invisible is exactly what I propose we do … in a manner of speaking. Those suits you're wearing are remarkable pieces of kit, which — and I know you'll appreciate this particularly Challis — come ready installed with full active camouflage.

'I can control them from my suit which has in-built command functions, or you can voice activate them independently. You simply say 'camo on' or 'camo off' to control them.

'A word of warning though, they're not 100% foolproof and won't cloak you completely. They work by absorbing light, bending it around the wearer, so that to all intents and purposes you become part of the background. They're not quite as effective when you're on the move and the power drain is considerable, so they're only good for short bursts.

'However they should be sufficient to fool our fishy friends long enough for us to reach the observatory unmolested. Any questions?'

We looked at each other and for a moment I thought the major really had really lost it, but seeing our scepticism he whispered 'camo on' and just seemed to shimmer and disappear before our very eyes. Moments later, he was back again.

'Fuck.'

'Impressive, no? Well we're all low-ish on charge, but we should have just enough to make it to that bridge which leads to the observatory.'

'Sir, why didn't the marines use this to evade the Devils?' said Haines.

'Good question and one I've been pondering myself. The ambush was sudden, brutal, intense. It's almost as if the Devils knew where to find them. Perhaps they didn't have time to activate it, but if it was planned, then...' He frowned, lost in thought.

'But that will have to keep for another time. We've plenty to be getting on with here, so let's concentrate on the job in hand. Visors down, follow my ghost closely and on your lives, not a sound.'

We snapped our headpieces into place, the major gave the nod, all three of us spoke the words and winked out of existence.

The heads-up display now showed faint, transparent outlines where the major, Challis and Haines had stood just moments before and when we moved off, it was as if we had become ghosts, spectres with no physical presence at all. The major broke cover and marched purposefully out into the open and following him, my HUD suddenly swarmed with red target icons. It was as if he were striding out onto the battlefield naked, amidst a blare of trumpets, exposed for all to see. I waited, waited to hear the agitated bleeps, clicks and chirrups of discovery and then the frenzy of the onrushing horde. Yet there was not a sound, nothing except the high pitched whine of the wind reaping the snowy ground.

It was weird. We followed him, tentatively at first, for it went against every instinct a soldier has. It was as if we had entered a kind of ghost world, become disembodied wraiths, haunters of that snowy steppe. We stayed close, nose to tail, following in the major's tracks, dripping with that mix of adrenaline and terror you always feel before battle.

The Devils were strung out across the plateau, sweeping across its frozen length in long loose lines, but small splinter groups foraged here and there, as if they were seeking something or someone very specific. The major's instincts were bold, faultless though and he guided us with an infinitely steady hand, knowing exactly how to slip through those living nets without arousing suspicion, as if he were playing some vast deadly game of hide and seek, all of his own.

Several times we had to pause to allow the Devil patrols to sweep past and despite our apparent invulnerability, my weapon was constantly readied, tracking them as they flopped and croaked by. At the slightest sign of discovery, I would have cheerfully opened up and blown them to whichever particular level of hell is reserved for the Devil dead.

They were tense, nerve-jangling manoeuvres and the minutes passed like hours, but finally, we seemed to have evaded the bulk of the searchers and made it to a position where the rocks narrowed and the land rose up steeply onto the path which lead to the observatory. A small detachment of Devils had been stationed there, a half dozen or so, but from our hidden vantage point, I could also see the squat outline of a shaman amongst their number. It was an ugly bastard, even uglier than the rest of them and that's saying something, its body marked with ritualistic tattoos and its neck adorned with strange necklaces and charms. It leant against one of those gnarled seaweed-encrusted staffs they use to focus their sorcery and at its belt dangled several gilded human skulls.

Keep left, keep low, keep quiet. The major's orders appeared as text on my HUD and while the devils lolled and stretched, we snuck our way around to the side, sticking to the major like shadows. A strong wind blew up, whistling down the path, stirring up the ground frost and bringing with it fresh flakes from above.

Our progress was painstakingly slow, for we dare not betray ourselves by even the slightest sound and we padded in each other's footsteps like particularly dainty cats, high stepping across glass. Now we drew level with their lines and I could smell them, their foul salty odour which assaulted the nostrils, permeating even through the visor. In repose, those strange, turtle-like faces were as alien and unfathomable as ever and their bulbous eyes, wide and unblinking, were utterly unreadable.

A few more steps and we were passed them. Now it was their ridged backs and sharp spines which faced toward us as we gained vital ground and began to inch up the hill toward the path. Bringing up the rear, I turned, pacing backwards, keeping my eyes fixed on them as we headed gingerly toward higher ground and our goal.

We had progressed some thirty yards in this crablike fashion when the shaman suddenly stirred and came to life. It levered its squat bulk upright and perched on its hind legs, its head sweeping from side to side as if seeking something. For long moments it continued this pantomime, still facing out toward the plateau but then it barked out a long malevolent croak, like a rusty iron gate swinging in the wind and now its accompanying braves snatched up their weapons and agitated, began to stomp and fidget, eyes wide, crests rising on the alert.

Suddenly, one of the braves flung out a flabby paw, its spear indicating the ground where we had trod and now the shaman's head inclined upward, its nostrils scenting at the cold night air, as if sniffing for prey.

The wind! The wind whistling down from above was carrying our scent to them and the brave had spotted our tracks outlined against the snow! I dialled the rifle to full auto and felt its reassuring bite in my shoulder. But as I looked down the sight, in the split second my attention had wavered, the shaman had raised its staff and sent a shimmering bolt of cold fire which shattered the ground above us, throwing up ice shards and muddy slush. The detonation sent Haines flying and left the major and Challis scrambling for cover.

Red lights lit up all over my HUD and a warning tone screeched something about failing systems, but I was too focused to pay them any heed.

'Weapons free! Weapons free!' I heard the order, but my first burst had already ripped the shaman's guts apart and it fell, ichor spilling in black torrents onto the snow. *Aim, squeeze, fire, aim, squeeze, fire,* my training insisted and my second burst caught the two rear-most charging braves, heavy calibre bullets tearing through their hides, spinning them crazily before they dropped. My attention switched, seeking more targets but none were left, just a mass of steaming shapes in the snow.

A quick glance behind me showed Challis' smoking barrel and the major helping Haines to her feet, no longer ghostly outlines but solid and substantial in the moonlight.

'Camo's dead, that spell has killed it,' said the major calmly. 'No use sneaking around now, we'll have to make a run for it. Come on!'

The HUD's tactical display lit up with multiple threats to the rear and we double timed up the steep slope, breathing hard, making heavy work of it as the sleet and shale slid beneath our boots, snagging and tripping us. Something, probably a spear snaked past my shoulder and I turned and blind fired, sending a burst toward the group of braves that had come leaping up the incline after us.

I couldn't even stop to see if I'd hit any as some ten yards ahead, Haines stumbled and fell, sinking into the snow, almost spent. There wasn't time to argue, so I simply swung my weapon onto my back, seized her by the scruff of her neck and hauled her to her feet, while Challis and the major laid down covering fire.

Scrambling up that last steep incline, while spears and bolts rained down on us was probably the hardest fifty yards of my life. I collapsed beyond the stones at its summit in a heap, sucking oxygen in like it was manna. Haines promptly rolled onto her side and puked.

Vision swimming, I lay on my back and drank in several more deep breaths before managing to rouse myself. Challis and the major were with us now, firing back down the slope which was already littered with Devil dead. Yet a far greater body remained below, working their way up in the face of our withering fire. Behind us, a gun-metal suspension bridge stretched across the chasm, its flimsy looking structure leading directly to the walls of the observatory on the far side.

'Are you quite all right Sergeant?' said the major, without turning.

'I'll live.'

'Good, take my place for a moment would you?'

I quickly slapped another magazine into place, dialled the selector back to single shot to conserve ammo and slid into the firing position. These Devils were fast and agile, scouts maybe, hopping from rock to rock, bounding between cover. Challis and I were in a commanding position and had an almost perfect field of fire down slope and we exacted a heavy toll, making them pay for every single inch of ground they gained.

However, at the very bottom of the slope, far beyond our range, a group of chieftains and shamans had congregated and were now conferring animatedly — it wouldn't be long before they brought their big guns to bear. A few volleys of those shamans' battle magic would pin us here, suppressing us and we wouldn't be able to withstand the inevitable rush which would follow. Either that, or they'd just land a lucky shot and blow us straight to smithereens. I glanced to where the major was kneeling by the bridge supports.

'I hope you've got a plan sir, this is about to get decidedly hairy.' As if to confirm my suspicions, a fizzing bolt of cold fire arced up into the night sky and exploded some twenty yards below us, kicking up rocks and earth.

'That one was just a range finder.'

'Almost there, you must buy me a few more moments,' said the major.

'We'll do our best.'

Breathe, pause, squeeze. Combat takes on a strange automatic quality in situations like that, time seems to slow as you pick your target, aim, feel the recoil pull in your shoulder and make sure the target stays down.

More battle magic streaked out now, multiple searing balls of cold energy, homing in on us, falling like flares and when they hit, the ground exploded, showering us with debris, forcing our noses into the dirt. The scouting braves used that small window to make more ground and even with Haines adding her firepower to our defence, we had to fire like maniacs to stem the advancing tide.

'They've got our range sir! Next one will be right down our throats.'

'Almost there, almost, hold, hold!'

Several balls of cold fire snaked out from the Devils' command group, describing a long lazy arc which could only end one way. This time, I was the one shouting the orders.

'Grenade launchers! Give them one round each, then back to the bridge!' We switched to the under-barrel launchers, which burped their projectiles with a deep satisfying pop, and then, not even waiting to see where they hit, we ran for our lives.

The ridge where we had been just moments before dissolved in a haze of white light and crackling energy and now we scrambled onto the bridge.

'Well done Sergeant, don't wait for me, get across and don't spare the horses!' shouted the major, shooing us onward, making a final adjustment, then following hard on our heels.

Lungs protesting, we sprinted across the length of the bridge, the sounds of our boots echoing hollowly on the metal floor plates. A crosswind gusted fiercely, tugging hard and the bridge itself swayed and bucked, but I've never been so intent on getting anywhere in my life and we thumped across and slid into cover. We took up our firing positions just as a horde of Devils came surging over the crest.

'Shit, there's so many,' said Haines and her voice was not panicked, just matter of fact, stating the obvious.

'We'll never hold them sir!' I shouted targeting the vanguard, which was now spilling onto the bridge.

'Don't worry,' said the major. 'You won't have to. Heads down!' Then he touched his index finger to the device on his wrist.

CHAPTER FIVE

A Rummage in the Archive

THE OBSERVATORY WAS A WRECK. Large holes had been blown in the walls and the main doors were hanging off their hinges as we walked inside. The lobby had been thoroughly ransacked and recently too from the looks of it, desks, consoles and scientific instruments strewn across the floor in the beams of our rifles' torches. There were bodies too, human and Devil, but nothing moved and when, after several long moments, all remained still, I let myself relax a little.

I was still shaken after the blast outside. The major's hastily planted explosives had briefly turned night into day, the detonation dissolving Devil, bridge and hilltop alike and leaving in its wake a greasy mushroom cloud which billowed up into the night and remained burned in the retina. The shockwave had thrown us back, sucking the breath from our lungs with a concussive force which would have shredded unprotected ears. Mine still rang.

When I was finally able to pick myself up and survey the damage, a good quarter of the bridge had been lost and the remains were still creaking ominously, shedding girders and steel support wires into the expanse below. I scoped out the hill top opposite and the position we held not five minutes ago. But it was barren, empty and there was not a sign of life on the other side. That was one way of keeping the Devils' heads down.

'Drastic I know.' said the major, 'but rather them than us heh?' It was a sentiment which was difficult to disagree with.

'So here we are Major, what now?' I said turning over one of the bodies with the tip of my boot. It belonged to a female solider, regular army, not exactly the kind person you'd expect to find hanging around a deep skies observatory miles from the front line.

'Looks like the Devils have cleaned this place out, I wouldn't hold out much hope of finding anyone here … alive at any rate,' I said.

'Looks, can be deceptive Sergeant.' The major replied. 'I have a feeling we might have a little more luck nearer the main array.'

'There'll be no need for tramping mud around in there *Mister* Seraph,' said a rather peevish voice. Our rifles came up as one, torches sweeping for the source of the sound but we found only darkness. 'Trust you to make a mess of everything as per usual. What do you mean by bringing those creatures back up here and who gave you permission to blow up my bridge?'

'Omelettes and eggs, Miss Dandridge, omelettes and eggs. Can't make one, without breaking the other,' said the major.

There was a derisive snort and then a rather severe looking old lady detached herself from the darkness. She had a lined face and sharp features and wore a set of tweeds that might first have been in vogue during the middle of the last century. Yet her watery blue eyes fair blazed over her bifocals and she strode forward indignantly, rather as if she had discovered something deeply unpleasant deposited on the sole of her shoe. Despite her relatively small stature and rather frail looking appearance, the words that most readily came to mind were 'pocket battleship'.

'And would you and your companions *kindly* stop pointing those dreadful things at me young lady?' That withering gaze directed itself my way and rather shamefacedly I lowered my weapon without demure. It was like being bollocked by a particularly severe nun.

'A rare delight as always Miss Dandridge,' said the major. 'Now please, be nice to Sergeant Stokes and her men, Corporal Challis and Private Haines. We've travelled rather a long way to see you and experienced some very trying circumstances en route just to get here.'

'Don't attempt to flatter an old woman Seraph. I didn't receive any word, if I'd known you were coming…'

'You'd have baked a cake? There's been no communication from this facility in over a month, I was beginning to get worried.'

'Ah yes, well, it'll have been that long since those disgusting creatures overran us. I'm afraid our poor little garrison couldn't fend them off for very long.' She nodded at the bodies scattered around.

'And the archive?' said the major meaningfully.

'Naturally, the archive remains intact,' she said testily. 'That is my responsibility and one I take extremely seriously. '

'As to my silence, well the protocols are quite explicit. If overrun, batten down the hatches, stay dark and await relief. Sensible advice given the dependability of our

50

current political masters, I would have thought?'

'Indeed,' said the major. 'But perhaps we should continue this discussion, somewhere a little more private?'

'Oh very well Seraph, if we must, follow me. But please … and this is vitally important, when the lift comes to a halt, please make sure you use the mat and wipe those muddy feet, hm? Nothing worse than soldiers trailing dirt and filth around my nice clean floors.'

'We'll do our best,' said the major tipping us a covert wink.

A short while later, after Miss Dandridge had ushered us through a cleverly concealed door (which we would never have found in a million years), we entered the lift and descended what seemed like hundreds of feet into the heart of the mountain.

The lift car initially deposited us in a huge underground chamber that mixed coal-mine chic with Sixties' Bond-villain aesthetic. After we had carefully removed our filthy boots under Miss Dandridge's eagle eye, she led us a short way through the underground complex to two changing rooms where we were instructed to 'scrub yourselves clean and change into something more suitable, while I see what I can make of those rather expensive looking combat suits.'

Major Seraph shrugged, unwilling to confront this apparent force of nature on this issue at least and so Haines and I headed into the Ladies' changing room, while Seraph and Challis disappeared off into the Men's. While Haines giggled and wriggled at the unfamiliar sensations, I was soon bathing in the unaccustomed luxury of a scalding hot shower with scented soap. The hot water beat down, washing away grime and sweat and dirt and after a long and intensely pleasant dousing, we found clean towels and neatly pressed fatigues waiting for us outside.

Miss Dandridge reappeared and finger-summoned us through a series of long, rather sterile corridors until we took a final turn and came to the door which led to her private quarters. Inside was an altogether cosier affair, the cold steel and concrete replaced by wood panelling, tasteful pictures, shelves of knick knacks and trinkets. A log fire burned snugly in its hearth, lending the room a warm, red glow. On the table, a full afternoon tea had been laid out with sandwiches, scones, jam and cake piled around the circumference of an enormous tea pot. Haines' eyes boggled and she almost leapt toward the food, before my restraining hand held her back.

'No, that's quite all right, please do help yourselves, tuck in,' said Miss Dandridge. 'But remember, *manners Miss Haines*, young ladies do not scoff their food, pace yourself, please.'

Soon we had all piled our plates high and were lolling around in the delight-fully comfortable arm chairs. It was quite the high tea: Haines already had jam stains around her mouth which had spread half way up her skinny cheeks and she was being watched by Miss Dandridge who eyed her with an air of indulgent amusement. After enjoying this spectacle for a while, the old lady suddenly placed her cup and saucer on the table and then addressed the major.

'So to business Seraph, to what do I owe the somewhat dubious pleasure? What really brings you knocking on my door?'

'Oh you know, a good tea is so hard to find nowadays, so I thought I'd show the troops what an old fashioned one was made of. Splendid cake by the way.' Miss Dandridge glared at him.

'Stop pissing around Seraph. The real reason please.'

'Well, there's no buttering you up is there? Very well, I need to consult the archive. Why else?'

'And you have authorisation for such a venture? I'll need to see it please.'

'Ah, no, not exactly authorisation as such, but I did bring the price of admission,' said the major, reaching into his backpack and producing a couple of bottles of what appeared to be a very high quality Polish vodka. 'Your favourite tipple, I believe?'

'Well, you always did know how to treat a girl Seraph, I will say that for you,' said Miss Dandridge her eyes suddenly glittering avariciously, but then her lined face contracted as she frowned.

'But I can't just let you go poking about in the archive willy nilly. What would our masters think, even ones as questionable as the current shower?' Her skinny arms reached out to grasp the bottles, but the major continued to hold them just beyond her reach.

'Oh I don't think they would need to know especially Miss D. Besides, the infor-mation I'm after is ancient, obsolete, you could say it's old enough to be practically de-classified already.'

'Are you saying this isn't an officially sanctioned mission?' asked the old woman suspiciously.

'I'm not saying anything of the kind,' replied the major. 'I'm just saying that the information I need is old, practically redundant. If you must know, it relates to the Dreadnaught programme, there's just a few points in the files I would like to clarify, that's all. Hardly worth troubling anyone senior over such a trivial matter, I'd have thought?' He appeared to study the bottles' labels intently, but kept them tantalisingly just beyond the old woman's grasp. 'Besides there wouldn't be any way for you to contact them in any case, would there, what with your coms being down?' the major observed dryly.

'Dreadnaught? But that really is old hat, dates back well before the Flood. Was it even commissioned?'

'I don't believe so. none entered service, so this is just for curiosity's sake, a loose end I'd like to … tie up. But old hat indeed, as you say, so it couldn't exactly hurt to let me take a little look now, could it?' The major clinked the bottles together meaningfully and this finally seemed to tip the balance.

'Oh very well, very well,' said Miss Dandridge peevishly. 'As long as you promise me, *promise me mind* on your oath, that you'll confine yourself to Dreadnaught and not meddle with anything else while you're in there. Your solemn word mind.'

'You have it,' said the major, handing over a bottle. 'Now, while the sergeant and her men finish this excellent repast, perhaps you'll kindly do the honours and open up the vault?'

So while Miss Dandridge bustled off to attend to the major, we sat and stuffed ourselves stupid, until our seams almost burst. I don't think Haines had ever seen such rich food before and she held her stomach in mock agony and groaned, although it didn't prevent her from simultaneously wolfing down a final jam tart. Even the normally taciturn Challis leaned back and pronounced it a 'fine spread' before slumping in front of the fire and beginning to snore gently. Moments later, Haines had joined him in the land of nod. curled up in her chair, the firelight reflecting on her pale features. She began to dribble a little from the corner of her mouth.

I sipped at my tea and spread my toes before the flames, full and content. Life surely, couldn't get any better than this? I was wrong, for not long after, Miss Dandridge reappeared with a tray bearing ice, tonic and glasses.

'This takes me back, no lemon I'm afraid, not so easy to get hold of nowadays, but I'm sure we'll make do. You'll join me of course? Girls together, hm?'

'Absolutely.' I said and in a couple of moments the vodka had been opened, mixed and a tall, fizzing glass was in my hand.

'Cheers.' We clinked and the frankly delicious drink was soon burning a virtuous trail down the back of my throat, leaving behind a decidedly pleasant afterglow.

'That's the stuff,' said Miss Dandridge drinking deep. 'Warms the cockles, hm?'

'Definitely, can't remember the last time I had a proper drink.'

'Well, what's the point in fighting to save civilisation, if you can't take a moment to be civilised?' she said rhetorically and upended her glass. Before I could reply, she had swiftly set up two more.

'Bottoms up.' She took another long draught and smacked her lips. 'There's a tonic for the troops, quite literally in this case,' said Miss Dandridge, already eyeing the bottle again. Yet instead of reaching for it, she said, 'So what's really brought you here my dear, trailing along on the coat tails of the illustrious Seraph?'

'Well, he needed a hand and I suppose I had nothing better to do. It's funny, they always say 'never volunteer' but there was just something about him, something that … well convinced me I suppose, that I should come along. It was nice to feel needed for a change.'

'Oh, he can be very persuasive when he tries my dear, even if you don't quite realise it at the time. There's many a fine fellow who's followed our Mister Seraph into the cannon's jaws without quite comprehending what they've fully signed up for.'

'Including you Miss Dandridge?'

'Please, do call me Hettie. Oh I'm no soldier, not any more dear, just a humble archivist now, though there was a time…' she let the sentence trail off into the firelight.

'Besides I've no appetite for all that nonsense nowadays and it's far too messy working in the field, far too little opportunity for study and reflection. In any case, the intervening years have been rather less than kind, age has most definitely withered me and custom certainly staled my infinite variety … if I ever had any, that is.'

'Can I ask you Hettie? Why do you call him mister rather than major?'

'Oh, he picks whatever rank he pleases my dear, I can never keep track. Far easier to use the civilian honorific.'

'Have you known each other long?'

She laughed and applied further ice and tonic to another generous refill. 'Oh, only for forever and a day. He can be an awkward sod, though underneath it all I'm quite fond of him really, like one is with one's most wayward but gifted child. Don't let on though,' she tapped the side of her nose confidentially. 'I'd hate for him to think I was going soft in my old age.'

'Forgive me for asking Hettie,' I said. 'But what is Dreadnaught?'

'Ah, splendid, concern for the mission and of course your men, sign of a good leader that, but I'm sorry my dear,' she slurred slightly. 'Not for me to say. Clearance you see and you either have it or you don't, and unless I'm very much mistaken, you don't, do you?'

'Not so's you'd notice. They don't just hand it out to sergeants, especially ones from the militia.'

'Thought so. I'm afraid the illustrioush Mister Seraph will have to share it with you in his own good time. Strange, s'completely forgotten programme, obsolete, never made it past the drawing board, or so I thought.'

'So why's he so keen to look it up?'

'Can't think what he wantsh it for and honestly he probably wouldn't tell me anyway dear. I've shaid too much already probably. Operational shecurity and all that, beyond the wit of a mere archivist, no doubt. No, no, not the done thing at all.' Miss Dandridge's eyes half closed and she appeared to be dozing, but then her rather frail, liver-spotted hand snaked out and she took another long pull of her drink and came back to sudden, vivid life. 'Can tell you one thing though, if he's involved, it'll be important, always is. Critical, vital to the war effort, no doubt.'

'We certainly need it, it's hell out there and not getting any better.'

'I'd give you a pound to a penny it's something to do with that island though,' she said grimacing. 'I don't like the look of that place at all, something wicked this way comes. Mark my words, it means us no good.'

'You think so too?'

'Oh I've no doubt, that's no Lyonesse or Avalon rising out of the waters of legend to help us in our time of need. But we'll survive, we always do and we've weathered worse than this, the Kaiser, Hitler, the Americans, seen 'em all off. Not bad for an obshcure little group of islands off the coast of Europe, hm? I've no doubt the result, in the end, will be much the same.'

'And the major?'

'Oh he's a scamp, goes his own way, does his own thing and sails a bit too close to the wind if you know what I mean, always has done, always will. But if push came to shove there aren't too many I'd rather have in my corner. If he's up to something and he always is, then you can depend on him to see it through to the bitter end.

'Now, way past my bedtime so I'll bid you goodnight my dear, sleep tight. I shall shee you in the morning.' Miss Dandridge nodded, courteously refilled my glass then tottered off, taking the remainder of the bottle with her.

I awoke slowly with a dull, insistent ache knocking on the front of my skull, then, panicking at the unfamiliar surroundings, I sat up with a start and wished I hadn't. I sank back into the same armchair I had dozed off in and grimaced. It had been so long since I'd had any booze, I'd quite forgotten the unfortunate after effects. Still, apart from the persistently throbbing head, I felt well rested, if a little stiff. My sleep had rarely been as long or as deep recently, not a single thing had interrupted the dreamless oblivion I always craved, but so rarely found.

I lay still and quiet with my eyes closed, listening to Challis snore and wishing the headache would bugger off, but a pungent and insistently delicious smell began to tease my nostrils and almost involuntarily, my mouth began to water.

Shaking off my lethargy, I roused myself and followed the delightful smell and the growing sizzling sounds and discovered Miss Dandridge in a kitchen a couple of doors down, brisk and disgustingly efficient for someone who must have put away the best part of half a bottle on her own last night.

'Good morning Sergeant, though you've slept through nearly most of the day. I trust the Full English will be acceptable fare?'

'God yes, but where on earth do you get the ingredients?'

'Ah, we have *deep* freezers here, from whence came the bacon and sausages etc. As for the fresh eggs, well, there's only one place to get those. I keep a few chickens in one of the more obscure archive rooms. Persuaded the old CO, god rest him, that it was a good idea to always have fresh provender on hand, in case of emergencies.'

'Well, I won't argue with that.'

The delicious smell soon drew a blinking, yawning, scratching Challis, with Haines trailing in his wake. But Miss Dandridge dismissed my glare with a wave of her hand, bade them sit down and we were soon tucking into the heartiest of fry ups. Eventually we leaned back from the table replete, to Miss Dandridge's evident satisfaction. Haines was still mopping up bacon grease with her bread. I'm sure she'd have licked the plate clean if I'd let her.

'Ah, good morning Seraph,' Miss Dandridge hailed the major who had materialised in the kitchen doorway.

'Good morning.'

'Breakfast?'

'Just a cup of your always-delicious tea, thank you.'

'Very well,' she said pouring him one out, then rather sternly adding, 'I trust you found what you were looking for?'

'I did, a tribute to your consummate skills as an archivist. I have read long and deeply and to our great advantage.'

'Now then Seraph, desiccated old women are immune to flattery. What else are you after I wonder?'

'Nothing I assure you Miss Dandridge, nothing at all really, other than a quick word … in private if you'd be so kind. Sergeant, how soon can you be ready to move out?'

'Well, it depends sir, on the suits and how quickly they…'

'You'll find them in the locker rooms where you showered,' said Miss Dandridge. 'Clean, recharged and folded properly with the appropriate creases. I've also packed some additional supplies which you'll find in your packs. Now then Seraph, let's you and I go into my study and parley while the young people sort themselves out.'

Some twenty minutes later, a different lift had delivered us to a small chamber where an apparently featureless rock face confronted us.

While the major and Miss Dandridge conferred, we had found our suits returned as promised and so spotless that they might have been used on a dress parade. I wondered idly if Miss Dandridge had been up all night attending to them — or if perhaps she had unseen helpers?

While we changed, I attempted to earwig in on what the pair of them were discussing but could detect little, apart from muffled noises, though at one point I'm sure voices were raised and I heard the major exclaim 'It's the only way'.

Yet when they rejoined us, they seemed friendly enough as if any cross words had quickly been forgotten. Or perhaps they simply didn't want to row in front of the 'children'.

Miss Dandridge fussed over a control panel and a portion of the blank rock face which made up the wall, detached itself and swung inward. It revealed a concealed alcove which just happened to be at the exact spot behind the waterfall, where we'd begun our ascent up the chimney, almost twenty four hours ago.

Major Seraph sighed, 'You might have saved us no little time and a great deal of trouble, if you'd opened this up in the first place Miss D.'

'Well, I didn't know you were coming did I? Besides, a girl can't have you knowing all her little secrets now, can she?'

'I suppose not. Well, good bye then.'

'*Au revoir* rather,' she corrected a touch fiercely and then turned to me. 'Take care my dear, I hope to see you again and soon. Please do stop by on your way back, if...' She suddenly broke off, letting the sentence dwindle away and giving the major a most distinctive look.

Framed there in the rock door she waved us off cheerily, the other bottle which the major must have surreptitiously slipped her, only partly concealed behind her back.

Our way back from where? I wondered, but didn't have time to ask before Haines said.

'Sir, will Miss Dandridge be all right in there all on her own? What if the Devils come back?'

'Oh well, even if by some remote chance they did, then managed to cross to the observatory, find their way to the secret lift and penetrate to the very archive itself — then it'd be them that I feel sorry for, not Miss Dandridge. She's more than capable of taking care of herself, has done for years. You needn't worry about her, she'll still be around when this mountain is worn down to a hillock.'

CHAPTER SIX

Bondage

W E MADE OUR WAY through the shrouds of dusk to find the *Saucy Sally* exactly
where we had left her, concealed beneath camouflaged branches. It scarcely
seemed possible a whole night and day had passed since we had begun our journey
up to the observatory and the hidden archive beneath it, but now the gloaming of
another dusk lit the sky, as the cloud-cloaked sun prepared to retreat over the horizon.

We had scouted the area carefully before emerging from the chimney's sheltering
rocks, but there were no signs of Devils anywhere. Perhaps the major's pyrotechnics
had scared them off? I doubted it, it was more likely the survivors had simply retreated
to gather reinforcements and would be back soon and in greater force. I didn't doubt
the major's confidence in Miss Dandridge though. For all her apparently advanced
age and frail demeanour, there was a seam of steel that ran through that old bird, a
vodka-fuelled one possibly, but I had no doubt she would still be there, tending that
archive, long after we were all dust.

So we cast off and with the major at the helm, threaded our way through the
mountain gorges, aided by the stiff current which hurled us giddily through sections
of white water, until the steep mountain sides began to flatten out into the gentler
slopes of hillier land. Eventually we rejoined the intersection with the main branch of
the river, and I was not sorry to quit that mountainous land, for it was a bleak, wild
place and I was glad it was now behind us.

However, as we swung around a bend of the main watercourse, the land dipped
again and now we could see straight out to sea. In the far distance loomed the island
dominating the surrounding waters. It seemed to have grown larger in our absence,
swollen and bloated and lit up against the encroaching darkness. Mist and fog banks

curled around its rocky mass, hinting at strange alien geometries, imbuing it with a loathsome life. Weird flashes of green and blue light arced up into the sky above it, a portentous display of atmospheric pyrotechnics. Great waves emanated from its rocky shores, turning the surrounding seas foam capped and white, as they seethed and bubbled. Even from this distance, you could feel that strange all-pervading low frequency hum it exuded. Despite myself, I suppressed the shiver which had crept unbidden up my spine.

'Impressive, isn't it?' said the major. 'A certain unholy magnificence if you look at it from the right angle.' I couldn't tell whether he expected an answer or not, but I supplied one anyway.

'And what angle is that?'

'Ah, quite so, there is no right angle, yet it is has a certain horrible fascination for those who study such things.'

'And what do your studies reveal, Major?'

'Nothing conclusive as of yet, though even a layman's — or rather a layperson's eyes — must see its malign influence is spreading. Tell me, what do you make of it?'

'Well I'm no expert, but if I had to hazard a guess? Trouble. They control the seas and coastline, we're clinging onto the higher ground — a rather uneasy stalemate which has probably gone on too long as far as they are concerned. If I was them, my next move? Establish a forward base, a bridgehead from their world to ours, somewhere to launch the next phase of their invasion.'

'A convincing hypothesis Sergeant,' said the major. 'What it lacks in mystical analysis, it makes up for in cold hard pragmatism. It would seem you apprehend a deal more than our so-called masters' tacticians and forward planners.' And with that he returned to his own quiet, contemplation of the distant phenomena.

We chugged along in silence for a while, making slow progress for the major steered us close to the bank, taking advantage of whatever natural cover he could and keeping the engine on its lowest and stealthiest setting.

We ran silent in the closing darkness and our journey took on an otherworldly quality under the baleful gaze of that place. Under its spell, strange thoughts and fancies seized the mind and lingered and were not easily dismissed. For a while it seemed to me as if the island itself were watching us, like some vast, antagonistic organism, a floating consciousness, which monitored our progress with contempt for the painfully insignificant species which crept along at the very fringes of its perception. The barren landscape also took on a hostile, unearthly quality and in the villages and abandoned hamlets I seemed to see the ghostly outlines of Devils plundering, raiding and killing.

'Sergeant.'

Overhead, the stars span and whirled in bizarre, unfamiliar patterns careering across the velvet heavens, but these were alien skies, unfamiliar suns, at once cold and boiling, white hot and blue-frozen, uncaring and callously indifferent to the destinies of those they looked down on below.

'Sergeant?'

They seemed to exert a dread influence like a palpable energy, a crushing pressure, heedless of our concerns, indifferent to our lives, no respecters of age or gender, a great malign force, a crusher of souls, dooming us to an existence of servitude and death…

'Sergeant Stokes!' I felt something shaking my arm and then I was back in the boat, dazed and blinking. The major had a look of concern on his face.

'Apologies Sergeant, careless of me. I had quite forgotten that thing's capacity to overwhelm an unprotected mind. Here, this should help.'

He looped something over my head and hands still shaking, I held up the object to examine it. It was a small, round, silver pendant with three interconnected spirals which seemed to glow faintly in the dark, like those old novelty watches. Challis and Haines were already sporting identical companions.

'A triskelion,' the major said. 'An ancient ward against dark powers, you should start feeling better … well … any moment now really.'

He was right, for all at once those macabre images seemed to be dispelled, banished like gossamer in the sunlight and my mind was clear, sharp and my own again.

'What the fuck? What just happened?'

'The island appears to be getting stronger, growing in power, its malign influence spreading even further, though I'm surprised it has reached this far, this quickly.' He smiled at Haines who was clutching hers protectively. Challis nodded.

'I don't see you wearing one major?' I said.

'Thanks for your concern, but there's really no need. I have a certain, how can I put this … natural resistance to such blandishments. Now if we're all feeling restored?' A round of nods. 'I think we should swiftly move along.'

So we continued our progress in silence and while the island drew closer with every moment and loomed larger in both sound and vision, it no longer held the same dominion that it had exerted before. Whether those triskelion symbols contained an actual enchantment or perhaps it was the major's mere suggestion of one which reinforced our own will and determination, but from that moment on, my mind and my thoughts, dark though they may have been, remained very much my own.

The *Sally* slipped through the head waters and we threaded our way down the river, darting from bank to bank, bobbing from cover to cover, weaving a contrary course all of the major's own choosing. We had to put our trust in his steersmanship for none of us could have negotiated those wild eddies and currents, the many vagaries and twists of the waters, with his skill and determination.

Naturally I ordered everyone to keep alert, eyes wide, sweeping the banks for any sign of activity but in that strange moonlight, the landscape now took on a surreal quality as if we were journeying through some ethereal realm, sterile and cleansed of life.

But always on the horizon, the island, like some sinister pilot star. Despite our new found protection and a determination not to gaze on its unholy form, it still preyed on the mind, even when you weren't looking directly at it, like a distant itch you're unable to scratch.

Yet the mind is a curious and contrary thing, on one level able to focus on immediate danger while below the surface it churns and processes myriad detail. We had survived the episode at the observatory, by the skin of our teeth no doubt, but we had done so like proper soldiers and that was no small source of pride.

But what next? The major had clearly unearthed something of interest rootling around in that archive. But what was Dreadnaught and what did he intend to do with it? Miss Dandridge had said 'It'll be important, always is. Critical, vital to the war effort no doubt'. For the major maybe, but how could we three possibly help?

Where indeed were we even heading now?

'Sergeant.' I was pulled from my speculations, back to the present by the major's urgent command.

'Sir?'

'Trouble ahead. Heads down now and not a peep.'

'I don't see…'

'They're there, don't worry.'

The major steered the *Sally* towards the shore and the protective shelter of a cluster of willows, their long drooping branches parting to enfold us. He cut the engine and allowed us to drift in until we nestled against the bank.

'I still don't see anything, sir.' I whispered over the com.

'Patience Sergeant.'

We waited, long tense seconds turned into long tense minutes. Just as I was on the point of wondering what had spooked him, I began to hear it too: a regular insistent boom breaking the silence, the beat of a distant drum, but one that was drawing ever closer.

Their scouts appeared first, a small advanced guard of Devils lightly armed with tridents and nets, sweeping along the bank of the far shore, lurching and skittering in that disjointed way they have when they want to move quickly on land.

The beat grew louder and then the main body of the column began to emerge, washed by beacons of torchlight. At first it was difficult to believe the evidence of one's own eyes, but the visor helped, zooming and enhancing the image and then, then, there could be no doubt.

It revealed a long, winding ribbon of profound despair, captive humans, almost exclusively women and female children chained together like animals, shuffling along in their hobbles, while the accompanying escort employed whips made of twisted strands of kelp to goad their plainly terrified captives. A massive bull of a chieftain oversaw this long chain of woe, stalking along the line emitting crude burps and keenings, while two braves beat out the relentless pulse of the march on a drum head which looked like it was made from human skin.

It was a profound, almost unreal spectacle, but the most horrifying thing of all was that interspersed amongst the braves, there were unbound human figures assisting those Devils carrying torches which burned and crackled, poking, chiding and mocking the captives, playing a full part in this loathsome spectacle. The whole sorry slave train was heading toward the distant shore, and ultimately toward the island.

There were rumours of course, rumours of human collaborators, but there were always rumours in war and I had never seriously believed that there would be any who would betray their own kind this way. I felt bile rise in the back of my throat.

'Those are not our kind,' whispered the major, answering my unspoken thought in that unsettling way he had. 'Look closer.'

Through the swaying fronds of the willow, I zoomed in closer on the unchained humans, noting the uniformity of their narrow heads and flat, smooth, almost featureless faces. They had unusually pallid skins and a strange cast around the eyes, that seemed to have more in common with the Devils rather than their captives. Hybrids, Innsmouths as some had dubbed them, the long rumoured half-human half-Devil spawn, offspring of an unholy cross-species mating.

'Fuckers,' whispered Challis softly, raising his weapon as I did mine. 'Dirty collaborating hybrid traitor scum...'

'Stand down Corporal! You too Sergeant!' hissed the major.

'But sir...'

'There's nothing we can do for them now, *nothing*. Stand down, *now*, I mean it.' His eyes blazed furiously and his command brooked no argument but beneath the surface anger, there was an undercurrent of pity. He too felt the horror of that despicable sight, but had managed to master himself with an iron-hard self-discipline that belied his fey appearance.

Reluctantly, we lowered our weapons.

Still furious, I watched those things, Devil and hybrid whipping that chain gang onwards to whatever foul fate awaited them

'I understand your anger,' said the major quietly and his voice sounded hollow, disconnected. 'I share it, but if we intervened now, we compromise this mission and I can't allow that. Even if we were to prevail and that's by no means certain, we'd stir up many more, bring them down on our heads and condemn thousands more to the same fate — or even worse.'

'And what exactly is that fate, sir?' I asked bitterly, wanting him to say it.

'A slave line, made up of women and children, corralled by hybrids? I don't think you really need me to fill in the blanks do you Stokes?' said the major wearily.

We watched the line pass silently from our hiding place, feeling impotent and worthless. Beneath the visor, the salt of my tears had grown dried and crusted, long before we had seen its end.

The wee small hours of the morning found us back at the estuary, where the fresh water of the river mingled with the bitter salt of the ocean. The major turned the tiller so that we headed out into the open water now and paralleled the coastline, the island slinking away to our left, occupying our peripheral vision rather than our main eye line. It was no small relief not to have to look at that accursed place directly and wherever we were headed, I was glad we were no longer on a collision course with it.

The horrors of the slave line and my inability to do anything about it still lingered, preying on my mind. Yet the bracing sweep of the winds slowly began to blow it away, though I knew the revenant would continue to haunt me. If ever I was tempted to show Devil or hybrid even a shred of mercy, that memory would sustain me: they deserved none.

Scattered islets dotted the waters of this shallow archipelago, the last high-lying remnants of dry land before the rising waters had claimed this last frontier of old Wales. We threaded our way through that bleak chain of island fragments, still partly hidden from the direct gaze of the island, which glowered at us when it could from across the intervening wastes.

We steered on a slow, steady heading, navigating the swells and breakers which rolled against these long forgotten shores which had probably not seen a free human face in years. Here and there the remains of that old pre-Flood life broke through the surface, the rusted, decaying spars of a pier poking up through the waters, its gaudy funfair attractions bleached white, like ancient bones, by the intervening years. Near to where the original shoreline must have once stood, the upper floor of a hotel held its nose just above the waves, its rotted roof collapsed in on itself. A sign that must have originally spelled 'The Grand' was reduced to the outline of a mere handful of letters.

The wind started to blow up, carrying the shrill cries of gulls as they whirled and dived for fish and as if to reinforce the gloom, great sheets of rain suddenly began to erupt from the skies, splashing the *Sally's* thwarts, pattering against our waterproof suits.

'Heavy weather on the way, sir,' shouted Challis pointing at the squall which had suddenly blown up. It overtook us quickly, the wind fierce, salt water breaking over the gunwales to slosh around the bottom boards.

'Noted!' bawled the major, as he wrestled with the tiller and I hailed Haines over the rising wind to start bailing out, which she attempted to do by upending her helmet and turfing the accumulated water overboard. Full marks for improvisation, though her efforts were like trying to put out an inferno with a snowball.

Now flashes of lightning began to streak across the night sky and the waves scaled accordingly, sending us bucking up and then tearing down their steep peaks and troughs. The driving rain stung and flayed our faces and the major ordered us to batten down the hatches, visor up and cling on for all we were worth. Amidst a welter of squawks, the gulls suddenly wheeled, turning tail and began to flee inland, heading for the safety of the shore. The major's eyes narrowed.

'This is no natural squall, something's got it in for us and no prizes for guessing what! Hold on, hold on for your lives!'

The *Sally* pitched and yawed crazily and we struggled to stay onboard, while the major steered a precarious course, keeping the *Sally's* bow pointed into the suddenly vertiginous foam-capped breakers. We climbed and plummeted maniacally and in between the sickening lurching motion, I kept catching glimpses of that horrible isle which seethed at us from across the waters.

Now the concentrated malevolence of that dread place was directed fully upon us and it really did take on the aspect of a sentient thing, a bloated, ancient consciousness hurling all its ire and malice at our paltry, unprotected souls.

Whirlpools began to form off the bow, churning up the water, gaping like throats, leading down to the ocean floor and they churned and boiled, threatening to swallow us whole, dragging us down into the depths and our doom. The major wrestled the floundering, bucking *Sally*, her advanced technology helpless against the elemental power of the angry ocean.

Above, great spinning water spouts reached up to the storm-lashed skies, vortices tearing and rending, the wind stinging like a wire whip. The noise was tremendous, like nothing I had heard before or since, as great walls of water loomed over us and came crashing down, threatening to capsize us at every moment.

Yet somehow, instinctively, inexplicably, the major managed to keep us alive, fighting for every inch of precious headway as he guided us, skimming and tacking around the whirlpools' gaping maws.

It was as if the sea itself had become fury, but the major gunned the engine again and it wailed and protested, but turned, groaning, slowly, oh so slowly, toward the shore.

Lumbering like a barge, the lithe hull of the *Sally* twisted and bucked as we skated between two enormous whirlpools and were spat out the other side. I thought we must be nearly safe, or nearly dead, since there didn't seem too much to choose between the two.

Then something smashed against the side of the boat, sending us whirling so that I couldn't tell left from right or up from down. Wallowing, the *Sally* righted herself and I could see the distant shore again and now, surely, we had passed beyond the diabolical reach of that thing?

I heard the major shout 'Brace yourselves! Brace! Brace!' and I grabbed a gunwale, flattening myself against it and that's when I saw the great grey-green wall of water towering over the bow. It seemed to fill every inch of the sky, like that wave from long ago and my mouth tried to form inarticulate words, as if they could protect us from its malice.

I saw the major's arms extend to meet it and they glowed with a force of light, a fragile, shimmering penumbra formed above us beneath the great mass of the wave. I just closed my eyes, not daring to look and then the water broke over us with a force that was indescribable. I remember the green-grey darkness, the bitter taste of salt filling my lungs and I can remember thinking perhaps drowning was not such a bad way to die — then nothing more.

CHAPTER SEVEN
Stranger Shores

CONSCIOUSNESS CAME SLOWLY, wavelets lapping damply against my cheek and the churn of the shingle sounded like the workings of a giant hour glass inside my head. Everything hurt, it was just a question of how much and what took priority. Head, it was most definitely head, which felt as if it had been hung from the pendulum of Big Ben in old lost London. I opened salt-crusted eyes and blinked groggily into the early morning half-light, wishing I hadn't. Haines was stretched out unmoving a few feet away, while beyond her, Challis was energetically hacking up gobbets of sea water.

'Ah Sergeant, you are alive after all. Good. Feeling any better?' The major's voice enquired politely.

'Not really.' I said spitting out a quarter mouthful of sand and dribble.

'Pity,' said the major, 'but no time for dilly-dallying I'm afraid, we've got to get moving.'

I tried to lever myself up from the cloying sand, but my arms appeared to have lost all strength and simply wouldn't support me. Groaning, I sank back, face down.

'Here, let me lend you a hand.' The major's fingers grazed my temple and although I recoiled, startled by the touch of his flesh, what followed was a pleasant, cooling sensation. In a matter of moments, my head had cleared, my eyes refocused and even the aches which had shot through my body seemed to recede. In a few moments more, I managed to stand, a little unsteadily it must be said and swaying groggily, surveyed my surroundings

While I got my bearings, the major was already at Haines' side, his hand upon her brow and a light seemed to suffuse her grubby, elfin features. She gave a great heaving sigh and sat bolt upright, looking bewildered. Challis was already on his feet, shaking

66

himself down and checking his weapon, though whether he'd needed the major's assistance I couldn't say.

We had washed up on a long, almost featureless expanse of shingle-strewn beach which stretched off into the distance beneath the leaden skies of a granite-grey early morning. Nearby, the solitary rusting corpse of a Challenger 2 main battle tank lay pitched on its side, the only landmark on this bleak shore. This mighty piece of armour had once ruled the battlefields of men but its outer steel and ceramic shell had been no match for the creatures' sorcery. The turret had been virtually melted in two, exposing charred innards and its 120mm main gun lay snapped and broken, impotently resting across the remains of its body.

The sea remained stormy and unsettled, but the island was hidden amongst the veiled shapes of the archipelago. Beyond the shoreline, small, steep cliffs led up to a dense, shadowy expanse of woodland.

'How in hell did we survive that giant wave?' I asked shakily. 'I thought that was the end of us.'

'Sheer luck,' said the major. 'Or maybe you're tougher than you look, which I must say I've always rather suspected. I'm afraid our gallant little *Sally* wasn't quite so fortunate.' He indicated the remains of our craft which had been rent from bow to stern and was now just so much high tech matchwood.

'How long have I been out?'

'Not long, but we must get moving immediately. That thing,' he waved out to sea, 'was behind that attack or I'm a Dutchman … and the creatures won't be far behind, looking for survivors. We need to get going, right now, are you all fit and ready?' Nods all around, although the sickly greenish tinge was still in the process of draining from Haines' face.

'Right, come on then, let's find a way up those rocks and head for the shelter of the woods. We should be relatively safe in there. After that, we'll get our bearings, take stock and plot our next move.'

With that, the major was off, loping up the slopes as if he hadn't a care in the world and was taking an agreeable stroll somewhere far flung and tropical. Haines followed blithely in his wake, but I lingered for a word in my corporal's shell-like.

'Luck my arse,' said Challis, as we peeled ourselves off the beach and began to climb up the rocky heights. 'That wave should have finished us. If it hadn't been for … well whatever the hell he did with that light, we'd most definitely be food for the crabs now.'

'Light?' I said, half-remembering, as Challis continued, sounding the closest he ever came to impressed.

'Weirdest thing I've ever seen. He extended his arms and next thing I know it was like we were encased in a sphere of light, 'bout the only thing that saved us from being smashed to pieces. Guess all that talk about the White Witchman's magic wasn't just talk after all.'

'I guess not,' I said as my memory began to restore itself and I half recalled that glowing protective penumbra.

'Wonder what he has in store for us next?' grunted Challis.

'What indeed?' I wondered and the question was directed as much at myself as my taciturn corporal.

We had vacated the beach not a moment too soon and I scampered up the last few yards, sending small rocks skittering before Challis lent a hand and hauled me up and over the edge. I flattened and watched three long lines of Devils emerge from the surging surf. Not much doubt it was us they were after either, for a pair of fugly looking chieftains and a shaman hopped straight over to the remains of the *Sally* and bent over it, clicking and cheeping, while their braves spread out to search the shore. Our tracks led up to the edge of the cliff, but then became lost on the sheer rock surface. However it wouldn't take the Devils too long to figure out where we had climbed up and they'd soon be on our trail again.

'Okay if I leave them a little parting gift?' enquired Challis.

'Rude not to,' I said, 'after all the trouble that thing went to, to speed *us* on our way.' A nod from me and he was quickly deploying micro-charges and rigging a trip wire. I went to join the major who had perched up by the tree line. Haines was by his side, sighting down the length of her weapon.

'Want me to take out those chieftains, Sergeant?' she hissed, suddenly all piss and vinegar. 'I can, either one, or both, or just the shaman, or all three, take your pick.'

'Easy tiger, Challis is preparing a little present for them down there by the cliff top, so don't go springing it prematurely. Let's maintain the element of surprise.'

The major nodded his approval. 'Very important, half the battle sometimes. Stand down for now Haines, though of course, the sentiment is thoroughly appreciated.'

'Yes sir,' she said, obviously a little disappointed. The blood lust slowly receded from her face, until she was just a normal teenager again. 'But I owe them for wrecking the *Sally* and I *will* pay them back,' she said determinedly.

'That's the spirit Haines and don't worry, you'll get your chance. Now Sergeant, once the corporal's finished, let's head inland and lose ourselves under the trees. The creatures won't be able to track us so easily in there and we can throw them off the scent with any luck.'

'Well, we won't be able to count on the suits to evade them,' I said, 'the batteries seem almost dead after that dousing. I'd have thought they'd have made these things waterproof?'

'They do, but being in the vicinity of any supernatural force or active magic drains them too. Well, we'll just have to keep our wits about us and make sure we cover our trail.'

'And after that, sir?'

'After that, I suggest we lay up somewhere and secure ourselves a spot of breakfast. I'm rather peckish after this morning's exertions and you must be positively starving.'

Three hours later and we had left the wreck of the *Sally* far behind and found ourselves marching along beneath a welcoming canopy of spreading branches. This forest was old and ancient, smelling of earth and loam, densely packed with mature trees, and interspersed with deep patches of ferns and undergrowth. It had been easy to fold ourselves straight in and vanish into its green and gold foliage, 'wrapping ourselves in the skirts of the earth goddess' as the major had rather quaintly put it.

We had scarcely got underway when a large and rather gratifying explosion signalled that the Devils had discovered Challis' parting gift. Even under the shadows of the canopy, the rising column of smoky aftermath was visible from afar. 'That should give them pause for thought at least,' said the major and soon, following his instructions, we had criss-crossed, doubled back and concealed our trail so thoroughly that with any luck, any pursuing Devils would take hours to pick it up again — if any had survived Challis' surprise that is.

By mid morning a weak sun had emerged through the surrounding grey, patches of dappled light broke through onto the forest floor and we might have been strolling through some sylvan idyll and a million miles away from danger. The Devils and all their unholy depravations seemed far far behind us and the major evidently believed so too, for he leapt up onto a fallen tree and seemed to take the air, scenting it like a foxhound. Apparently satisfied, he hopped back down and said, 'This will do nicely. They appear to have given up the chase, so, at ease and make yourselves comfortable. I don't know about you but I could murder a cup of tea. We should probably take stock of what food supplies we have left too.' He slipped off his backpack and upended it and we all did likewise, sending ration packs and foil containers tumbling onto the forest floor.

'Hm, a reasonable enough cache, but hardly the breakfast of champions, hm?' said the major.

'We've had worse, much worse, in our time, sir.'

'A young artillery officer of my acquaintance once observed that "an army marches on its stomach."'

'He never commanded the militia I take it?'

'No, I don't believe he ever did, but the point remains valid. Now Corporal Challis, you strike me as a man who knows how to live off the land?'

'Sir.'

'Well, I've a feeling if you head over that way, you might very well find some rather appetising wild game. Be a good fellow and bring it down without making too much noise, hm?'

'Sir.' Challis nodded and shouldered his rifle.

'Oh and take Haines with you,' said the major. 'I'm sure she could learn a thing or two from an old hand?'

Challis looked less than thrilled at that prospect, but waved a hand for Haines to accompany him and as he stalked off, she followed with puppyish enthusiasm.

'Now, let's see about that tea,' said Major Seraph, quickly gathering twigs and kindling and arranging them into a neat stack. He produced an object which unfolded into a large Billy can and moments later the fire was lit, water added and a proper brew was on the go.

'Only powdered milk I'm afraid, but there's sugar, chocolate and ah, even some cigarettes too. Please do help yourself.'

'You certainly know the way to a girl's heart, major.' I took a smoke and breathed in a couple of delicious lungfuls, while, in extremely short order, he produced two steaming mugs of the requisite. I sipped the strong, sweet, expertly brewed tea and smoked some more, well satisfied. It had been a long while since I'd tasted such luxury out in the field and unbidden, a small tear formed in the corner of my eye. I looked away.

'The simple pleasures, hm? I often think that while we're still capable of making a decent cup of tea, there's hope that civilisation might not entirely be lost.'

'Permission to speak freely, sir?'

'You don't need my permission Stokes, please ask away.'

'When we were out at sea, what exactly happened back there? The island seemed as if it were hell bent on destroying us, like it was alive, a living thing.'

'Not a bad summation.'

'But how is that even possible? An island? Alive?'

'These are strange days and the Devils are an old and particularly strange race, steeped in millennia of arcane sorcery. Before the Flood we were complacent, squabbling amongst ourselves, blind to the many warning signs, but at least we still had teeth back then and they had cause to fear us. Now the old rules no longer apply and entities like that island can manifest themselves unhindered, without fear of retaliation.'

'But what is it exactly?'

'I'm still not entirely sure of its true nature yet, though I have my suspicions. You were partly right when you said it was a bridge from their world to ours, and it's certainly that, but a product of their sorcery, a breeding ground for their unholy experiments, a physical incarnation of their dark god's dreaming? It could be any of those things, or perhaps, all of them. Yet that little display of petulance on the open water was instructive. It starts to perceive us, our mission, as a direct threat to it and the more it shows its power, the more it reveals its true purpose.'

'Which is?'

'A locus, a focal point for whatever dark design is coming next. I can't say for sure, but I think you were on the right track when you said it was a staging post, a preliminary base camp for a wider invasion. What I can tell you is that it's getting bigger, growing, expanding its influence. It's already larger than when it first appeared. As for being alive? Well perhaps not in the strictest sense, but it would appear to display a degree of sentience certainly.'

'Shit. That doesn't sound good.'

'No, but we have other equally pressing concerns to ponder. Consider this mission, it has been dogged by misfortune at almost every step. The marines: ambushed in the middle of nowhere. Coincidence? Possibly, but I don't trust coincidences and don't much believe in them. Furthermore, why were there so many Devils waiting for us at the observatory? It is almost as if they knew we were coming. I'm able to keep a very low profile in the normal scheme of things, even without these clever suits, but this reeks of something more than just simple chance.'

'What? Who could do such a thing? Why would anyone want to sabotage our mission? Aren't we all supposed to be in this together?'

'Why indeed? Yet I think you already know the answer, you've seen it, witnessed it at first hand, helping herd along that slave line. Not all hybrids are as readily identifiable as the ones we saw.

'No-one outside of the highest levels was supposed to know about my mission. However, I've no doubt now it was a set up, meant to fail and I'm supposed to be currently occupying a position face down, lying in a ditch with the unfortunate captain and her men. Perhaps that was the … If only I hadn't left them to… ' His voice tailed off, as if he were pondering something deep and impenetrable. But when he hadn't spoken for a while, I prompted him again.

'So what now? Where do we go from here?'

'The parameters have changed radically, this no longer a simple reconnaissance operation to reconnoitre and determine its intentions. That thing needs to be stopped and I think I've got a pretty good idea of how to go about it.'

'Dreadnaught?'

'Ah Miss D, delightful old soul, but a touch indiscreet when liberally plied with the sauce. Yes Dreadnaught indeed, the answer's there if we can find it...'

'What is Dreadnaught, sir?'

'I ... actually, perhaps we should postpone that particular discussion for another time. Now, please don't react in any discernable way when I tell you this, but I believe we're being watched.'

It took every ounce of my self control not to snatch up my weapon, but I took another soothing drag of my smoke and sipped quietly at my tea. 'Who? Where?'

'About fifty yards to your left. Human ... not one of ours.' I flicked the butt and casually ground it into the loam, breathing out the last lungful of the smoke.

I could see him now too, in my peripheral vision, an indistinct figure observing us from around the trunk of a distant tree.

'A feral,' I said, 'let me take a furtive shufti.'

'Yes, I believe he is. Cautiously though Sergeant, he's just watching ... for now.'

I yawned expansively, casually flicking down my visor and taking a peek out of the corner of my eye, at where the distant figure lurked.

'Threat, sir?'

'I don't believe so, he seems harmless, mostly anyway. I don't perceive anything particularly ... hostile, though I'm sensing something ... fear, curiosity and greed, yes greed, He wants something, wants something so badly that it's overcoming his natural timidity ... ah, and there it is. Of course. Would you mind lighting up another cigarette?'

I raised my the visor, tapped the pack, extracted another and applied the match.

'Waft a little over his way, if you'd be so kind.' I exhaled, letting the smoke spiral and coil toward our visitor.

'Done.'

'Now, don't do anything to startle him, just let him come to us.'

We continued to talk in low voices as the figure drew closer, edging from tree to tree, reluctant but still captivated by us apparently. Now he hovered on the very periphery of our improvised camp, eyes watching us intently, torn between cupidity and coyness.

Now we'd succeeded in reeling him in, the major casually turned and invited him into our little tea party as if it was the most natural thing in the world.

'Ah, hello there, do come join us. No need to be shy, would you like a cup of tea?'

'Tea? Tea? Tea? Where'd you get that then? Ben haven't had a cuppa in years.'

'We've plenty to spare, if you'd like some?'

'Couldn't, mustn't, shan't.' His fingers gripped the bark and he seemed on the point of bounding away.

'Perhaps a cigarette then?' said the major and the creature's rheumy old eyes lit up.

'Fags? Fags? Fags? Ain't had a smoke in donkey's. Shouldn't, bad for you, everyone knows.'

'But oh so delicious too,' I said, smiling and exhaling a nicotinous blue cloud his way. His nose wrinkled in a strange mixture of revulsion and delight and he hovered for a moment, torn between avarice and flight.

'Here, take one.' I offered the pack and that seemed to tilt the balance and he scurried into the clearing, hopping from one foot to the other as he waited for the light. He took a long lingering drag and then tilted his head back, exhaling into the canopy above.

'Gargh, that's the stuff.'

Our 'guest' was a rather peculiar specimen. He was old and grubby, clad in a covering of crude evil-smelling furs which he'd evidently sewn together himself with rude stitching. A small collection of rusty bread knives was thrust through an improvised string belt and he clutched a primitive, though no doubt effective, bow in one hand.

Underneath this startling collection of *haute couture,* he was so gaunt and rangy that it looked like a combination of cat gut and gristle was all that was holding him together. Long, rank hair which may once have been white but was now streaked with filth spilled from underneath a squirrel skin hat, gimlet eyes peered out from beneath a sprawling monobrow.

He grasped the cigarette in the crook of a claw-like appendage that might have once been a hand, and both eyes and voice carried more than a requisite portion of crazy. He did a little dance and breathed the smoke in greedily, burning through a significant portion of the cigarette with each dank inhalation.

'Good I'm glad to see you are enjoying that. I'm Major Seraph and this is Sergeant Stokes. What's your name?'

'S'Ben, Old Ben, some call me Odd Ben ... Weird Ben ... Pervy Ben.'

'Well, nice to meet you Ben,' said the major politely.

'See you got a girl. Don't see 'em too often an' all. 'ow much? Got game to trade, rabbits, squirrel, nice juicy mole, delishus! 'ow much? Just one go, won't take me long...' His rheumy eyes switched from the cigarette and leered suggestively at me. Without further ceremony, he slipped a hand inside the furs in the vicinity of his groin and began to rub himself vigorously.

Disconcerted, I reached for my FS knife intending to deter him with some none-too-gentle dissuasion, but a look from the major made me pause. The major configured his fingers in a peculiar gesture and whispering under his breath, intoned a phrase that human vocal chords didn't really seem made for. The effect was immediate and evidently rather severe.

'Ow, ow, ow! Bloody hell! Me nut sack is on fire!' howled the old degenerate, hopping and screeching. 'Make it stop! Make it stop!'

'Very well,' said the major. 'But only if you promise to behave yourself?'

'Promise, *promise!*' The creature pleaded piteously.

'Very well.' The major uncrossed his fingers and Pervy Ben's torment ceased, leaving him bent double and rocking on his haunches.

'Now Ben, I have a few questions which you will answer for me...' The creature stopped his sobbing for a moment and looked up, seeming ready to spit rage and defiance. The major simply raised his fingers again and the old wretch subsided, cowed.

'Always the same, you buggers from the great iron fish, bullying Ben, luring him in with promises, hurting him, no good reason f'rit.'

'Intriguing, you think we're from the 'great iron fish' then?'

'Bound to be innit, with your girl and guns and those fancy suits. Where else would you be from, 'round these parts?'

'Tell me what you know about the great iron fish.'

'Can't, promised not to, made me swear didn't they, didn't you? More 'n my life's worth if I breathe a word ... you're just trying to trick Old Ben.'

The major raised his fingers again and the old giffer hurriedly began spill his guts.

'But can't do no 'arm, seeing as you're from its belly too, right? So I seens it ain't I? Ploughing along on top of the waves, always at night, always in the dark. You lot think no 'un notices, but Ben does, sees it all, sees all sorts that don't belong in the world: fish men on the beach, the wild uns in the woods and the king in his castle. And now the island, the terrible singing island, that takes men's bodies, families, souls 'n all.' Genuine tears began to suffuse his eyes

'Interesting,' observed the major his eyes narrowing, which plainly terrified the old man.

'Told you all I know, promised you wouldn't hurt me. Promised!'

'Relax,' said the major calmly. 'Now Ben, you and I are going to have a nice little *tête-à-tête* and once we're done, you'll be free to go on your way, no harm done. We'll send you off with some nice treats too, load you up with tea, food, even some cigarettes ... everything you need, everything you desire.'

He placed a hand around the old man's bowed shoulders, gently raised him up and sat him down on the trunk beside me.

'Now relax, this won't hurt, not even a little bit.' The major closed his eyes and placed a hand on either side of — but not quite touching — the old lecher's temples. There was a singular moment when a strange stillness seemed to spread throughout the forest.

'Not the brain pan! Not me brain pan guvnor, I begs ya! I can't spare any more brain cells...' Old Ben plainly terrified, tried to pull away, but was held there firmly, gripped by some unseen force. When the major opened his eyes they were opaque, without pupils, like they had rolled back up inside his head. Instead, witch fire burned in the sockets and his long pale hair stood up on end, writhing like it was alive. The white fire coursed along the tips of his fingers enveloping Ben's head, and the old man gave a long rasping shudder, convulsing.

The major's eldritch gaze bored into the old man's brain and he held him there for a long timeless space, seeming to suck him dry and then the old man's body slumped, sagging and the major laid him down gently, inert on the sward. Gradually the witch fire subsided, crackling and fizzing and then the major's pupils returned and he was himself again. You struggle for something to say when you see weird shit like that performed. The best I could manage was,

'Fuck me, that was intense.'

'Quite so, peering into another mind is a delicate — not to say risky — pursuit at the best of times and in this case, a none too pleasant one either. Ben's brain pan is not the most salubrious of minds to go rummaging around in, even temporarily. Yet it was instructive Sergeant, highly instructive.'

'Care to share?'

'For the moment I must decline. I should take a short while to consider what I've learned and how best we might use it, but it's promising, I will say that, highly promising.' Sweating and even paler than normal, the major stood, somewhat shakily.

'I believe I have taken everything I need from this old degenerate. When he wakes, give him what I promised. I think I need to take a little stroll to clear my head.'

'Yes sir.'

'And Sergeant.'

'Sir?'

'Not a word to others, for now.'

'Yes sir.'

CHAPTER EIGHT

Sons of the Dragon

O UR HUNTING PARTY RETURNED a short while later with a small muntjac deer slung over Challis' broad shoulders. Haines was as excited as a kid on Christmas morning. Funny how we never celebrate that kind of thing anymore isn't it? When did we lose that particular urge I wonder? Probably about the same time calendars and diaries became irrelevant. When your day largely consists of: trudge, hide, forage, fight, survive, there's little reason to keep track of the passage of days. Chances are you may not be around to mark off many more.

This rather gloomy train of thought was interrupted by Haines bouncing into the clearing like a hyperactive toddler, proudly proclaiming how she had stalked and hunted the creature almost solo, 'with just the tiniest bit of help from the corporal'. His raised eyebrow told a slightly different story, though as she rushed through her tale, he seemed content to let her take the laurels.

However when Challis began to butcher the deer, sliding his knife up along its belly to spill its entrails and clean out the lights, Haines gave a couple of dry heaves before retreating to watch, horribly fascinated, from a safe distance. Guess she had a little way to go before she becoming a fully fledged woodswoman.

'Fresh meat girl,' said Challis. 'This'll keep you going. Come here, you should learn how to cut it up, expert hunters need to know that kind of thing.' But Haines wrinkled a sceptical nose and moved not a single inch from her position as Challis' expert hands made short work of the carcass. Soon he had butchered it neatly and was cooking several smaller joints over the fire, giving off a most delicious smell which had all our mouths watering. I squatted beside him.

'See anything else out there?'

'No, but not likely to with madam stomping around the undergrowth like Godzilla. This one,' he indicated the deer, 'must've been the only stone deaf creature in the entire forest. Why?'

'We encountered a feral, revolting old wretch…' I filled him in on the delights of making Old Ben's acquaintance, then concluded, 'The major also demonstrated a brand new information extraction technique for me.'

'What did he do? Carve little pieces off the dirty old bugger? Wouldn't have thought the major had it in him.'

'Didn't need to, used some spooky magical shit. Sucked the intel directly out of his brain.'

'Freaky.'

'But effective. Seemed to take a bit out of him though, he's off in the woods gathering himself together again.'

'So what do we know?' said Challis, turning the meat thoughtfully. 'Any word on where we're headed yet?'

'Not exactly, though something seemed to spark the major's interest … wouldn't let on though, still playing his cards very close to his chest.'

Challis noted my hesitation. 'What's the matter, don't you trust him?'

'It's not that … I know he wouldn't have saved us, if he didn't need us, but…'

'What's he saving us for?'

'Exactly. But I know it's got something to do with Dreadnaught, that thing he found in the archive.' Challis took a moment to assimilate this fresh information, then said.

'Hm, don't know much about that. I do know a lot of good people can die around a man like the major, someone with a higher purpose, seen it before.'

'Precisely.' I agreed.

'Thought you didn't particularly care about what it cost?'

'Maybe I'm starting to. I don't want us to become just footnotes in whatever particular crusade he's currently waging.'

'Well, there's no turning back now, even if we wanted to. We're miles from our own lines, deep in uncharted territory, I'd say we're kind of committed.' Challis raised an eyebrow.

'Balls deep,' I replied.

My misgivings were partially buried under several sizzling joints of roast deer and we tucked in heartily, stripping the tender flesh away from the bones with relish. Major Seraph, having returned from his brief sojourn in the wilderness looked refreshed, but refused his portion, urged us to 'eat up' and kept watch while we made pigs of ourselves. When we had finished, Challis carefully wrapped the remaining meat and the juicier cuts of offal and stored them away in our backpacks. Haines licked the ends of her fingers clean and held her belly, grinning, 'Mmm, never tasted anything so good.'

'Makes a change from ration packs and wild mushrooms, no?' I replied, kicking over the traces of the fire.

'Hunger assuaged, inner self renewed I take it?' asked the major. A round of nods. 'Good. We move out in five, Sergeant.'

'Yes sir. Where are we headed?

'Oh, I think we'll just follow my nose as per, it doesn't usually lead me too far astray.'

So we spent the first part of the early afternoon marching at a gentle pace. Weak, watery sunshine broke through the leafy branches which reached up like fingers into that pleasant canopy of diffuse dappled light. The rich forest greens, deep browns and reddy-golds, redolent of the change of season, were a vibrant, airy palette, a million miles away from the grey desolation which was our daily bread.

This ground was high enough above sea level so that no flood water had ever penetrated this far and the dry, loamy scent was as welcome as it was half-remembered. Reacquainting myself with the sights and smells of this tranquil place was a delight, like a return to a forgotten Eden. No wonder crazy Old Ben roamed here, who wouldn't choose to live in a place like this instead of the garrison towns, concrete bunkers and underground tunnels we called home?

The forest was teeming with life as well, birds sang and whistled in the trees, insects clicked and droned, dragonflies swooped and dived, lazily weaving between patches of wild flowers. It was like something from some old forgotten Disney film and Haines jumped a mile at the first butterfly she encountered, looking at it open-mouthed as if she'd never seen the like before. Being born after the Flood, she probably hadn't. I struggled to remember the last time I had experienced such bucolic beauty. It had been a lifetime ago, long before the Flood, when I had last walked in woodland like this, shepherding another child, tiny eyes filled with wonder...

So we continued our progress through this woodland idyll, heading towards, well, wherever it was we were headed. Challis was on point, often roaming far ahead and out of sight as he scouted the forest for pathways or signs of danger. I listened with half an ear as Haines chattered, greeting each new Arcadian wonder with delight, but my eyes were elsewhere, constantly scanning the tree line and beyond.

The major appeared to retreat into himself, as if he were with us in spirit alone now and his focus was elsewhere, his mind roaming far beyond the confines of this sylvan realm. Distant and distracted, he answered with short, curt orders when any decision needed to made, then his saturnine brows would knit again, returning to contemplate whatever problem he currently wrestled with. A strange man, if man indeed he was, for after all we had seen and experienced recently, I was beginning to believe that some of the outlandish tales surrounding him only told the half of it.

It was late afternoon and the autumnal sun had begun to lose the last of its watery power, shadows sweeping across the loam, when I saw something out of the very corner of my eye, over to our right.

Perhaps it was just a stray gleam of light or an incongruous shadow, but something over there was not as it should be. I gave it a moment before causally glancing over. Nothing, yet you quickly learn to trust your senses, for you have little else to rely on and my instincts told me something was amiss. Haines prattled on oblivious about some new marvel, while I subtly slid the visor down to surveil what I had seen.

'No need Sergeant, he's been following us for a while now,' said the major quietly. 'One of Ben's 'wild 'uns possibly? '

'A feral? Give the order and Challis will make sure we're the last thing he'll ever track.'

'I'd rather not, not yet at least. Feral or not, he's still human, notionally on our side.'

'I'd like it a lot better if it was more than just 'notionally'. Ferals are trouble sir, full stop. They'll kill you, skin you and eat you as soon as look at you — though that'd be the least of your worries if you're a female and captured alive. No telling what flavour he is … sir.'

'A persuasive point Sergeant, though perhaps put a touch forcefully, no?' An arch of his eyebrow indicated Haines, whose eyes fair boggled.

'Don't break stride, keep walking as if we're continuing our idle chit-chat,' said the major. 'No need for panic just yet. Not all ferals are hostile, in fact, I've known one or two over the years who you wouldn't be shy of introducing to the king.'

'How terribly civilised, sir. But I can't say I've ever had the pleasure of dining with his majesty, so you'll forgive my scepticism. Besides, they almost never travel alone. What if he calls his friends for help? I doubt they'll be bringing cucumber sandwiches and a pot of Earl Grey.'

'Too late for that I'm afraid. He had a colleague with him earlier, who is now long departed. If he's gone to summon help and there are more on the way, there's probably no stopping them now. Besides, my point still holds true, they're still human, possible allies. They might even be able to help us, if we tread carefully.'

'Well let's make sure we tread very carefully indeed, sir.'

So we continued on our way as the light began to fade and the shadows lengthened. When Challis checked back in, I quietly appraised him of the situation and his preferred solution was as uncompromising as mine. Still, orders are orders, so we both had to just grin and bear it, but it didn't sit easily. That feral dogging our tracks was like a rogue flea you couldn't quite scratch and I had to fight the urge to turn and try and catch him unawares.

We ate up a mile or two more, but our insouciance apparently made our shadow grow bolder, for now, instead of following at a discreet distance, he began to parallel our course and it was possible to catch sporadic glimpses of him through the tree line. We affected not to notice, but I quietly thumbed my safety off and tracked him, even as he followed us.

~

All at once, the major seemed to snap out of his reverie and ordered us to pick up the pace and as we increased our stride and fought our way up a muddy leaf-strewn ridge, it didn't take long to discover why. Our lone follower now had an accomplice, several accomplices in fact. Although they were still a little distance away, perhaps a quarter of a mile, you could see they were armed and their outlines fair bristled with weapons. The visor brought further details, seven or eight wild looking men and women, clad in fur, feathers and scrounged steel, their exposed flesh sporting tattoos and tribal markings. A hunting party and no doubt who they were hunting.

'I see them too Sergeant,' said the major.

'Seems like he's found some friends, sir.'

'Yes, well, I suppose if I found interlopers stomping through my territory, I might well be tempted to seek them out and have a quiet word, especially in these troubled times. Perhaps it's time we had a little chat with out pursuers?'

'A chat? I wouldn't recommend that sir. An ambush possibly, they don't look like they have any guns. Play it right and we could bring them all down quickly, quietly, with a minimum of fuss.'

'Indeed, and what of the other four hunting parties who are sweeping up the valley? They'll be on us soon too and we can't possibly ambush them all. We won't outrun them forever.'

'Four hunting parties, how could you possibly…?'

'Oh, I have my methods. No, better to bring this to an early and peaceful resolution if at all possible. Call Challis in. We'll wait for them at the top of that ridge there and see what they have to say.'

'Sir, if I could…'

'I'm aware of your doubts Sergeant and fully appraised on your opinions on ferals, but we're going to do this. Make ready.'

'Yes sir.'

As you can probably tell, I wasn't exactly enamoured with the major's plan, evade or ambush would have been my preferred options, but he brooked no argument and he was the ranking officer. So a short while later, we had assembled in the clearing just beyond the top of the ridge, while the major explained his intentions.

'Now, this may turn confrontational but let me worry about that. No matter what the provocation, what you see or what you think you see, do not react and do not open fire unless I give an explicit order. Understood?'

'Sir.' All three of us affirmed.

'And don't look so concerned, remember just keep calm and stay focused. Feral or not, they are just people after all. Wild looking people true, but fundamentally people all the same. Any questions?'

None were forthcoming, so we arrayed ourselves according to the major's instructions, in a loose line behind some fallen trees on the fringe of the clearing. Once we were in position, Major Seraph simply strolled into the middle of the glade, sat himself down upon a tree stump, drew that asymmetrically bladed *Khukri* of his and began whittling away, sharpening a stick to a fine point as if he were on his holidays.

Minutes passed, the light ebbing away with every passing second and I checked and re-checked my weapon: safety, scope, magazine. Challis remained stoic and unmoving on my right, while on my left Haines was twitchy. I could see her fingers shake slightly as she gripped the handguard of her weapon.

'Haines.' I whispered but she seemed too pre-occupied to notice.

'Ellie!' I hissed and this time it got through. She glanced up and I could see the anxiety written on her face.

'Easy girl, remember your training. Just breathe easy and await orders. It'll be all right. Okay?' She nodded earnestly, but without real conviction and I was just about to reassure her some more, when the first of the ferals appeared over the brow of the hill.

He was a small man, wiry and bearded, clad in wool and leather and carrying a bow with an arrow ready nocked on the string. When he saw the major, he scuttled sideways, flattening behind a tree. Peering around the trunk, the string was at his cheek, ready to loose, but the major paid him no heed whatsoever and just sat there continuing to whittle, producing a small pile of delicate shavings as he brought the stick to a pronounced point. The scout kept the arrow trained on him, but when the major began to whistle rather tunelessly, the man's dark bushy features relaxed a little, he lowered the bow and gave a waved signal behind him.

Soon, more figures had materialised. They were a savage looking crew, dressed similarly to their pathfinder, though more heavily armoured. Most wore the same plaid patterned cloak fastened with a pin at the throat or chest, and they sported a motley collection of scrounged armour and crude iron helmets like something out of a bad version of the Dark Ages or a *Monty Python and the Holy Grail* re-enactment.

There was nothing remotely funny about their weapons though, they were armed to the teeth with an array of lethal looking spears, knives, clubs and improvised axes, which they carried with a grim familiarity and ease. The one crumb of comfort, if any were to be found, was their grisly collection of keepsakes: some had gills and fins hanging off their armour like trophies, while one wore a necklace made of a string of Devil eyeballs.

Silently, they parted to reveal a strapping fellow with an array of gaudy jewellery who strode forward boldly. Blue eyes brooded beneath dark brows set over a long, drooping moustache and beard which had been braided to adorn his florid features. Beneath the rim of an ornate helmet with metal cheek pieces, he was arrayed in burnished, scale-mail armour and from the richness of his garb and his general swagger, it wasn't too difficult to identify him as their leader. His voice was loud, clear, commanding, though it was difficult to say whether he spoke in anger, or these were just his natural robust tones.

'By whose leave do you walk in the lands of the Sons of the Dragon?'

The major, appearing to notice the armed band for the first time, laid his whittling to one side and stood up. He held his leaf-bladed *Khukri* in one hand and the yellow head and green stalk of a daffodil in the other, though god knows where he had produced that from. The major answered him in a language that was lyrical though unfamiliar, but a small prompt appeared on my HUD, reading:

>> Welsh language detected — Translating:

'A free man walks where he will,' said the major. 'If his heart is honest and his motives are true.'

'Well well now, a bard is it?'

'Not exactly, though I've known a few. My name is Major Seraph.'

'I am Owain Glyndŵr, ruler of these lands. So Major, you're a magician too it seems, able to produce spring blooms in autumn?'

The major nodded, 'Well 'Owain Glyndŵr' you must be one too. You're looking remarkably hale and hearty for a man who died over six hundred years ago. As for this? It is just a symbol, yet symbols are important in these troubled times, don't you find?'

'No bloody kidding boyo. What are you going to pull out next, a leek and a rugby ball?' This witticism was embellished with scoffs and guffaws from his fellows.

The major, his back to us, was unperturbed. 'You say magician, well some have called me that, others know me simply as the White Witchman.'

Suddenly his hands shifted and *Khukri* and daffodil were gone, replaced by glowing spheres of light which detached from his palms and hovered before him, throwing light and shadow skittering across the clearing. They span and whirled, eventually coalescing into a stylised red dragon. At this the backing band's laughter died, they muttered darkly and a couple stepped backward looking spooked.

'Never fucking heard of you boyo,' said Glyndŵr seemingly unimpressed.

Now the dragon ascended, hovering behind the major shoulders, roaring and spewing flame. Glyndŵr, to his credit, didn't even flinch.

'Steady,' he said to his men 'This isn't bloody Tolkien you know and cheap illusions and party tricks do not make him fucking Merlin. Now tell me *magician*, what brings you and your little party of soldiers back there, tramping through our woods? The truth now, I'm done pissing about.'

'And who are you exactly to claim these woods as your own?'

'I'm the last true prince of fucking Wales, that's who I am. Now out with it.'

'The exact nature of our mission is … classified, but I'll happily share intelligence or any supplies we can spare.' He gestured to the Devil trophies which adorned the dragons' armour. 'It would seem we share a common enemy.'

The leader spat. 'Intelligence. Pff, fat lot of good that would do us. We know all we need to know about fighting the *gythreuliaid* thanks very much. Besides, your kind abandoned us long ago, why would we need your help now? We're quite capable of fending for ourselves.'

'Very well,' said the major. 'Then it would seem we would have little left to discuss. We'll be on our way.'

'Maybe, maybe not, *mainly* not. As for sharing anything you can spare,' the man chortled and a nasty gleam entered Glyndŵr's eye as his beard split in a broad grin. 'Well, I think you'll do a lot more than that. Those fancy suits and guns would be better in the hands of real warriors, rather than those scrag ends you have masquerading as soldiers back there. A militia bitch, a little girl and a spade, I don't call that much of an army.'

'They're all man enough, believe me,' said the major. 'And there I was thinking this was a land renowned for its hospitality. Not a very polite way of greeting guests.'

'You're not our guests and we levy a tax on all interlopers who trespass in our woods — double for army scum. Just be glad I'm offering you a choice, so save yourselves the trouble and hand them over now and you can be on your way. Afterwards I'll even set you on the right path, can't say fairer than that now can I boyo?'

'Oh I think you can and I must warn you *mrawd*, we won't hesitate to defend ourselves if you try and take them by force. You may have the numbers, but we've got the guns and honestly, they're the least of your worries. For someone who professes no love for the army, trying to flank us mid-negotiation is a classic, if rather underhand military tactic.'

My eyes slid left and there, looming over the ridge and bearing down on Haines' corner was another dozen heavily armed fighters. Instinctively, she tightened her grip on the rifle to cover them, but they were now advancing at speed.

'Hold your fire, hold your fire!' I shouted desperately, already seeing where this was heading, but they kept on coming, makeshift armour jangling, their heavy tread an ominous rumble in the gloaming.

Difficult to say who fired first. The muffled retort of Haines' silenced rifle seemed to come at exactly the same time as the first arrows whistled through the air. But then everything seemed to happen all at once and it didn't really matter any more.

Haines' initial volley folded their first rank and it stumbled and faltered in a welter of blood, heavy impacts resounding as the first bodies hit the turf.

My shout of 'weapons free' was almost superfluous by then for Challis was firing now too, the stilted thud-thud as each shot found its target and the flank charge dissolved in a heap of the dead and dying. I flicked an eye back to the major, who had caught and parried a vicious sword stroke from the man who called himself Glyndŵr. Two of his companions dashed forward to help their leader, but I dropped them with as many shots.

That peculiar battle state descended on me, the mix of adrenaline and sedation where everything seems to slow right down and speed right up at the same time. As the major and Glyndŵr contended, sword against *Khukri,* I sighted, ready to take the shot that would fell the warlord.

There was a furious exchange of blows, metal rang on metal, but the major's back was to me and they moved so fast, I couldn't get a clear target. Glyndŵr was a big man, strong and powerful and he swung his sword in great scything arcs, attempting to batter down his opponent through sheer physical strength. But the major was no slouch either, quick like an eel, all lithe grace, parrying or slipping the tremendous blows with languid ease.

Our weapons fire had driven the main body of Glyndŵr's men back, but behind the ridge the ferals began to mass again, gathering beyond their leader and from the sound of it, reinforcements weren't far behind either. The major seemed to sense it too, for he gave ground, drawing Glyndŵr on as he fell back towards us. I aimed again, exhaling, breathing slow as the warlord came closer, so close now I could hardly miss. My finger tightened, began the slow squeeze which would bring his death, but abruptly, I heard the major's voice, though my com remained blank.

Hold your fire Sergeant, do not shoot!

I hesitated and in that instant, Glyndŵr launched a mighty overhand blow which would have cleaved the major from forehead to breast bone. But in a blur of motion he was gone, moving a hair's breadth ahead of the edge which would have split his skull, sidestepping like liquid quicksilver. As the flashing sword point buried itself in the turf, the *Khukri* slashed once and Glyndŵr went down, grunting and clutching at his sword arm, which was now decorated with a crimson slash of blood.

In the blink of an eye the *Khukri* was gone and the major was clutching something in each hand which looked like a oversized test tube. He smashed them both together and hurled them to the ground and a billowing, choking cloud erupted across the clearing, enveloping friend and foe alike. Suddenly out of the miasma sprang the major, sprinting towards us.

'Bit too close for comfort that. We'd probably best not tarry!' he shouted, vaulting over the fallen trunk. 'The smoke won't hold them for long. Let's move!' That was one order I wasn't about to dispute and so, shouldering my weapon, I dragged Haines to her feet and pushed her bodily forward as we fled into the arms of the forest.

We ran at the double for a long, timeless space, constantly urged on by the major, piling pell mell away from the clearing as fast as our legs would carry us. Branches and brambles tore at us like claws but we ran, until lungs burning, we could run no more. Then we slowed and stopped in the gloom, bent over coughing and heaving like puppets whose strings had been cut. Finally, we had a chance to look behind us. There was no sign of immediate pursuit.

'Take a minute, and drink,' said the major offering his canteen. 'It won't take them long to regroup and then they'll be after us like hounds after a stag.'

'My fault sir, I should have anticipated ...' I said between dry heaves, trying to take the focus away from Haines, who had the decency to look shamefaced.

'No matter now Sergeant and don't worry Haines, you did the right thing. They're about the most hostile friendlies I've ever come across and Glyndŵr's as stubborn as his historical predecessor. Pity, I was hoping I could persuade them to ... but no matter, no matter, spilled milk and all that.'

'Doesn't look they're going to give up easy,' whispered Challis, nodding back towards where we had come from. Flickering torchlight bounced off the trees' shadowy boles about a quarter mile away and then the long, shrill blast of a horn rent the night air. 'Looks they've brought some new friends too.'

So began the pursuit through that benighted forest, the Palladian idyll of the day transformed into a place of dark and terror by night. You can't keep sprinting outright for too long and soon we had dropped into a steady lope, although my pulse drummed in my ears and my arms and legs felt heavy and leaden. The suits were far too drained to cloak, but at least there was enough juice left to power the visors' low light function, though the night sight gave the place a manic green glow, like an emerald version of hell.

More horns sounded to both left and right, answering the first and soon it felt like the whole forest was hunting us, a giant snare that was slowly tightening around our necks. We struggled and stumbled, always moving, hardly daring to look back as the blasts came closer and closer, but the major was always at our side, ready to lend a hand, steady us, drive us forward. Footsteps sounded so close behind us, I thought they almost had us and I glanced quickly back over my shoulder and was rewarded by almost inhaling an arrow, which dug into a nearby tree with a resounding thud.

I was almost too weary to raise my weapon, but Challis dropped the pathfinder, drilling a round through his kneecap so that his screams would draw the others and we plunged on, not caring about what noise we made now, led by blind instinct as much as the major. The ordeal seemed to last for hours, I'd no way to tell and no time to check, the brief moments of lucidity punctuated by short brutal encounters with scouts and pathfinders who attacked us singly or in small groups. We simply kept going, shooting and hacking our way through, leaving as many wounded as we could to slow down the pursuing Sons of the Dragon.

I was bleeding now, a deep gash in my arm courtesy of a scout's axe and my face was scratched to shreds. Arrow shafts lodged in his suit's armour made Challis look like a hedgehog and even the serene Major Seraph was bloodied and battered, though I don't think any of the blood was his own. Haines was the only one left unmarked, though whether that was sheer luck, I didn't even have time to check.

Fuck it, they were persistent, why wouldn't they just sod off, give up and leave us be? But I already knew the answer, that prick Glyndŵr wouldn't let it go: not only were we a rich prize, but we'd belittled and insulted him in front of his men. It didn't matter how many lives it cost, he would run us to ground, or die trying.

So we ran for our very lives, dragging ourselves beyond the edge of endurance, beyond thought, beyond the weariness and fear which dragged at us like quicksand, until we became automatons, consisting of raw nerves and reflex muscle responses. I believe I had even started to hallucinate towards the end, the eerie jade low light of the visor becoming populated by prancing goblins and leering monsters rather than our actual, very real foes.

We burst into another clearing to be confronted by another group of ferals and I totally lost it, fatigue, desperation pushing me beyond my limits. There was a short, whirlwind volley, blood spurting, bodies falling, strobing horror and the next thing I remember, I was smashing the gore-encrusted butt of my rifle into the ruin of a feral woman's face, again and again, long after her features had been obliterated. The skull cracked and split under the blows and I watched, disembodied, as I tried to grind it into the turf, shouting and howling like a mad woman. I only stopped when the major physically wrenched me away.

I lay back, chest heaving, leaking great sobs, eyes raised to the heavens. I was spent, Haines was dead on her feet and even the indomitable Challis looked like he couldn't manage another step without collapsing. We were at the base of a sharp rise, clustered rocks around a hollow cleft, leading into a narrow defile and darkness.

So this was it, this is where we would make our final stand, this is where the mission ended and we died — quickly if we were lucky and slowly if we were not. I would save one bullet for Haines and one for myself, before any of those fuckers could lay hands on us. Challis? Well Challis would take care of himself.

The major, preternaturally tireless, must have sensed it too, for after an evaluative look at our surroundings, he regarded our breathless, prone forms. I tried to rise, but he waved me back and said quietly.

'So we come to it, at bay and rocked back on our heels, ready to take a standing count.'

'Sir, if we…'

'No, no need, you've gone above and beyond anything I could rightfully expect of you. Now it's my turn. I'll be damned if I'm going to let the mission end here.'

'What can we do, sir?'

'I want you to head into that defile, work your way deep into it and lose yourself in the shadows. With any luck, they won't spot you as they come through. I'm going to give them plenty of reasons not too.'

'And you, sir?'

'Me? Oh I intend to lead them a merry chase and draw them far away from here — and you. Once I'm gone, keep heading north by north west…'

'You're … you're a-abandoning us?' said Haines breathing hard but unable to keep the emotion out of her voice.

'Only temporarily, don't worry Haines, it won't be for long, I'll be back as soon as I can. But if we stay together now, you'll all be taken and I can't — I won't have that.'

'Sir…'

'No, remain here and stay in cover. Once I've drawn Glyndŵr's men off, your orders are to evade further contact and continue heading north by north west. I'll set a waypoint in your suit, Sergeant. Follow it like a guiding star, your destination is a day or so's march away give or take, when the forest starts to thin and meets the sea. When you come to it, you'll know where I mean, biggest thing around for miles, you can't possibly miss it. Now, into the defile and make yourselves scarce.'

'But Major…' This time it was I who interjected. 'I can't let you…'

'I'm sure I don't need to remind you who issues the orders here Sergeant … and who has to obey them.'

'We're a long way from home, sir. I can't just let you sacrifice yourself…'

'Touching, but I assure you there'll be no sacrifice required on my part. I'll be fine.'

'But what about the mission, we don't even know what it is, how will you even find us? What about…?'

'No time to argue Stokes you'll just have to trust me … again. Get your men into cover and I mean *now*. The ferals are almost upon us.'

Weary to my bones and almost too tired to form the words to argue, I hauled myself to my feet and dragged Haines up into a standing position. Then all three of us half scrambled, half fell over the rocks, positioning ourselves back within the protective shadows of the defile. The major stood alone in the clearing for a moment watching us, then he gave a great lop sided grin, followed by a hasty thumbs-up and with torches now encroaching just beyond the tree trunks, he was off, bounding like a great hound into the night.

Torchlight slowly began to lick against the outer circle of the trees, then seep across the ground, throwing long shadows as the first scouts broke cover, the whites of their eyes wide, glowing in the green glare of my night vision. They scanned the clearing for signs of our passing, but the earth was unyielding here and finding nothing of consequence, they waved the main body forward. The were thick on the ground now, perhaps a hundred or more, a ragbag collection, some in heavy armour and weapons, some woad-coated and semi-naked, their flesh glistening in the gleaming bands of torchlight. In strode Glyndŵr and it didn't take a genius to spot he wasn't in the mood to hand out medals and ribbons.

He roared at the scouts to make their report and gave their leader, that same terse, wiry little man with darting eyes who had first found us, a hefty cuff around the ear, evidently not liking what he heard. Their language — even in anger — was fluid and lyrical and fortunately my winking HUD provided a ready translation.

'…I couldn't give a shit if you've been running all night or how hard the ground is. Pick up the trail again and find them. Those suits and guns will give us an even better chance against those other bastards, hell they might even finally break the stalemate with Gwae … hello, shit on a shovel man, why the hell do I waste my bread and salt on the likes of you?

'Jones the scout, Jones the fucking imbecile more like. Dew dew, it's staring you in the face man, if they've not scampered up that culvert like rats up a drainpipe, then I'm a fucking blind man.'

He directed the tip of his sword to where we crouched at bay and my mouth went dry, as if I'd swallowed sand. The sharp end of the blade seemed to point straight through me and in that moment I knew we were finally lost, dead and buried, no matter how many of them we took down, they'd rush this position, overwhelm us, outflank us, and we simply wouldn't have the strength or the firepower to fight them off. Well, if we were going down, that bastard was coming with us and I raised my weapon until Glyndŵr's head filled my sight like a swollen jack-o'-lantern. The scout was mumbling something peculiar about 'not treading the path to the castle', but Glyndŵr's earthy, bearded features twisted into a snarl as he exclaimed.

'Fuck that, they won't come this close. Well, what in the name of Tom Jones' balls are you waiting for man? Get after them before they...'

But he didn't have time to complete his sentence, for in that instant an explosion detonated in the centre of the clearing. For a moment the intense flash whited out my night vision, but when it cleared, Glyndŵr's men were scattering for cover, apart from a couple who were rolling on the ground, attempting to beat out the flames which licked at their clothing.

This thunderbolt was followed by a sustained burst of gunfire which succeeded in sending the rest of the remnants scrambling for cover. Four rifles sounded full auto, echoing our own weapons exactly. Shit, where had they come from? Had the major somehow summoned the seventh cavalry?

I scanned the top of the ridge and there, there he was, with three other soldiers, dressed in the exact same suits as ours, wielding the exact same weapons as ours, arranged in the exact same combat stance as ours, intent, as they poured suppressive fire into the clearing. The sustained volley whistled over the ferals' heads, screaming through the canopy, but my brain must have been firing slow, for I couldn't think. Where the hell had they come from?

Moments later the firing ceased and then the major and the three marines stood outlined above the dark of the ridge, backlit by the first embers of dawn. The ferals were too astonished to move for a moment and then slowly, oh so slowly and very deliberately, the major raised a gloved hand and gave them a long, lingering and extremely brazen middle finger. Then he turned, nodded to his troops and they disappeared below the rise of the ridge.

'Bastards! Well, what are you waiting for? Get after those fuckers and make sure you take them alive! I want that long-haired bastard whole, do you hear me, whole!' bellowed Glyndŵr and in moments he and the rest of his feral army were sprinting after them, leaving us completely forgotten.

'I thought we were fucked there,' said Challis, suddenly coming to life. 'Where the hell did he get the reinforcements?'

'No idea, but while he's got their attention, let's get going while the going's good. We have our orders.'

'Guess we do,' grunted Challis, helping Haines to her feet. As we made our way up into the enfolding dark of the culvert, I wondered if I should tell them that the troops accompanying the major, were not troops at all, but three perfect facsimiles of us?

CHAPTER NINE

Up the Rabbit Hole

W<small>E STUMBLED ONWARD</small>, so worn, so wearied from the pursuit that we had to lean on each other and use our rifles like walking sticks to make any progress. The walls curved over us, as we trudged up that long, dark, featureless tunnel and overhead, the first spears of light began to creep across the sky. We continued like that for a timeless space, blind, disconnected, as if we were trudging up the birth canal of the earth mother's womb.

The suit batteries were all but spent now, so I powered everything else down but kept the com channel open. Nothing, not even the comfort of a static ping, but perhaps the defile's high walls were damping the signal? More time passed as we dragged ourselves along that endless corridor and then real light began to bleed in from the true dawn and the sinister atmosphere and hideous black shapes of the night resolved into a neutral, indistinct grey.

We had been marching, if you can call that fatigued, incoherent stumble a march, steadily upward for a good half hour, when we found a sudden break in the defile. The steep sides had tumbled down in a shambles of earth and loam and here the sheer walls became a little shallower. I motioned the others to a halt and they collapsed in a disorderly heap and I followed them, sliding onto the leaf-strewn floor in my exhaustion.

After a few minutes lying there on my back, I managed to summon enough strength to scramble up the side, until wheezing, I was eventually able to heave myself over the lip. I stood and scanned the forest in the steely post-dawn light. The trees were densely packed here, difficult to penetrate, but I expended a little of my meagre remaining energy into the suit's sensors and looked toward where the major had last been heading.

I still couldn't see anything, so tentatively, I tried sending a pulse over the com channel. I waited, watching for the slightest flicker of movement on the waveform, but it remained stubbornly static.

Perhaps the major had given them the run around and managed to lose them? Perhaps he'd used those unsettling doppelgangers to send the ferals on a wild goose chase?

At that particular moment, I didn't have any real fear for the major, he seemed nigh on indestructible and I was certain nothing the ferals could do could harm him. I was sure he would evade Glyndŵr and his mob and would return to find us as promised. Then we would simply resume our mission, hell, he'd given his word hadn't he? The signal might be dead for now, but it wouldn't be too long before he'd reappear, that lopsided grin on his face, that familiar drawl in his voice…

The explosion rent the forest like a living thing. I saw it fractionally before I heard it, a searingly bright flash perhaps two miles away. It gouged a great fiery wound into the wood, scattering the thickest trees like kindling, flaying off branches and foliage and generating a fireball which unfolded like a bright fist being uncurled. This imploded inward, consuming itself and the sound wave followed hard in its wake, a scudding boom like a titan's retch, before the last remnants of the accompanying pressure wave dissipated, washing over me. The cataclysmic detonation brought Challis and Haines scrambling up the slope and we watched together as a great oily mushroom cloud gathered itself into the sky and then hung above the canopy like a smoking wreath.

'Fuck,' opined Challis, 'reckon that was the major?'

'Who else?' I said, stabbing the com button repeatedly. But the signal was flat, not even a glimmer disturbed the channel now.

'Is he … is he dead? Sergeant, do you think he's dead?' said Haines, scarcely able to give voice to what we were all thinking.

'Not sure what could have survived that. But if anyone could, it's the major,' I said, but she must have sensed my uncertainty.

'But he promised he'd be back, didn't he?' She insisted. 'He wouldn't lie to us, not now, would he?' Haines' eyes were tearing up.

'He wouldn't child,' said Challis gently throwing an arm around and pulling her to him. 'Reckon he's lured those ferals in, tricked them, caught them in a trap, then made his escape. Made them pay for chasing us and then some. That's all. He's probably watching from a safe distance and working out how he can get back to us, even now.'

He raised a questioning eyebrow toward me, but the channel stubbornly remained dead. I shook my head.

'We'd best keep going,' I said. 'The major will want us to be on time for that rendezvous,' though the words sounded hollow, even to my ears.

We trudged on through the grey of a new day, following the sunken course of the depression, but my heart was in my boots. Periodically I moved to higher ground and tried the com again, but it was silent, not even the ghost of a signal to say we were anything but alone.

Challis' reassurance might have satisfied Haines who mooched along with her usual blithe nonchalance, but I wasn't so easily comforted. That explosion would have fragged anyone and anything unlucky enough to be caught in the immediate radius and if there were survivors, I wasn't counting on the major being one of them. Even someone of his tremendous sagacity, cunning and extraordinary powers wouldn't be able to outrun a blast wave like that. Where the hell had he got ordinance of that magnitude anyway?

It was then I noticed that a small directional arrow had materialised in the corner of my HUD. It pointed north west, destination unknown.

We half slid, half scrambled our way down the defile and back into concealment, but the aftermath of the explosion continued to nag at me, like a dog worrying at a bone.

Perhaps Challis was right? Maybe the major had set some kind of trap and Glyndŵr's ferals had just stumbled blindly right into it? Perhaps the major had planted it as a distraction, throwing his pursuers off the scent with a spectacular pyrotechnic display? Worst case? The major had been run to ground and desperate, had detonated it as a last resort, taking them with him.

My mind ran through all sorts of scenarios, weighing and evaluating, but none ended particularly well for the major or indeed us for that matter. Here we were, miles into the hinterland, days — might as well have been years — away from our own lines or any form of safety, on a mission whose former leader's remains were now most likely falling gently to earth in a cloud of ashes.

And what of that mission anyway? The major had underlined its importance, emphasised its vital nature, described it as a true game changer. The way he had positioned it was as a chance to strike back at our most hated enemy and turn their plans to cinders.

But he had never disclosed any specifics: not our destination, nor our goal or indeed what it might entail, he had not revealed even the slightest detail, just one word Dreadnaught and what the fuck did that mean anyway? All we had accomplished was moving from point to point on a schedule of his own devising and now he had (perhaps posthumously) launched us on a trajectory towards a vague target in the middle of god knows where.

All I had to trust in was his word and that blinking directional arrow — though that could have been pre-programmed. Right now there was little comfort in either.

Were we just supposed to blindly keep going and unpuzzle this enigma on his word alone? He was an extraordinary man no doubt, by turns brave, infuriating, otherworldly and condescending but how could he have left us — left me — hanging like this?

These were questions it seemed that would be best answered by the finest military and strategic minds of the age, not a despairing NCO from the reserve who'd foolishly gotten herself involved above her rank and way above her abilities — sold on a now increasingly hazy concept of revenge. This wasn't so much out of my league, as out of my universe.

Trust him? I'd like to take him by the throat and shake him, if he wasn't already most likely as dead as the proverbial dodo.

Why had this mission fallen to us, fallen to me to command and what could we three possibly achieve without him? What were we supposed to do with this poisoned chalice the so-called White Witchman had handed us?

We pushed on, I detached, lost in my reverie, until Challis dropped back and said quietly, 'Been a while since we've eaten or rested. If we're going to keep going, we'll need some of both.'

I sighed, but was glad to be presented with something tangible to tackle, a problem which was easily addressed.

'You're right, we've earned it. Find a safe place, no fire, but break out some ration packs and let's all take a breath while I try and work out what the fuck we do from here.'

'Yes sir.' Challis' deliberate use of the ranking honorific didn't go unnoticed. Fuck me if he wasn't right. For better or worse, I was in command now.

We shambled along for another thirty minutes until Challis found a secluded spot where we could duck out of the defile and rest up in a small, concealed clearing. Despite my constant backward glances, we seemed to have thrown off any immediate pursuit. Glyndŵr and his gang had either gone up in that explosive burst of hard light themselves, or now believed our doppelgangers had perished alongside the major. Either way it seemed no-one was coming after us right this moment.

Here seemed as good a place as anywhere, so I gave Challis the nod and Haines let herself fall to the ground wearily, then lay back with her eyes staring vacantly up at the sky. Challis ripped open a couple of ration packs and passed one to her. I rootled around in my pack for food, but instead my hand closed on the crumpled packet of cigarettes the major had donated to me. I took it out and lit one, keeping a wary eye back on where we had come from, but savouring the smoke as it trickled its way down into my lungs.

Shit I was tired, near exhausted, the crown already hanging heavy. I sat and smoked numbly for a while, while the others began to mechanically chew their way through their rations. I should have been starving, ravenous, I honestly couldn't remember the last time I had eaten, but I didn't feel especially hungry, even now. I was just conscious of the ache in my feet and the weariness in my mind.

We sat like this for a while, I don't know how long with not a word spoken, the background sounds of the forest filling in the gaps. This reverie might have lasted for five minutes or fifty, I lost track, but the next thing I knew, Challis was squatting next to me and waving a ration pack.

'You should eat something.'

'I should.'

'...and you may not want to smoke those all at once either.'

I had another cigarette in my hand ready to light and must have been chaining them, one after the other. Three discarded butts lay crushed on the floor.

'Hm, well seems unlikely I'll live long enough to die of something smoking-related, but thanks anyway.' I took the ration pack, tore off the top and bit into it, watching the vapour stream out and barely tasting the rehydrated shepherd's pie.

'True enough, but you might want to save a fag or two, you know, in case things ever get *real* stressful.' He grinned and I forced a smile.

'Shit, perhaps you're right. Difficult to say when that might be though, hm? It's been such a stroll in the park so far.'

'True.' He smiled then looked hesitant. 'Emma, can I offer you some advice?'

I raised a quizzical eyebrow. When he used my first name, it meant something serious was coming, but I nodded him on.

'You're in charge now and that can sit heavy, but it don't mean you have to decide everything right this second. I know the major might be gone and it seems like we're fucked all ways to Armageddon...

'But food, a little sleep, give your mind — give yourself — a chance to rest. It'll bring a whole new perspective ... sir.' Challis straightened up and threw me a lopsided salute, something which I don't think I'd ever seen him do in all the years we'd served together. I almost laughed out loud, half amused or half hysterical I didn't quite know.

But then I got up, stood to attention properly and returned it.

'You're right. Thank you, *Corporal*. Remind me to recommend you for a promotion to field marshal if we get back.'

'When we get back,' he answered firmly. 'You know you can try, but I'm not sure my shoulders could bear the weight of all that extra brass.'

Sunlight streams through the trees, a drowsy summer's day. Childish giggles, a ball bounces lazily across the grass, 'Mummy, look at me, look at me mummy!' attention-seeking, almost on the verge of a tantrum, but when I look, he beams, smile like a ripe banana, then brows knit in intense concentration for the run up, uncoordinated limbs flailing then hoofing the ball in a random direction.

Surely this is the cleverest, bravest, most skilful boy that's ever been born? Destined to become a footballing superstar, those chubby little legs pumping furiously will one day be worth millions, billions. I sigh contentedly and gather him up into my arms. For long seconds we are one, mother and son bathed in sunlight, but then he pulls away, eager to be free, ready to chase that damned ball again. I let him go, because in the end, you always have to…

Weak autumnal sunlight prised open my eyes and reluctantly, I returned from my halcyon dream world to cold, hard wakefulness. Suddenly and urgently aware, I sat bolt upright and peered around blinking. Haines lay stretched out like a kitten, her mouth open, muttering something softly in her sleep. Challis was nowhere to be seen, but something had triggered my survival instincts and I rose quietly, snatched my weapon and roll-slithered into the nearby undergrowth.

I hissed at Haines, but she was insensible to my whispered reveille and cursing, I threw a twig at her. It bounced off her nose and she mumbled something incoherent and turned over, burrowing deeper into her blanket. *Christ Ellie!* Breath followed hard breath, one after the other, charging as the adrenaline began to surge, but the only external sound was Haines' placid snoring. Nothing moved and I started to think that perhaps I had imagined the sound, some strange collision of the dream and real worlds.

Then I caught an unfamiliar scent on the breeze. It was savoury, salty, like an intimation of the ocean and I hunkered down even further and brought my weapon up to bear. Tense seconds ticked by and again, I wondered if my imagination was playing tricks on me, but then I heard them, soft footfalls, coming from just beyond where Haines lay. I eased my safety off and dialled up to full auto. Where the fuck was Challis? He was supposed to be on watch, my dependable right hand … but then my suit display lit up with his call sign.

>> I'm close by, I see them. Stay where you are.

I was just about to mouth a furious reply when the figure emerged from around the bole of a tree and slid quietly into the clearing. He didn't look like one of Glyndŵr's thugs, being a striking, dark haired man-child of perhaps seventeen or eighteen. He wore plain camouflage fatigues and carried a sword on his belt and a bow in his hand, but didn't look especially ready to use either. Pale blue, rather watery eyes shone with a keen intensity as he regarded our small camp and then encompassed the sleeping Haines. Softly, he paced over to where she lay and stooped, a single hand outstretched to the recumbent figure.

'Touch her and I will open fire!' I barked the words and then everything seemed to happen at once. His hand had hovered inches from Haines' face, ready to brush against her skin, but at my challenge he leapt back like a cat and froze, those sharp eyes searching, scanning, but betraying no undue fear or alarm.

Haines, wakened by my shout, started to rise but only succeeded in sitting up and looking sleepily confused.

'Step away from her. Do it now and slowly, or I will be forced to fire,' I said in more even tones. The figure regarded my hiding place with a curious tilt of his head, but took a couple of paces back, hands raised in a placatory gesture.

'As will I,' whispered a female voice beside me, as the tip of an arrow imposed itself on the fleshy part of my cheek. Cursing inwardly at being caught cold, I was about to lower my weapon when Challis' even tones drifted down from the tree tops above.

'Easy now or you'll be dead before you can draw that string back any further missy. Now I suggest we all calm down, lower our weapons and start talking, before someone gets hurt.'

Slowly, palm open, finger off the trigger and weapon pointing to the ground, I stood up. Challis was perched in the lower branches of a nearby tree coolly covering us all. By my side was a girl just older than Haines' age, easing off the string of her bow, her dark Amazonian features an echo of the boy's own.

'Well, a talking bush below and a tree-spirit above, truly these are the end of days, what wonders this new age brings. Perhaps these woods are enchanted after all?' said the boy, a knowing smirk crossing his face. Haines scrabbled to her feet, looking for her weapon but failing to locate it.

'Easy Haines, this little stand-off is over,' I said, eyes locked meaningfully on the boy.

'Oh absolutely, please, let me make the introductions,' he said, grinning. 'I'm Arthur, the young lady who was ready to send an arrow through your head is Boud-icca, my delightful sister.' The girl scowled while he gave a bird-call and a small group emerged from the trees surrounding the clearing. They were a hardy looking bunch of young men, dressed in similar garb to the siblings. A group of clean, presentable looking teenagers lurking in the woods in these strange days? That was remarkable enough in itself.

'And these are … well, the rest of us,' concluded Arthur.

'I'm Sergeant Stokes, man upstairs is Corporal Challis, sleeping beauty there is Haines.'

'Charmed.' He twinkled at Haines who blushed crimson. 'So ... Sergeant Stokes, what brings you to our ... well, our literal neck of the woods? Long time since we've seen soldiers up this way ... long time since we've seen anyone we don't know for that matter.'

'Could ask you the same thing.'

'Us? Well, they're our woods — didn't I just say that? But no, the reason we find ourselves abroad today is that we saw something light up the sky earlier this morning, just after dawn. A big explosion, not exactly a common occurrence around these parts, seemed like the kind of thing that merited investigation. Your doing by any chance?'

'Not us,' I answered, which was factually if not strictly correct.

'I see. Well you must forgive our ... cautious reception. Despite their beauty, these woods aren't the most welcoming of places, especially to strangers.'

'So we've gathered. We ran into some rather hostile ferals earlier.'

'Ah, so you've encountered Glyndŵr and his mob I imagine? Don't play very nice do they? Not exactly Robin Hood and his merry men. They take from rich and poor alike and give, well, only unto themselves. Not exactly your classic fairy tale outlaws.'

'So I understand, they demanded everything we had with a fair degree of menace, but when that thing, whatever it was, detonated, we managed to give them the slip.' I said. 'We've spent the last few hours putting as much distance between them and us as possible.'

'Interesting. They don't usually venture this far north, or rather we've taught them not to. Still, if Glyndŵr and his band are abroad and in strength,' he glanced at his sister, 'there's probably more to this than meets the eye. That explosion interests me too, it's ... but perhaps we should return home and lay all this before Father?'

'I've an idea. Why don't you accompany us, back to Gwaelod?' He waved vaguely to the north. '...As our guests of honour, naturally? We've got food, drink, humble enough fare, but you're welcome to share it. We have shelter too, comfortable guest quarters and high walls to keep us safe. You'd be welcome to stay as long as you like, rest up, recuperate, get your mojo back before continuing your journey. We'd welcome some news of the outside world as well, it's been a while since we heard anything beyond the whispers of the forest.'

It was the best offer we'd had in a while, the *only* offer we'd had in a while that didn't involve death threats or handing over everything we had, including our dignity. Despite looking reasonably handy with those weapons and their natural youthful swagger, they didn't appear to be much of a menace, a bit too eager to please if anything, especially Arthur, although that might have something to do with Haines' hitherto undiscovered charms. However there was something underlying his easy manner that still made me cautious.

I hesitated, but there didn't seem a great deal to lose if we were heading in that direction anyway. I checked the HUD arrow, it still continued to point due north west, virtually the same direction Arthur had indicated.

I had a sudden thought. Perhaps this was the path the major had actually intended us to take? Even if it wasn't, Arthur and his friends would be able to share some intel with us, point us in the right direction at least. It certainly wouldn't hurt to have some local knowledge, get to know the lie of the land.

'Perhaps you'd like some time to think about it, discuss it amongst yourselves?' he said. 'We can't wait too long, but we can spare a few minut…'

'I think you've mistaken this for some kind of democracy Arthur. I'm in command here.'

'I see. Well…'

'Thank you for your kind offer, we'd be delighted to accept. Please, lead the way.' He looked a little surprised, but then smiled winningly, though I noted his sister didn't appear to share his enthusiasm.

'Yes ma'am.'

CHAPTER TEN
Sushi

A S SOON AS WE GOT UNDERWAY I could see I had seriously underestimated them. They may have seemed like little more than kids, but they were clearly no fools and moved through those woods like something out of *The Last of the Mohicans*. I don't think a crack team of SAS snipers could have done any better.

Arthur and Boudicca remained with us, but the other half dozen fanned out to scout ahead and kept in touch with a variety of bird and animal calls, which amused Challis no end.

We made good ground, quickly and quietly traversing a series of hidden paths and concealed byways that we wouldn't have spotted in a million years if we'd been on our own. Arthur cast the odd surreptitious glance at Haines when he thought no-one was looking, not salacious, merely curious and intrigued, although the one time I caught him red-handed, he had the decency to look a little shamefaced and turn away. But his eyes always crept back toward her — he'd bear watching that one.

After another half an hour Arthur sidled up and fell into step beside me. 'So, sorry to insist and I know it's perhaps a little forward of me to ask, but can I press you again on what exactly does bring you to our neck of the woods Sergeant?'

I wish I knew, I wish I knew, I thought, but wasn't about to open that particular can of worms in front of our brand new — and still apparently friendly — acquaintances.

'I'm afraid I can't discuss the exact nature of our mission with you Arthur, you understand?'

'Oh, but you are on a mission though? Exciting. Mind you, I should have guessed with those weapons and all that gear you're sporting. I've never seen guns or armour like them, they must be state of the art.'

'They are, or at least they were. They're beginning to look a bit battle-scarred now, kind of like their wearers.'

'I've never met a marine before,' he said and my eyes must have narrowed a little. 'Sorry, I couldn't help but notice that insignia. When I was little, I used to hear such stories about the marines: strong, fearless, always in the vanguard, the first to fight. Father once told me a single marine was worth five ordinary soldiers.'

'Father?'

'My father, he leads our community.'

'I see. Well he's right, the Royal Marines are a regiment with a long and noble tradition.'

'Oh, I know all about the Leathernecks. 'By Sea, By Land' is your motto. Formed in 1755 at Chatham, though you can trace their history all the way back to the Duke of York and Albany's maritime regiment of foot...' he continued to recount the history of the regiment in far greater detail than I would have ever known or even guessed. I interrupted him before he asked me something specific I wouldn't have the answer to.

'You seem to know a great deal about the regiment Arthur.'

'Yes, I have all the knowledge but lack any real experience, that's why I'm so delighted to meet some real soldiers, finally. One more question if I may? What does it take to earn the right to wear that uniform?'

He was full of unsettling questions this one, his intelligence bright and burnished like brass, but I played it by the book.

'As any real soldier will tell you, it's not the uniform that counts, it's the man or woman inside it.'

'Of course, of course.' He nodded sagely, as if I had imparted the wisdom of the ages rather than one of the oldest soldiering clichés in the book.

'She must be a mighty warrior to have earned her place in your ranks, especially for one so young.' He nodded at Haines who was slouching ahead of us, porting her weapon more like an umbrella than a lethal killing instrument. It was a good job he probably couldn't tell the difference.

'Hidden depths, that one.' I replied. He nodded thoughtfully and at that, I was relieved to let our conversation peter out.

Another hour or so and we kept steady and true on our course which stayed roughly north by north west. The HUD indicator hardly flickered off station and it seemed oddly fortuitous that our new friends were leading us exactly where we were meant to be going, or at least as close as made no odds.

So far so good, circumstances dictated I could happily follow orders by just keeping in step with Arthur and his chums and it sounded like we would find a safe haven when we got to Gwaelod, whatever the hell that was.

But how should we play it when we got there? We wouldn't exactly be able to fend off their questions with vague assurances and hiding behind 'orders' forever. And how long should we wait? Should we go looking for the objective and what exactly were we supposed to do if we found it? Would we even recognise it if we saw it? Perhaps Arthur and his people would know? But that would mean we'd have to disclose elements of our mission and perhaps even our ignorance of it? Should we let them in — even partially — on our darkest secrets? How much should we tell them? Could we even trust them?

My mind whirred, there were more questions than a specialist subject round on Mastermind and I had no ready answers. Intermittently I sent a silent ping out on the com, hoping against hope that the major's reply would come bouncing back and provide some answers, but I received only silence in reply. It would be so much easier if the major was here, so much easier if he was still alive, but if he was, he wasn't answering. Damn.

It was during one such unsuccessful transmission, that two of Arthur's companions suddenly appeared back amongst us. There was a hasty whispered conference and then Arthur beckoned us forward eagerly. Motioning us to absolute quiet, we snuck low and then wriggled into position on a ridge overlooking a shallow bowl in the wood below.

'Look, see, there they come. Tramping through Gaia herself with all the grace of a herd of cattle,' said Arthur as a line of perhaps two dozen ferals skulked through the young trees. Daylight appeared to have robbed them of much of their menace and now they looked like what they were; a group of thin, ragged clutchers-on, their crazy streaks of woad and mud-spiked hair no longer intimidating but strangely pathetic in the harsh light of day. Arthur emitted a long low bird call and I could see a frisson of excitement pass through his companions.

'What are you doing?' I whispered urgently.

'Oh, we mean to kill them naturally,' said Arthur casually as if he were discussing biscuit preferences for his morning cuppa. 'They have violated our territory and their heads will decorate the trees and swing in the breeze as a warning to the others.'

'I'd prefer to avoid an engagement.' I said. 'And when I say 'prefer' I mean I don't want one, full stop. No point in stirring them up even further, or giving away our current position.'

'Dead men tell no tales,' said Boudicca looking daggers. 'You are a curious soldier, Sergeant. There is great honour in killing one's enemies. Why would we leave them unmolested?'
'I was taught the greatest battles are the ones you don't have to fight,' I replied laconically. 'There's nothing to be gained and plenty to be lost by attacking those people.'
A look passed between the two siblings and then Arthur said, 'As you wish, you are

our guests and we will respect your wishes in this matter.' Boudicca's narrowed eyes and locked jaw pronounced her own verdict on the matter. Yet at Arthur's expertly whistled birdsong, the others melted back into the foliage again as if they had never been there. Below, the ferals tramped noisily on through the forest, oblivious to the fate which had so nearly descended upon them.

Now the sky began to brighten, the spaces between the trees grew wider and a salty note entered the air, which told even a dry boots like me that we were fast approaching the coast. Arthur seemed subdued and Boudicca especially so and double sulky after being denied a chance to slake her blood lust. So our journey had passed in a rather cautious resentful quiet, like two boxers who had begun to feel each other out in the opening rounds, but then, afraid to over commit, had retreated into watchful defence. The otherwise deafening silence was occasionally broken by Haines' oblivious, tuneless humming.

We had left the ferals far behind now after a couple of hours solid marching. The distant sounds of the sea had drawn ever closer, lapping just over the horizon as the boles of the trees started to thin out and the rising breeze brought the brittle shriek-rattle of the gull's call.

Up until then I had allowed myself to relax a little, observing our host's laid back demeanour but still relying on my keen eyes and Challis' impeccable nose for danger, yet nothing had disturbed our onward journey. However, as we drew ever closer to the sea, I couldn't help but tense up, listening for the Devils' whistles or chirrups or that distinctive lurching sound they make when they venture onto *terra firma*.

However it seemed our hosts did not share my misgivings. Arthur, Boudicca and their companions could have been out taking a meander through 257, 144 (the map co-ords for the 'navel', the furthest inland you could get from the sea) for all the attention they paid. The siblings strolled along without an apparent care in the world, weapons casually slung over their shoulders, a picture of complete insouciance.

Tempting fate it seemed to me and I didn't like it one bit. It went against every inch of our training as well as every instinct in my being, especially since the rocky top of the coastline was now actually in sight and beyond it, the first blue ribbon of sea, glinting in the offing. Each step that dragged us back toward those limitless depths and the nameless island which squatted over them, filled me with a dread I could hardly name. Despite the impression it might give — a supposedly fearless marine getting windy near water — I was just about to say something when the pair stopped dead, as if they'd suddenly caught a whiff of the Gorgon's breath.

Their companions sensed it too, stiffening and then stretching and scenting at the breeze like wolves. Their eyes sought each out and there seemed to be an abrupt, wordless communication pass between them, then a round of nods, a silent collective assent and then they dispersed into the woodland, disappearing in the blink of an eye with a speed which bordered on the uncanny. Moments later it was if they had never even been there.

Arthur and Boudicca came stalking back and addressed our plainly mystified faces.

'More interlopers and this time it is the creatures from the sea who intrude upon our heartlands,' said Arthur. 'It is curious, they rarely tread Gwaelod's soil nowadays, for we have taught them many a harsh lesson. We must repeat the dose once again it seems.'

'I thought we agreed we were avoiding engagements on this little outing?' I asked.

'Glyndŵr's men we might overlook, as a courtesy to you, our guests, the creatures we cannot,' said Boudicca, eyes gleaming and clearly spoiling for the fight she had been denied earlier. 'We cannot allow this violation to go unchallenged, Sergeant. You can help us, or not, as you prefer.'

'My sister is right Sergeant. Regretfully, we cannot ignore this incursion. Yet there are a mere two dozen, easy pickings. Please, allow me to escort you to a place where you may observe. We would be honoured if you would study our approach and perhaps offer us some guidance, once we have dealt with them.'

'You kids … taking on a warband? You'll need our help,' said Challis.

Boudicca smirked, 'I assure you we will not. Keep yourselves out of the way, watch and you may even learn something.'

'I'm sure my sister means no disrespect, Corporal Challis, especially to such a group of renowned warriors,' said Arthur glaring at her. 'However, we are used to fighting together as a group and it may complicate matters tactically if we mix our forces. However, I'm sure we would very much appreciate you providing us with a tactical reserve, acting as the anvil to our hammer, should any escape.

'I know the ground here well. If you would be gracious enough to accept, I'll station you up there, near those ferns with a commanding field of fire. You can then observe or participate at your discretion and we can operate without interfering with your lines of fire, or you, ours.'

I looked to Challis, who raised an eyebrow. Clearly they were intent on taking down this Devil warband and little we could say or do would dissuade them now. I shrugged and bowed to the inevitable.

'Lead on then,' I said.

Which was how we found ourselves a short while later overlooking a narrow clearing perhaps fifty yards above the cluster of rocks which crested the cliffs leading down to the shore. It was an almost perfect spot for an ambush, trees hemming in either side, funnelling a path down the centre and the ground rose steeply up to the position where we were camouflaged in a thicket of ferns. We were well hidden, practically invisible from the direction from which the Devil warband would apparently approach.

'We'll keep things simple,' Arthur continued solemnly. 'I wouldn't dream of dictating tactics to such a formidable group of fighters as yourselves, but please, hold fire until they are all above the cliffs and well within the clearing so we can bait our trap. Once it is sprung, you may fire at will. Is that acceptable Sergeant?'

'It's your home ground, so it's your decision,' I replied. 'But if those fuckers suddenly come up at the double and threaten to overrun us, we'll have to take them down. Otherwise, we'll await your move.'

'Excellent. Agreed, thank you, Sergeant. Now, let us be about the business!' he said with relish. Despite his impeccable manners and easy grace, those eyes burned intently, showing he was every bit as elated as his sister at the prospect of battle.

In moments Arthur too had melted away, disappearing like a shadow at noon and we were left to our own devices. Despite our entrenched position and superior firepower, I suddenly felt rather exposed up there. A few kids taking on an entire warband? Even with the advantage of surprise, surely that was too big an ask? It was their funeral perhaps, but had I allowed myself to be too easily manoeuvred into this? We would be safe enough up here if the Devils came, but why were Arthur and his companions so keen to give battle?

Minutes, perhaps seconds passed, time takes on a different meaning in those situations. They say the waiting is the hardest part and maybe it is, but not so hard as the killing and dying in my experience. Still, in that situation all you can do is keep your eyes wide, your ears open and your breath even. Courage? Coolness under fire? No, it's patience which is ultimately the soldier's greatest virtue.

I checked my safety for the umpteenth time, then the various ranges with my scope, still nothing. Then the first faint sounds began to drift up toward us from beyond the cliff top.

The first of them crested the crag, slithering elastically on all fours over the rock until its hind flippers came to rest on the sward and there it squatted like a bulbous, loathsome frog. Its neck swivelled to examine its surroundings and those wide, soulless eyes encompassed the clearing without blinking. It stayed like that for a little while, simply looking, then turned and gave a low sibilant chirrup to its fellows below. More of them clambered up to join it, but as they assembled, I noticed those fishy bastards' behaviour was unusual, bordering on the remarkable even. You never see fear written on those expressionless mushes, their faces are not exactly configured for emotion, but these ones moved with a caution and a vigilance I had rarely seen before, almost as if they were afraid of what they might encounter up here.

Curious, most curious, but those fleeting observations were quickly forgotten as, lumbering over the cliff top to complete the incursion, was the ugly bulk of a shaman. But no ordinary shaman this, its huge misshapen form was wrapped in a seaweed shroud decorated with shells and anemones and its head topped by a wreathe-crown of interlocked starfish. One fore flipper clutched an intricate barnacle-encrusted trident, inscribed with unholy runes instead of the usual gnarled staff. A warlock! One of their holy elect, Devil royalty practically, a vile, evil spellcasting son of a whore that could cut swathes through bone, blood and even armour with its enhanced sorcery. Holy fuck, we were in deep shit now, pray to god that Arthur and his companions had sense to leave well enough alone and let that evil bastard pass unmolested.

With any luck its ancient, rheumy eyes would miss us entirely and the rest of its warband would pass into the forest unhindered and there they could cut down the trees, piss on the flowers or stamp on the butterflies for all I cared — as long as we were far far away when they did it. I glanced over at Challis and Haines, finger over my lips, but it wasn't necessary, both of them knew exactly how to play this — silent as the grave. If we got out of here with our skins intact, well, it would be one for the books — surviving an encounter with a warlock would arm you with a story which meant you'd never have to pay for a round of drinks ever again.

The warlock gaped, opened its cavern of a mouth and emitted a low bassy croak and then its braves formed up around it and advanced into the clearing, still wary it seemed, as if they were expecting trouble. God alone knows what they feared, a warlock was generally reckoned to be worth a battalion in a stand up fight. I'd seen hardened soldiers, good fighters, break and run in terror, preferring to risk being shot as deserters, rather than face one of those waddling horrors.

But in spite of the raw, salty stink which wafted up toward us, it looked like Lady Luck might be smiling on us for a change, instead of perpetually pissing in our cornflakes. Instead of coming straight for us, the warlock gave a low grunt and pointed its trident, signalling its escort to move away at right angles to our position and they began to lope off in that direction. I let out a long-held breath silently, I would not be sorry to see the back of this particular band of demons.

And, fuck me with a feather, sir, if I didn't get my wish as well, though not quite in the way I expected. I was still sighting down my weapon, watching them shuffle off into the woods, when the distinctive whizz-whine of a volley of arrows ripped through the air. The rearmost half dozen Devils, fully one quarter of the patrol, just crumpled, sporting arrows buried deep in their brains or pierced through a single eye socket, so that they folded into the turf with barely a sound. It was done so quickly, so quietly, so calmly, that the ones in front didn't notice for long seconds. I should have sworn, or shot, or both, but I was so staggered by the sheer audacity of it, that my mouth simply hung open and I gave no order.

Impossibly fast, another volley erupted into them and another six dropped, arrows piercing their flesh, hurled hand axes splitting skulls asunder. They looked like gutted fish dying on that forest floor, flopping weakly as the life drained out of them. Now, with a series of whoops and war cries, Arthur and his companions dropped from the trees upon the startled creatures, slamming into them with the force of a hammer blow. Four more were felled in the blink of an eye, cut to pieces, knifed or bludgeoned from above with a precision that bordered on the uncanny. Then Arthur and his companions were amongst the Devils, the fierce light of battle seeming to play around them like a halo.

Fuck me, but they were quick too, fast as quicksilver, literal blurs of motion as they unceremoniously hacked, carved and sliced, reducing the Devils to a mere collection of limbs and assorted body parts, slick with foul, black blood.

They were so fast the eye could barely follow and all I saw was snapshots, strobe-like vignettes: one of the companions, a dark haired, rather quiet seeming lad wrapped his legs around a Devil's neck and twisted, flexing his thighs so that they exerted a force that exploded its eyes clean out of their sockets. Another dropped, lopped off a Devil's arm, rolled and ducked past its clumsy spear thrust, then slashed open its bowels spilling blood and gore, before burying twin knives in its neck. Boudicca, preferring to strike from range, fired a staccato succession of arrows, which pierced another, pinioning its flippers to a tree, where it struggled, waggling ineffectually.

It was like the Devils were moving in slow motion as the companions wove and danced through them, striking and evading with a speed, precision and savagery that was beyond natural. It looked like a dance, a cruel, deadly ballet and for once, the Devils were on the receiving end of a close quarters beasting they wouldn't forget.

Before the Flood I used to be a big fan of sushi and the way they carved up that patrol reminded me of an expert sushi chef, a master *itamae,* blades striking with an accuracy and grace that was nigh on superhuman. Who the hell were these deadly, stupidly gifted adolescents who could degrade an entire warband in the blink of eye?

The last brave fell to Arthur's sword and now the warlock was turning, manoeuvring its lumbering bulk to face the audacious man-child who confronted it, standing there bold as brass, completely undaunted. Its eyes registered hatred, its mouth twisted with rage and the trident glowed, a cold fire pulsing through its tangs as it brought its *magika* to bear. Arthur just stood there, immobile, as the concentrated energy surged, a cone of eldritch magic which passed straight through him and then beyond, splintering trees and vaporising all in its path.

Shit! That poor, brave, stupid boy, why had he just stood there and taken it? Oh well, fuck the consequences, I gave the order and our volley smashed into the warlock's hide, the sheer force driving it back, making it recoil. Some of our rounds bit deep into its flesh, tearing off ragged slices, but most simply bounced off its ancient, barnacled hide.

The warlock staggered under our volley though, giving ground, then it rallied, summoning more of the foul magic through its rune trident and I barked 'incoming, scatter!' Yet as we scrambled to find fresh cover, impossibly, I saw Arthur rise from behind the creature.

How the hell he got there? How had he evaded that blast? I couldn't fathom unless somehow he'd somersaulted clean over it. A cold, callous joy filled his face and then his blade swung, a blur of shining silver, biting through the creature's wrists, shearing both flippers off and causing its trident to fall, the cold fire remnant hissing and sputtering as it died on the forest floor.

The warlock roared, croaking its pain, but in a moment that too was silenced as the tip of Arthur's blade appeared, driven through the back of its neck, straight through its fishy brain to bisect that great pitiless mouth.

It fell then, just another empty sack of flesh and guts, sliding to the floor with a long drawn out wheezing sound as it expelled its last breath. Arthur placed his foot on the back of the creature's neck pulled his sword free with a great sucking sound and then began to meticulously wipe the blade clean of the warlock's dark blood.

Rather sheepishly we wandered over to join him and the rest of the companions as they reassembled amidst the carnage of the field. Everywhere Devil corpses were stretched across the floor, yet the companions had escaped without a scratch and the blood that splashed and spattered their clothing was not their own. Just one Devil remained alive, wriggling helplessly where Boudicca's arrows had nailed it to the tree.

If I hadn't witnessed it with my own eyes, I would never have believed it and I hardly expect you to, sir. A warlock and an entire warband reduced to its component parts in what? Under thirty seconds? That kind of thing just does not happen.

'Well that was rather enjoyable,' said Arthur grinning as he sheathed his blade. 'A little light exercise really sets a fellow up for the day.'

'You certainly have a gift for understatement,' was about all I could manage.

'I want to thank you Sergeant,' said Arthur.

'What for?'

'I never dreamt I would fight shoulder to shoulder alongside his majesty's marines, this has been a most singular honour.'

'Can't say we did much of the fighting.'

'Nevertheless, we shared the same field, the same perils, the same victory. Oh, but it is glorious day!' said Arthur enthused beyond measure, his boyish face lit up by excitement as he bestowed a beaming look at Haines. The rest of the companions seemed to share his enthusiasm as they grinned rather shyly at us. All except one.

'If you could spare a moment from your mutual admiration society?' said Boudicca, holding a long knife to the throat of the remaining Devil. 'What of this filth?' she enquired as the creature shrank back, flinching from her blade.

'Ah yes,' said Arthur blithely. 'Bind it, then blind it. I'm sure Father will wish to interrogate it and find out why they violated our lands. As for the others? Make a pile, roll them over the cliff so that they collect on the shore. The others must see the fate of any who dare trespass upon our territory.

'Now then Sergeant, a most productive day and it is only just past noon. After we have finished our work here, it's just a hop and a skip home and there you can rest, recuperate and be most welcome. I'm sure Father will be very glad to meet you too. I dare say we might scavenge up a bite to eat as well. All this exercise has given me something of an appetite.'

'Sounds good,' I nodded, still not quite comprehending what I'd witnessed.

We watched as the companions, laughing, joking and ribbing each other about their prowess in battle began to lift the Devils bodily, picking up the heavy corpses like they weighed no more than a bag of feathers. It wouldn't have surprised me to see them juggling the remains for shits and giggles. A frenzied thrashing and chittering came from the lone Devil survivor as Boudicca methodically carried out her brother's commands.

'Shit, incredible speed, superhuman strength, never seen anyone fight like that, leastways not anyone human anyway,' said Challis. 'Whatever vitamins they're taking I could use a course of the same treatment. Clearly there's more to this than meets the eye.'

'Roger that, but what?'

'No idea, maybe we'll find out more when we reach this Gwaelod? Tell you one thing though…'

'Which is?'

'Seeing the way they took those Devils apart, I'm kinda glad you chose not to pick a fight with these kids.'

'One of my better command decisions,' I said.

CHAPTER ELEVEN
Gwaelod

WE HAD WATCHED SOLEMNLY as they tumbled the bodies and their constituent parts over the cliff, to form a bloody cairn on the seashore below. The warlock's bloated, blood-soaked corpse went last, rolling and bouncing to rest on the gory heap, then Arthur affixed its head on top with a sharpened spike, a fitting capstone for that grisly warning. That grim task completed, we followed Arthur and his now ebullient companions as they led us along the line of the cliff tops, full of beans and bubbling with boasting and banter.

Now the restless pounding of waves upon shale was our constant marching companion and as we left the last remnants of the forest behind, we broke cover and emerged onto a headland overlooking the waters of a wide bay.

'There it is, Gwaelod, our home,' said Arthur.

From where we stood, we beheld a long, flat sandy cove which rose dramatically towards a high promontory. There, protected by the impressively steep set of cliffs, was a walled settlement, old and medieval looking, its buildings and houses constructed of flint and slate, gleaming and glinting in the weak autumn sunshine.

A formidable looking castle dominated the skyline, a massive white stone keep gleaming at its centre, while four solid red-topped towers pierced the azure sky above. It was like something out of a story book, its high walls and crenulated battlements forming an impenetrable barrier and its lofty situation making it seem damn near impregnable — or they would have, were it not parked directly next to the Devils' own element.

Even though the waters which washed up against that shore were calm, its proximity to the sea naturally raised my hackles and glancing back, way way back toward where we had come, there it was again, the island, materialising gloomy and malign beneath its mists and vapours. It seemed to have grown even larger and more menacing in the intervening time and although now subdued in the daylight, it still exuded an air of palpable hostility. I gave a shudder and involuntarily took a step backwards, as if stepping out of its line of sight.

'Do you fear it Sergeant?' I found Boudicca's dark eyes locked with my own and for a second words deserted me.

'With good reason,' said Challis suddenly standing at my side. 'We've encountered its wrath directly.'

'Interesting,' said Arthur, 'yet here you stand alive and unharmed. That must have taken some doing, you must tell us more of such a feat.'

'Perhaps another time. We survived … as much by luck as judgement, if I'm honest,' I replied, annoyed that Challis had given away more than I would have liked.

'I'm sure that's just modesty talking,' smoothed Arthur. 'Marines take a lot of killing, as you've proven. Come Boudicca, this is hardly the time to press our guests, we promised them food and shelter, not the inquisition.

'Now, once we're home and you're settled in, we can talk some more. Father will be anxious to meet you I'm sure, so follow and be most welcome.'

Arthur's charm and warmth papered over that needley little exchange and on the way toward the walled citadel he was full of stories and chatter, pointing out various features of Gwaelod, trying to put us at ease and make us forget Boudicca's obvious antipathy.

Despite his cheery chatter and rather callow attempts to impress Haines, doubts still gnawed at me. Was this what the major wanted? The HUD arrow, still pointing firmly on course, would seem to suggest so, but were we supposed to encounter these freakishly powerful adolescents or had he meant us to reconnoitre this place without revealing our presence?

Well, whatever he intended, that particular jack was firmly out of its box now and even if we wanted to, there didn't seem to be any easy way to refuse their hospitality anyway. Based on what we'd seen, they could most likely disarm us in the blink of an eye, sling us over their brawny shoulders and haul us bodily into Gwaelod whether we wanted it or not.

But we were also tired and hungry, still feeling the effects of being hunted all night by Glyndŵr and his men and that walled town was a haven where we could all rest and I could regather my scattered thoughts. It seemed another lifetime since we'd slept and we all needed some R&R. At least that's what I told myself to keep any lingering doubts at bay.

We walked along the top of the cliff and followed Arthur, Boudicca and their companions until we came to a path which led down onto the sand and shale of the bay. They all jogged down without a thought, much to our collective consternation but when Arthur saw us hesitate, he sidled back with a puzzled look on his face. Before I could say a word, Haines piped up.

'What are you doing?'

'What do you mean?' he replied.

'Going down there. We'd never risk walking that close to the sea.'

'Why on earth not?'

'Why? Are you mental? Because of the Devils of course,' she said.

'The Devils?' Now he looked really confused.

'The sea devils, the demons … you know, the walking fish: ugly, violent, prone to kill people and worse?' I said. 'You made a big pile of them back there.'

'Oh, you mean the sea creatures? Well, you've seen how we deal with them, there's no need to be worried, you're safe with me … I mean … us.'

'Yes but that was on dry land,' Haines persisted. 'You shouldn't go near the water, they'll drag you down to their undersea cities, kill you, or worse, breed with you, so that you're forced to carry a terrible hybrid baby. Then they…'

'Relax,' said Arthur smiling easily. 'There's a half dozen catapults and arbalests trained on that beach. They couldn't put a flipper out of the water before they were shot through. They're slow, ponderous, far too vulnerable on land, no match for us. Father has taught us all about their weak spots.' Haines softened but still looked a little sceptical.

'What about their magic?' I wondered, voicing a question that had puzzled me since we beheld the fortress. 'You dealt with that warlock like, well, like nothing I've ever seen before, but could your home deal so readily with a legion of their spell casters?'

'Our walls are high and well protected against the creatures' magic. Something in the stones Father says which makes their sorcery ineffective. There were attempts apparently at the beginning, when we first occupied Gwaelod, before I was born. But Father's no slouch with his defensive strategies and they paid a heavy price. Since then, they've left Gwaelod well alone.' For a moment he was very much in earnest, then his eyes flicked back to Haines and he grinned.

'Come on, follow me down, there's absolutely nothing to worry about. You can take off those heavy boots too and wriggle your toes in the sand. You'll never get a better chance.'

Haines looked at me, but I shrugged and then nodded assent.

'Go on then. She's in your hands Arthur … god help you.' He grinned and the pair of them bounded down the path and went scampering onto the beach like two colts in spring time.

'This gets weirder every minute,' said Challis as we watched them begin to — what can only be described as — frolic across the sands.

'No shit.' I said and meant every word.

So that was how we came before the walls of the fortress of Gwaelod, not hunted and pursued by our mortal enemies, but like a Victorian family taking a stroll along the esplanade after a paddle in the shallows. Practically the only thing missing was a bucket and spade. a round of ice creams and some striped bathing wear.

It was frankly just plain weird walking on that shore, as if we hadn't a care in the world, when every instinct and fibre of my being told me to run, flee inland and begone.

But after a short hike we finally stood before Gwaelod's walls and evidently we were expected, as I could hear sounds of bolts and bars being unfastened and a smaller portal in the ponderous iron-banded outer doors swung open.

The outer gatehouse was a reassuringly solid affair flanked by twin watch towers and it was heavily fortified, the flint and stones chipped and pockmarked as if it had born the brunt of some assault, though whether recently or from long ago, it was hard to say.

'Please,' said Arthur indicating the gap and waving us through. A heavy raised portcullis loomed above our heads and we found ourselves in a short arched tunnel with a second portcullis at the far end. Our footsteps echoed hollowly in that enclosed space and it was dotted with murder holes above and arrow slits on either side: anyone foolish enough to assault the castle via this route would pay a heavy toll for every inch of ground they gained.

Soon though, we had passed through that forbidding portal, the second portcullis had been lowered behind us with a reverberant clang and I began to drink in my first sight of the fortress town of Gwaelod. It was an old settlement, probably occupied since the Middle Ages, though now perfectly adapted to these troubled times. While a hundred half remembered movies told me to expect disease, burning dung and goggle-eyed peasants. it was actually rather clean, pleasant and well kept. There was a small market with vendors selling their wares, fresh fish and meat and stalls hung with flowers and bunches of cut herbs.

Medieval cobbled streets zig-zagged out in random winding patterns, forming an organic maze of stone-walled houses topped with a mixture of thatch and slate. Beyond, rose a second inner barbican and above that loomed the immensity of the central keep. On the nearest tower, an ensign flapped in the breeze. I didn't recognise the design though it looked like some kind of cartoon inventor flanked by a slightly downcast anthropomorphised dog.

The inhabitants were out in force to greet their patrol's return and its three additional curiosities drew plenty of stares. A heavily armed group was arrayed in front of us in the courtyard and their leader, a tall, rangy, bearded fellow who bore a more-than-passing resemblance to Arthur strode forward. He looked us up and down beneath arched brows before pronouncing.

'So, what news? And who are these *strangers* you've brought into our home?' He said the word with an obvious distaste he didn't bother to conceal.

'Where are your manners Rhodri? Is this any way to greet your brother or our guests?'

'Guests? Pffaw, infiltrators more like. Father won't thank you for bringing these undesirables inside our walls. What of the other matter?'

'The woods were crawling with Glyndŵr's men, it seemed rather senseless to slaughter all of them for no very good reason. Then we ran into the Sergeant here and her men, so it appeared more sensible to return and consult Father.'

'And what of you?' The rather splenetic Rhodri eyed us. 'Know anything about that explosion this morning?'

'It wasn't us,' I replied.

'Not quite what I asked.'

'Yet it's the answer you got,' I said, trying to keep my tone even.

'So what brings you so suddenly into our lives, our home?' Rhodri glowered.

'Not anything I'd particularly care to discuss in the middle of a courtyard,' I replied.

'Is that right? Well as Warden of Gwaelod I demand to know, especially before I let the SAS lite wander freely around within our walls.'

'For fuck's sake, calm down Rhodri,' Arthur said. 'I'll vouch for them, naturally.'

'Or is the Marshal's word not good enough for you?' interjected Boudicca, unexpectedly taking Arthur's side.

'On your word then *Marshal*, so be it.' The warden glowered and then turned abruptly on his heel, followed swiftly by the remainder of his guard.

'That was tenser than I was expecting.' I said.

'Forgive Rhodri, he has no great love for outsiders and even less so for the military. He's not exactly my biggest fan either. Thwarted ambition basically, as the eldest, he thinks he should be Marshal.'

'And what do you think?'

'I think it's time we get you settled before we lose our reputation as the region's premier tourist attraction.' He grinned and despite the nagging voice inside me, I smiled with him.

After that rather ambiguous welcome, Arthur and Boudicca showed us to a small, comfortably outfitted cottage in Gwaelod's first quarter and promising to return later, they bid us make ourselves at home, which we were glad to do. Food and drink was brought and laid out and we fell to heartily, tucking into the plain but nourishing fare, until finally pushing our plates away in contentment.

Challis shooed Haines out of the master bedroom which he said was 'reserved for the commander' and for once I didn't mind letting my rank do the pulling. In a short while they had taken a look around, stowed their gear and made themselves comfortable in the other rooms, but despite the cosy surroundings and warmth in my belly, I found myself staring out of our cottage window a little uneasily.

I quickly checked the HUD, the indicator blinked and spun, as if unsure of its direction or more likely, simply because we had finally arrived at our destination. This was surely the right place, but I still wasn't certain I had done the right thing in bringing us here. Arthur was friendly enough but that was in no small part because he'd taken a shine to Haines, but the rest of them? Well, they weren't exactly overflowing with the milk of human kindness judging by Boudicca's attitude and Rhodri's 'greeting'. Their abilities inspired awe when they were directed against the Devils, but they could just as easily be employed against us and despite our suits and weapons, there was little we could do to resist them here — or perhaps anywhere for that matter.

There was no denying these high walls would provide a strong refuge from the island though and that was important. The rest of the inhabitants seemed tranquil enough too, but I couldn't shake that feeling of unease. Had I meekly led us into a gilded trap?

'Command never gets any easier, you just make your choice and hope it's the right one.' Challis had suddenly appeared next to me, speaking in a low voice, while Haines rattled around in the room opposite testing out the bed by bouncing repeatedly on it.

'So who exactly gave you a direct line into my head?'

'Don't take a mind reader to work it out Emma, it's written all over your face. Truth to tell I was kind of wondering the same thing myself. A proper medieval castle, those extraordinary kids, it's not exactly something out of the training manual is it?'

'What is nowadays?'

'But look, better here than being hunted out in the open. Those ferals would probably have picked up our trail eventually and if not them, then what if we'd run into that warlock and its warband all on our ownsome? By bringing us here, you simply chose the least worst option. Sometimes, that's all you can do.'

'Perhaps, but what now? What if the major's dead or he doesn't come back? What do we do then? It seems like we've found the right place, but I still don't even know what we're supposed to be doing here. What if…'

'Look, sometimes you have to let things take their course, cross each particular bridge as you come to it. And I don't think we've seen the last of Major Seraph, he'll be back, that one, he wouldn't abandon us here. In the meantime, perhaps a little light reconnaissance will ease your mind?'

'Take a look around you mean, get the lie of the land?'

'Exactly.'

'Thanks Challis, I needed that.'

'My pleasure … sir.'

We left Haines at the cottage and her gentle snores were already drifting out into a drowsy afternoon, as we closed the door behind us. So began a rather rambling, random sightseeing tour which encompassed the whole of Gwaelod's first quarter. Everywhere we went, we were met by polite if curious looks, although no-one actually accosted us in even the slightest way. An hour or two's stroll while the sea breezes whipped in and the sun dipped in and out of the clouds was enough to get a pretty good picture of how things stood. As we stared out to sea on one of the outer battlements, there was plenty to mull over.

Gwaelod revealed itself to be an impressively self-sufficient stronghold. Well manned batteries of ballista and catapults bristled along its outer walls and if Arthur's assertion about them being proof against Devil magic were true — and there was no reason to doubt him — it was a formidable bastion, practically impregnable to conventional assault.

Inside, a couple of public wells provided fresh water which was drawn up by buckets, although there were plenty of reclamation and desalination units scattered around too. We spotted several wind turbines and even some photo-voltaic cells which had been angled to harvest the energy of the autumnal sun. Smaller penned off areas contained livestock and animals and there were many well-tended and cultivated kitchen gardens. Since you could throw a hook and line more or less straight off the battlements, you could probably pull up as many fish as you could stuff down your throat as well. Anyone intending to try and take this place by siege or starve it out, would be well advised to settle in for the duration.

As for the inhabitants, well they seemed a fairly unremarkable bunch, which was remarkable enough itself in these strange times. They were clean, well groomed and most presentable, when back in the safe zones everyone, civilian and military alike, wore their muck, grime and filth like a second skin. Gwaelod's honest peasantry were mainly dressed in practical attire, newly made and locally-manufactured, rather than the patchwork and rags you'd find on ferals or survivors. All these refinements and indeed comforts, told of a level of organisation and husbandry missing in even the so-called free towns, which clung like limpets along the spine of our flooded isle.

There were more than enough of them too, at least a couple of hundred by my rough reckoning moving around the settlement, engaged in various domestic tasks or about their everyday business. Groups of young lads kicked around a freshly stitched home-made football, young girls bobbed about running errands or playing hopscotch in the street, hammer clanged on anvil in a blacksmith's forge and the steady clack clack of looms beat out a constant, reassuring domestic rhythm.

A few middle-aged gossips and fishwives went silent and nudged each other giggling as we passed, though that may have been in response to Challis' imposing presence and handsome bearing. All seemed healthy, happy and content, a state which was downright unusual in itself. Didn't they know there was a war on? Evidently not, it seemed to have passed this prosperous, bustling place completely by.

There was only one fly lurking in this bucolic ointment and that was the bulk of the inner keep which loomed above the first quarter. Its gateway was awash with warden's men, who were heavily armed and armoured, their weapons a strange mix of the modern and medieval, though none the less deadly for all that. There were portable *carroballista*, hand-wound bolt throwers, what looked like some kind of steampunk rocket launcher and gently simmering cauldrons of pitch and tar, to complement the array of hand held pikes, halberds and crossbows.

Despite loitering for a while, we didn't see a single one of Gwaelod's ordinary denizens pass through that heavily guarded portal and even our low-key stroll past was met with unfriendly stares and the meaningful fingering of a few safety catches. Perhaps that bugger Rhodri had told them to expect us? Maybe not, but even as we hurried away, I found myself wondering why anyone would bother to guard an inner gateway so closely, when surely any real threat must come from outside?

But that random thought was soon forgotten as we climbed a staircase up onto the outer walls and took an amble along the battlements. The HUD marker continued its constant frustrating orbits, providing no guidance, but up here the gentle breezes and staggering view made any danger seem a million miles away. I sighed and watched the white crested waves roll in to pound the shore. Far away to the west, the island still lurked in the offing and although it rumbled and seethed sporadically, from this perspective, it now seemed remote and distant, perhaps a little impotent even.

Had we finally found sanctuary, a solitary bastion that could resist the horror and deprivations of the age? How easy it would be to shelter behind these solid, protective walls, proof against the threat of the creatures, the iniquities of the ferals, the burden of the survivors and the idiocy of high command? Had we finally found a place between the Devils and the deep blue sea?

These rather lyrical musings were interrupted by the rich baritone of Challis, who was staring far out across the waters.

'Interesting place this.' As ever, his powers of understatement were unsurpassed.

'Copy that: strong walls, formidable defences, self sufficient in water, food, even power. All the ingredients you'd need to ride out the apocalypse in absolute comfort.'

'True, but notice anything else that's weird?'

'That there isn't a queue stretching a couple of miles outside the gate?'

'Well, not just that, but don't you find all this a bit too fucking perfect?'

'You mean how did they manage to carve themselves out this little piece of paradise in the middle of the badlands?'

'There's that too,' said Challis. 'But actually, I was thinking more about the women.'

'Time and a place no, Corporal?'

'Very funny. What I'm saying is: plenty of kids, plenty of more ahem … mature ladies. But where are all the actual women? Not a single one of what you might call of — in old money — marriageable age. Odd, no?'

'Possibly, I hadn't give it much thought. But it isn't unheard of to hide your womenfolk away, there's a lot of bad men out there.'

'True, but fewer in here I'd say, so why hide them? Apart from yer fella's sister obviously.'

'Also very curious. I wonder…'

But any further speculation on my part was curtailed as the cold eyed subject of our discussion appeared alongside her more convivial sibling. Arthur, who had somehow managed to rouse Haines and persuade her to accompany him, came bounding up like an eager puppy.

'Ah, Sergeant, Corporal, there you are. I have good news, Father would very much like to meet you and he's decided to hold a feast in your honour, tonight, to formally welcome you to Gwaelod.'

'Very good of him, but it's hardly necessary to…'

'I know but he, we, I, all of us, we insist! It's a long while since we've had a chance to welcome guests from the outside world. I know Father will be eager to hear news of what's going on, as will we all and besides, your arrival is a cause for celebration. Please, don't deny us this privilege … and this pleasure.' They all looked at me meaningfully and I wavered. I was always more suited to the rigours of the front line than the niceties of diplomacy, but I suppose it would have been churlish to refuse, especially with all those expectant faces turned on me. Just one more burden of command I supposed. So I simply nodded.

'Thank you, we would be most honoured.'

'Excellent,' said Arthur. 'That's settled then. 'But if you'll allow one further indulgence. That impressive battledress is looking somewhat the worse for wear and not really suitable for a proper banquet. Ellie ... I mean Private Haines here was saying it's almost out of energy too.

'So, please let us clean and recharge them for you and perhaps we might also furnish you with some local garments a bit more well, becoming, to you ladies?' He raised an eyebrow at Haines who giggled nervously. 'With your permission, Sergeant, of course.'

'Well, in for a penny, in for a pound I suppose.' I sighed and nodded, bowing to the inevitable.

CHAPTER TWELVE

Tom, Dick and Harry

So it was that several hours later, as the shadows lengthened and night stole over the fortress of Gwaelod, Haines and I attempted to smuggle ourselves into some strangely unfamiliar apparel. On further reflection, I hadn't been at all happy about giving up the marines' suits, but they were nearly drained of juice and it had to be said, hardly formal attire, especially caked with mud, filth and not a few stray arrowheads. Arthur had arranged it so they could be charged in our quarters and he even provided a key for securing the cottage. Fortunately, the com system had its own battery and detached discretely so I was able to conceal earpiece and mic bud underneath my hair without any problem.

'What are these? Trousers, but only the legs?' Haines bafflement was writ large upon her face.

'They're stockings, you wear them under your dress.'

'What for?'

'To keep your legs warm I suppose, see you secure them with the garter and they tie there at the top with the ribbons. They are also considered to be quite ... alluring.'

'Alluring?'

You know attractive, sexy. By men mainly.'

'Oh, oh, I see,' she said blushing and turned away, probably believing I didn't see her secret smile. I ordered her to go easy on the booze and made a mental note to detail Challis to keep an especially close eye on our horny little private throughout the course of the evening.

It had been years, before the Flood, since I'd worn anything that could even vaguely be described as flattering let alone anything quite as decorative and becoming as the ensemble with which we had been provided. Haines and I had donned two velvet and brocade evening numbers which were both flattering and beautiful, fitted us like a dream and hugged in all the right places.

A vast bath had also been brought to our quarters and placed at our disposal and a wall tap brought a steady stream of piping hot water to fill it. For the second time that day, I pulled rank and sat and soaked in this unexpected luxuriousness for a blissful half hour. With the addition of hand-made soap and clean towels, it was just like being in a five star hotel at the beginning of a dirty weekend. I almost shed a tear with the sheer remembered indulgence of it all.

Haines had eyed the whole procedure with deep suspicion but when at last, my skin began to wrinkle, I hoisted myself out, towelled myself down and attempted to persuade her to give it a try. She immediately balked and bucked, more used to making her ablutions in a freezing river — if at all. Exasperated, I made it an order and after making a sour face, then tentatively dipping a toe, Haines at last took the plunge. However as the layers of grime, sweat and dirt had sloughed off her and a fresh deluge of hot water allowed her to feel the warmth and luxury, she became such a ready convert, that I eventually had to jokingly threaten her with a court martial in order to stop all the splashing.

Challis had tactfully made himself scarce during our ablutions, but just as we had finished putting on our evening wear and I was putting the final finishing touches to Haines' hair, a knock came on the door followed by Challis' dreadlocked head peeping around.

'Oh, I'm sorry to interrupt beautiful ladies, but I was looking for Sergeant Stokes and Private Haines. You don't happen to know where they've gone now, do you?'

'Ha, bloody ha,' I said. 'Mind you, you don't scrub up so bad yourself Corporal.' Challis had apparently found himself a berth for a similar wash and brush-up and wore a suit of elegant quasi-medieval finery like he was born to it. No doubt one of Gwaelod's ladies was already cherishing the memory.

'What about weapons? We can hardly take those along.' He indicated our rifles. 'But it don't feel right to go unarmed.'

'Knives in boots or wherever they can comfortably fit then,' I said. 'They can hardly object to those in these troubled times. Besides we'll need something to spread the butter. Make sure you take the com buds too, if we're separated I want us to be able to stay in touch. Okay, all set? Game face on? Let's go do this.'

Our feast of welcome was even more lavish than I had expected. We had been collected promptly by Arthur who pronounced himself delighted by our transformation and whose eyes lingered on Haines longingly, especially now she looked every inch the captivating young lady. We moved in close escort through the winding streets:

Arthur flattering and cooing at Haines, Challis squiring Boudicca and I attempting to make small talk with Alexander, the charming, rather earnest young man, who, earlier in the day had caused a Devil's eyes to pop clean out its sockets.

Our torchlight procession eventually took us to the inner fortress's main gate, where this time the guards gave us a much more deferential reception, raising their weapons in salute and clicking their heels. Above, the walls of the keep had been lit up with a series of rotating, coloured lights and this, combined with the starry skies above, gave the castle an enchanting air, as if we were walking through a living fairy tale.

Inside, we were ushered directly into the keep's magnificent great hall, all high vaulted roof, curving cross beams and rich tapestries — it positively dripped with medieval opulence.

There was evidently no famine or shortages here and course followed hard upon course, until the seams of my new attire groaned, threatening to burst. Delicious fresh baked bread, delicate cheeses, roast meats, platters of fruits and sweetmeats, all washed down with flagons of locally brewed honey and nettle ale, delicious fruit wines and golden horns of mead.

As guests of honour, we had been seated at the high table overlooking a merry throng, composed largely of Gwaelod's common folk down below in the cheap seats, while surrounding us were the cream of the companions. Arthur had skilfully manoeuvred himself into the chair next to Haines and was plying her with all manner of exotic sweets and titbits. I ate heartily but drank sparingly, as did Challis under strict orders to keep a close eye on my now giggling private.

But in truth, despite being hosted in the forbidding immensity of the central keep, this quickly became a highly convivial gathering. Between courses, we were kept well entertained: poems were read, songs — some rather risqué — were sung and a variety of jugglers, acrobats and comedians put the company in good humour and at ease. I must admit, amidst the warmth, laughter and candlelight, even I went so far as to start enjoying myself a little.

It was like being transported back through the centuries to a time of feasting, dancing and laughter, a text book medieval banquet. Even Boudicca seemed to have thawed somewhat and was making small talk with Challis, comparing lethal takedowns no doubt, while to my left, even Rhodri was wearing no more than a moderately low-grade scowl as he surveyed the hall.

However, of the mysterious Father, who had been so keen to make our acquaintance, there was no sign, though the high table's central chair was vacant and I presumed that this place of honour must be reserved for him. When I gently enquired, Arthur replied that our missing host was a 'slave to his work', opined he was probably just 'finishing up' and would most likely deign to bless us with his presence shortly.

As yet another course materialised, I politely declined a portion of blackberry and apple tart laden with honey and cream and decided I needed some fresh air and better still, a smoke.

Making my excuses, I rose on slightly unsteady feet, managed to half entangle myself in a curtained alcove but eventually found myself outside, on a handily unoccupied battlement. I removed the crumpled packet from the voluminous sleeve where I had stashed it, straightened out a creased cigarette and fired up my Zippo, enjoying the nicotine rush and breathing out a long cone of blue-grey smoke into the cool night air.

Below, the castle's mighty walls and tall towers were captivating in the moonlight and even the rumblings of the accursed island seemed distant and feeble, compared to the reassuring solidity which surrounded us. I let out a long sigh of contentment and possibly a small burp as well, as the wine glow stole over me.

'Is that a real cigarette?' A voice whispered from the shadows. 'So bad for one, yet so delicious. So many years since I ... yet one still finds oneself twitching. I don't suppose you could find it in your heart to spare one for a repentant quitter?'

'Sure,' I rattled the pack and extracted one, feeling benevolent in my warm contentment.

'Thank you, so kind, most thoughtful.' The flame from my Zippo made a small halo and he took the cigarette gently but eagerly, exulting as he inhaled the first lug.

'Ah, so wrong, yet so moreish,' he exhaled with satisfaction, greedily chaining several more puffs, then dissolved into a coughing fit, spluttering and hacking until he was almost bent double against one of the crenulations. When the fit had passed, he offered a thin smile and then inhaled the remainder in a series of deep pulls until it was smoked down to the butt, then placed the spent end into a pocket. Another fit seemed to be upon him, but with a supreme effort he mastered himself and instead deployed a dreamy kind of smile.

'Terrible habit, but when have we ever stopped doing something, just because it was bad for us?'

'True,' I said as I flicked my end over the battlement.

My new companion was a tall, angular looking kind of fellow, aesthetic and spare, with a shaved head and not an ounce of fat on his smooth, even features. He was dressed in a plain overall, topped by a white lab coat and spoke in an even rational sort of tone. Instinct seemed to tell you he was old, but his face seemed almost ageless, as if time had slid by him and simply forgotten to leave any discernable mark. His eyes were perhaps the only remarkable thing about him, alive and twinkling with a ferocious energy.

'You must be one of the new arrivals young Arthur brought back. Splendid boy that, kind hearted, thoughtful.'

'I am. Sergeant Emma Stokes, Emma.' I offered my hand, feeling surprisingly convivial. He didn't take it.

'I see, well I must say the marines' uniform appears to have undergone some significant changes over the years and all for the better, I might add.'

'This? No, this is a loaner, I...'

'Indeed? Well I suppose you know young lady what the penalty is for smuggling dangerous, filthy contraband like tobacco into Gwaelod?'

'What? But you just...'

'I'm sorry, I'm just pulling your leg. Appalling habit I know, but we have so few visitors and I have no one else to tease. Everyone here takes me so seriously, I'm sorry, I couldn't resist.'

'Jesus, you had me going for a second.'

'Relax, the penalty for such subversive behaviour is actually ... the freedom of the town and a guided tour of the keep.'

'Okay ... I suppose. Just one more thing. Who the hell are you?'

'Me? Oh, I didn't introduce myself did I? How rude of me, the mind plays such cruel tricks on the elderly. Most folks around here know me as Father, but that's not really appropriate for you, is it Emma? I used to have another name once, now let me think, what was it? Forgive me while I dredge it up from the back door of my increasingly fragile memory. Oh of course, that's it, please, call me ... Ken.'

And that was my rather bizarre introduction to 'Father' (I don't think I ever actually did address him as Ken) and after scrounging another cigarette 'for Ron, later Ron', he led me back along the battlement to a door concealed at the far end. Narrow circular steps led up into the interior to a darkened minstrels' gallery which overlooked the great hall below. The feast continued in full swing, the high table with Haines and Challis and the rest of the companions directly beneath us and the glow of candlelight and the many shining faces, gave it a warm, cosy vibe. It had been a long time, before the Flood, since I'd seen so many people looking quite so happy.

'Quite the place you've got here.'

He smiled, almost shyly. 'Yes, an oasis and a refuge in these dark times. We are fortunate indeed.'

'Fortunate is putting it mildly. How do you survive out here? How do you keep the Devils at bay?'

'The Dev...? Ah yes, the creatures. Oh we have our methods, our walls are high and strong, impervious to their magic. They leave us alone and if they don't...'

'If they don't?'

'Hm, well it's an old adage, 'show don't tell', so perhaps it would be easiest if I let you see for yourself? Now, let's move away from the edge, if they spot me up here, I won't have any peace at all. They'll shout and chant and hector me to come down, preside over the feast, insist on toasts and all sorts of nonsense. All very tedious and counter productive, a total waste of my valuable time, much better left to the young people. Now, I promised you a tour didn't I? Come this way, I think you'll find it all rather fascinating.'

A few minutes later we had made our way down, deep into the bowels of the citadel. We must have been well below ground level, judging by the number of steps, but you never would have known it. The clammy dankness and grim darkness you might have expected to find in the deeps of an ancient castle was nowhere to be seen. Everywhere we went was marked by immaculate masonry, with regular, almost unerringly perfect walls, all finished with a neat coating of lime wash.

Father kept up a constant stream of gossip and small talk, describing and itemising the minutia of life in the fortress, from the habits and peculiarities of its many inhabitants, to its carefully regulated crop cycles, immaculate dairy yields and even the production dilemmas faced in the composition of the various materials which made up my 'rather fetching dress'.

Perhaps it was the drink, perhaps I was just genuinely impressed, but hearing him talk like that was rather compelling and it was evident his vision, insight and intelligence ran through this community like a master thread, governing and regulating every aspect of its life. I listened, admiring, as he wove his web, until eventually we reached our destination at the bottom of a long spiral stone stairwell.

The walls and arched ceiling of this enclosed space was much like the rest of the castle's interior, but straight ahead, inset into the far wall, was a huge circular high-tech metal door which took up almost the entire span. It opened with a soft hiss and swung silently inward at our approach.

'Here we are at last, please, do come in Emma,' he stepped through and I followed him a little nervously. Was I about to enter some kind of weird dungeon or a freaky medieval torture chamber? The answer was no, instead we were in a bright, fluorescent-lit corridor, a long immaculately white hallway stretching out before us with modern doors lining either side.

'Well, this is not exactly what I was expecting.'

'A little different to the rest of Gwaelod, hm?'

'I'll say.'

'Well, I need a fairly sterile environment for my work and white always shows the stains.'

'I don't envy your cleaners.'

'You know, for that matter neither do I. But they do a decent job and rarely complain — now I've banned their union at least.' He grinned and dropped the cigarette butt he had smoked earlier. At this, a small robot thing scuttled out from some hidden cubby hole and began to meticulously sweep it up.

'Well, it seems you can get the staff nowadays,' I said, hoping to conceal the fact that I was actually rather impressed.

As the door closed behind us with a sigh, Father set out along the corridor at a brisk pace and I followed close on, trying to temper my curiosity but wondering just how I could politely frame the burning question of just what that so-called work entailed. In the end, I just decided to ask him outright.

'So what precisely do you research down … oh my good god!' But the rest of my questions remained unasked, as I beheld something so unexpected, I had never thought to see its like again.

We had just passed a long, thickly reinforced glass window and I had idly glanced down to see what lay below. For a moment I thought I must be looking at a picture or some kind of holographic projection, the next I must have double-taked like a gurning idiot.

Without thinking, I pressed my face and hands up against the glass, lost in wonder.

'Shit, is that real?! Is that really real? Where in the name of all that's holy did you get your hands on that?'

He smiled modestly, but couldn't keep a certain note of pride out of his voice.

'That? Oh it's real all right, really really real. Just a little something I picked up during the course of my travels. I used to roam much further abroad than I do nowadays, such a pity the work keeps me tethered here.' His nonchalance was somewhat undermined by the knowing wink he threw my way.

'Fuck me, if you'll forgive the vernacular.'

'I will, Emma, in this case I think it probably merits it. Your appreciation is noted.'

What I saw was quite simply staggering. Even though what I was looking at was as material and solid as you, I, or indeed this debriefing room, sir, I had to rub my eyes and almost pinch myself to make sure I was awake. I suddenly became very sober, very quickly.

'I shit you not' is a phrase that's become worn out from long overuse in the army, but in this case it was justified, I think that might be the very first sentence of my report if I ever get round to typing this up. To be honest, I can't think of anything more appropriate to presage the rest of my remarks.

What I was looking at was a dock, carved out from the living rock underneath the base of the castle. You could easily have mistaken it for the lair of some unlikely Bond villain or at least the set they built to film it. But this was no illusion, conjured for a spectacular movie climax, or an artfully contrived thwarting, but a fully operational naval dock.

And there, nestling in its berth in the shallows was the sleek, dark lines of what looked for all the world like the smaller sister of one of the Royal Navy's old Vanguard class boats.

'Meet the *Daedalus*, formerly HMS *Damocles*, a Dreadnaught class nuclear-powered attack submarine. She was thought lost with all hands before the Flood.'

'Isn't she a bit small for an attack boat?' I said but as I uttered those words, a particular penny suddenly and very firmly dropped.

'Small, but perfectly formed and every bit as deadly as her older siblings. When it looked like Scotland would vote to secede from the union back in 2014, it was decided to build a smaller, more agile class of vessel, one which would suit the shallower drafts of the proposed new bases in England and Wales.

'*Damocles* was a prototype, the first and last of her kind. Fortunately, when the creatures overwhelmed the naval bases and the rest of the fleet was lost in the deeps, *Damocles* was on the surface, undergoing secret trials. Through a rather circuitous process which I won't bore you with, we eventually managed to acquire her and now she's been reclaimed, refitted, renamed and I suppose you could say re-commissioned for active service.'

'How do you 'acquire' a nuclear submarine? Who are you, Captain Nemo?'

He smiled. 'With great difficulty I assure you, but there's little reason to dwell on the specifics now. Past history is well, past history. Suffice it to say she is mine now, lock, stock and launch codes.'

'How, why, wh…'

'I know, I know, a little overwhelming isn't it? You'll have to forgive a certain level of self-satisfaction on my part. It's not every day I get to show off my favourite toy to a fresh set of eyes, especially ones who are properly able to appreciate her.'

'Crew?'

'Long gone by the time she came into my possession, but Arthur and the others have been trained in her operation, though actually, she can be commanded by a remarkably small crew.'

'Fuck me, what would the government, what would the Navy say, if they knew you had one of these?'

The words were out of my mouth before I had a chance to haul them back.

'Oh, I doubt they'd be best pleased Emma.'

'No shit.'

'Well indeed, so quite possibly the worst thing to reveal her presence to one of their representatives, especially given the *Daedalus'* payload. Doubly so, if that representative happened to be a Royal Marine, no? It would be a case, as our American friends might put it of quite literally "telling it to the marines".'

'Hold on a minute…'

'Relax Emma, please, be at ease, I'm just teasing you again. I didn't bring you down here to make you feel uncomfortable. Besides, as for revealing things I shouldn't to the marines, well, as we both know, you're nothing of the kind.'

'What! I'll have you know…'

'Come come now Emma, this is hardly the time to dissemble. You may wear those rather splendid suits and display the requisite insignia, but you're no more a Royal Marine than I am. Don't worry, it's fine and I'm not here to judge, we're all forced to adopt uniforms, convenient masks to hide our true intent in these straightened times.' He spoke so gently, without a hint of reproach, but with such a degree of certainty, that there seemed little point in trying to maintain the fiction.

'How did you know?'

'Oh, not too difficult to discern. Your black comrade, Challis? A soldier? Absolutely. Experienced? Undoubtedly. He would certainly pass muster. You? Well, the same, with a few more reservations, but I'd still buy it … just about. As for the young lady, the delightful Ellie, whom Arthur seems so struck by? Not a chance. Besides, if I didn't already have my own suspicions, she rather let the cat out of the bag I'm afraid.'

'I see, what gave her away?'

'When she was down by the shore with Arthur, she revealed she was almost pathologically afraid of water. Hardly exactly ideal marine material, hm? And if she wasn't a marine, well, it followed logically that neither were the rest of you.'

'Damn, you appear to have us bang to rights.'

'Indeed, but don't worry, I won't hold it against you or ask any more inconvenient questions: what circumstances forced you to adopt those uniforms and what brought you here, is your own affair. I have always been more concerned with the future than the past. Now, let us proceed, we can always return to the *Daedalus* later. She is, though remarkable in many ways, the least of the many wonders I wish to lay before you.'

He waved me forward and as we walked, preoccupied, I barely heard the sound of our footsteps echoing hollowly along that corridor. Our cover, such as it was, was well and truly blown, but Father, apparently, could not have given less of a flying fuck.

Frankly though, that was the least of my worries. To meet someone who has a nuclear powered sub — even a small one — casually stashed in their basement is not exactly an everyday occurrence in these trying times. As you can imagine, my gob was well and truly smacked, sir. What can you say to that? I had nothing and if I wasn't mistaken, he had mentioned something about a 'payload' too. Could that thing still be carrying active warheads? My mind was churning, as he ushered me through one of that anonymous multitude of doors.

I was still so preoccupied, it was a couple of moments before I registered I was now in a laboratory, but not the kind of lab I had ever encountered before. Oh, there were benches and test tubes and apparatus and all the experimental paraphernalia which you might expect to find in a well-stocked, high-end research facility, there was all that and more. No, the most arresting and immediate sight was contained on the far wall, which held row upon row of large glass containers all hooked up via tubes and pipes. They bubbled and churned as they pumped various coloured liquids around a hermetically sealed network.

Perhaps that's what you'd expect to find in a mad genius' lair and to an extent, so would I. However, more disturbing was the fact that each of those bell jars contained the neatly severed head of a Devil. Countless bulbous-eyed, crested Devil noggins floated there, suspended in various coloured solutions or plain sea water.

Perhaps you'd think I'd be shocked and staggered and you'd be right, yet far more disturbing than the simple fact of them being there, was that a good half to three quarters of them still appeared to be alive! Impotent malevolence, madness, burned in their fishy eyes and there was a horrid fascination to the animation of their gaping mouths as they breathed, apparently without gills, their existence maintained by the wires and electrodes which pierced their flesh. It was one of the few times I ever detected more than a hint of emotion in those blank, impassive faces. A whole row appeared to have had the top portion of their skull removed and you could see brain matter, pulsing and changing colour, as it peeped over the bony ridges of the cranium.

I trust you'll believe me when I say I'm no shrinking violet, sir, but in that moment I could feel my stomach contract, spasming in a dry, heaving retch, that surfeit of rich food bucking and churning. With some difficulty, I managed to contain my nausea and refocus.

'Please don't be alarmed, they really can't hurt you.'

'Are those *things* alive?'

'Oh yes, quite alive, though safely contained. You've nothing to fear from them.'

'I think I need to sit — possibly lie — down.'

'You'll find a chair just behind you.'

My fingers found its edge and I sat back onto the high-backed lab stool without really looking, still transfixed by the macabre spectacle contained within those detestable bell jars. Yet the next thing I knew, I was jumping out of the chair and almost my skin as well, as something lurched behind me. I turned, blade drawn, ready to fight for my very life, for even in that instant I had recognised the tell tale sound of Devil movement.

'What the actual, *actual* living fuck?!'

My blade fell to my side and my fingers, numb, almost let it drop at a sight that surpassed even the remarkable horrors I had just witnessed. For there, shackled to the wall, held fast by weighty steel fetters and secured with looped chains were three live Devils, a chieftain and a brave, flanking the shaman in the centre.

Instinctively, I took a step backward as the shaman lurched toward me, straining at its bonds, but it was held fast and after a moment's struggle it subsided and sank back apathetically.

I was so stunned that I just stood there gaping, for how long, I don't know. We, and by that I mean the combined might of the regular army and the militia, have never succeeded in capturing so much as a single one of these things alive, as far as I'm aware. Yet, here were three living, breathing examples of our mortal enemy, bound, chained and helpless as newborns. More so, for now I saw that pieces of their bodies, their very flesh, had been removed, carved off with a precision that spoke more of the surgeon's knife than the fishmonger's cleaver. The brave's body appeared reasonably unmarked, although it seemed to be blind, there were just vacant spaces where its eyes should have been — could this be the creature Arthur and his companions had captured back in the battle in the forest?

The chieftain was missing various limbs: an arm, a flipper and even some of its back spines. One of its saucer-like eyes has also been removed and it squinted at me fearfully out of the remaining orb.

The shaman had been preserved intact, mostly, just one long, meticulously stitched wound stretching the length of its throat to its pallid stomach. Its body may have stayed limp, but its baleful eyes regarded us with a bitter hatred. Clearly these creatures suffered, hurt, hated when put under duress.

'Take your time, it's a lot to take in,' said Father.

'Yes, yes it is.' I stared at the three captives, long and hard. In spite of my long and carefully nurtured loathing for these creatures, I was surprised I found the sight both pitiful and a little pathetic.

'Impressive brutes at close quarters though aren't they?'

'I've seen more than enough of them up close and personal thanks.' I found myself taking a step forward, my knife still in my hand. At this, the chieftain shrank away from me, straining as far as its chains allowed. The shaman remained uncowed, its mouth twitching but making no discernible sound.

'Don't be alarmed, I've removed its vocal chords, it's quite incapable of triggering its magic,' said Father.

'So many questions, but let's start with why? Why the fuck have you got three live Devils, chained up like they were lab rats?'

'Lab rats? Why yes, a very insightful simile, but let me answer your question by going back to first principles: in order to defeat your enemy, first you must know him, intimately, thoroughly, completely. To achieve that, there is no surer way than studying him at first hand.'

'But how do you even go about capturing a shaman alive?'

'Oh, we have our methods, you may have observed my children have something of a talent for the more martial arts. One just needs to know where to strike to render them harmless, information easily derived from dissection and study of their central nervous system. A most fascinating endeavour. I've dictated an extensive paper on the subject, which I'm sure the military would find most fascinating.

'After that? Well one simply has to seize one's opportunity — making sure of course they don't revive prematurely — until one is quite ready. Our new arrival Tom is already getting used to his new surroundings. Richard, that's the shaman, proved rather troublesome in that regard, but we managed to settle it eventually with the correct dose of anaesthesia.'

'Richard? Fuck, you've named them?'

'Merely a convenient label, I can assure you, I have no emotional attachment to these creatures, they are test subjects to be used and discarded as I see fit. They merely needed identifying nomenclature, that's all: Tom, Dick and Harry seemed rather appropriate somehow.'

'This is some crazy, fucked up shit, if you don't mind me saying.'

'Not at all, I value honesty above all other virtues. I suppose to the untutored eye, or to someone who has only ever known continued defeat and withdrawal, my actions might be seen as questionable.'

'I'll say.'

'But the fact remains, if we are going to defeat these creatures, we need to understand them.'

'Defeat them? We're barely holding on and that by our fingernails. How do you intend to defeat them?'

'Oh, I'm so glad you asked,' he said, a crooked finger beckoning. 'Come this way and allow me to explain.'

CHAPTER THIRTEEN

Third Generation

THE SHAMAN WATCHED US as we left the lab, still staring its quiet, implacable hatred and I couldn't keep my eyes off it as we left that strange chamber. Captive Devils? If I hadn't witnessed it with my own eyes, well, even I wouldn't have believed it, much less you, right sir? But listen, indulge me a little further and then you can make up your own mind.

We walked down the length of the lab in silence. I was too lost in my thoughts to speak, too wrapt up to notice until I came to the far end where, Father, Ken, whatever, stood waiting for me by what looked like a small airlock.

He waved his hand and we stood aside as the mechanism rotated, while a beam of laser light descended from ceiling to floor, washing over us with a vivid green glow. As another airlock door rolled open on the other side, it revealed a vast chamber, pristine, blank, clinical though the effect was somewhat softened by very subdued lighting. It had been arranged like a hospital ward, though instead of beds, cylindrical tanks were stacked from floor to ceiling as far as the eye could see. Banks of consoles and monitoring equipment nestled alongside each stack, blinking and beeping. Dozens, perhaps hundreds of human foetuses in various stages of development floated contentedly in the viscous amniotic liquid, tranquil and placid in the low light.

'Well Emma, what do you think of my nursery?'

'I'm literally lost for words.'

'Staggering, strange, sort of beautiful isn't it? All those lives, all that potential, just waiting to be realised.'

'Hell's tits man, first the *Daedalus*, then the Devils, now this? What other marvels have you got hidden? The choir invisible hidden up your sleeve and the secret to eternal life in your back pocket?'

'Hm, closer than you might think Emma, but we'll come to that.'

'How on earth did you manage to put all of this together? The castle, the lab…'

'Before the Flood I was a humble scientist, a specialist in genetic modification. You may remember all that foolishness about GM crops, Frankenstein food, etc. etc. Fortunately I had nothing to do with any of that nonsense. I worked for the government and I can say, without fear of false modesty, I was one of the top men, perhaps the finest in my field this country has ever produced.

'I researched genetic answers to the questions posed by disease and injury, using the body's own processes, manipulating its genetic code, rewriting its DNA, harnessing its capacity for change.

'The human body is the most amazing machine ever conceived and I found that with the right stimulus, it could be made to fight off any disease, repair and renew its own flesh and organs, be programmed at the micro-cellular level to meet any challenge. The answer, as always, came from within.

'Even as our doom came upon us, I could already see the way the tide was turning: corruption, confusion, every one trying to defend their own little corner, still trying to make a fast buck or protect their own local patch, while the rest of the country drowned.

'Where this external threat should have united us, like the terror of the Blitz once did, instead, we were divided by all our usual stupid, petty little concerns.

'In truth I had been preparing for years, so when the big wave hit, in the confusion and breakdown of all central authority I was able to slip away, slide under the radar and appropriate enough equipment and resources to make a new beginning. With a small but dedicated staff, I eventually founded this place and slowly carved out this complex beneath the old castle.

'Freed from the ridiculous constraints of codes of ethics and abstract moral theory, I was able to begin a series of clandestine experiments which bore the most remarkable fruit, fulfilling the higher purpose I had long dreamed of pursuing. I began by changing my own body, forging it in the white hot crucible of technology, transforming it into something superior, better.

'Oh, there have been mistakes along the way, I'll be the first to admit, but we will not dwell on those today. Sacrifices must be made upon the altar of science and the survival of the species takes precedence above all other considerations.

'Here you see the third generation of my children *in utero*. You have already met their elder siblings, Arthur, Boudicca and Rhodri, Alfred, Alexander, Napoleon, Rodrigo, Charlemagne and Joan. Magnificent children, my own creations, the second generation of *Homo Ultra*, a race of supermen and women, made in my own image, who have far surpassed even my own lofty ambitions for them.

133

'They call me Father, for father I am to them, biologically, genetically, literally, in most cases. Each and every one of them carries at least a sliver of my own genetic code, as well as a selection of the best characteristics from my many loyal followers and helpmeets.

'I have engineered and cross bred many further refinements and enhancements into them over the years: strength, improved reactions, superior intelligence, but also ferocity, cunning, intuition, every augmentation honed and refined, burnished with a bright genetic sheen — until they were worthy of the title *Homo Ultra*.

'So I have laid my plans and been content to lie in wait, harvesting resources like the *Daedalus*, securing a home and base in this castle, gathering our strength, watching, waiting, while the rest of the land dissolved into chaos and anarchy.

'Once the final vestiges of the old order have been swept away, when the slate has been wiped totally clean, then I will unleash them. Their genetic superiority will make them natural leaders, conquerors if need be, and they have an inherent instinct to breed, to pass on their superior DNA. They will repopulate this island with their descendents, hurl the creatures back into the sea and reclaim it as our own.

'There were challenges naturally. The creatures were a threat early on but I discovered almost by chance, that something in the very rock of this place, made it impervious to their magic and when they dared to confront us, we punished them for their presumption. As for the feeble efforts of the ferals and troublemakers like Glyndŵr, well, they can hardly compete. They are like flies buzzing around the head of a god. I have only let them live this long for my own amusement and to provide some sport for my offspring, frankly.

'Time has gone by and I have watched my children grow and prosper and I have even learned how to accelerate their development, so that what once took a lifetime, now only takes a few short years before they reach maturity and are able to fend for themselves.

'We have hidden ourselves away for so long, kept our light firmly hidden under this convenient bushel, but our time is coming and it is coming soon. Come.'

He led me on, through those rows of assembled tanks, each housing a new life and I watched those tiny bodies gently rotate in their artificial wombs, blissfully unaware of the fate that was being wrought for them.

But perhaps he was right? How could we hope to beat the Devils, when we had to rely on our own feeble resources, fighting a war that we seemed destined to lose, if not now, then ultimately in the fullness of time? We could only retreat so far and if the flood levels continued to rise, where would we go then? Wales? Scotland? Make a break for continental Europe and the heights of the Alps to make our final stand? We'd slowly retreat back to ever higher ground until the waters finally overtook us. There we would make our end, a stark choice: enslavement or death.

All these thoughts swirled around my mind as we walked along, my eyes drifting to the tanks on either side, watching those babies suckling on their artificial umbilicals in the half light.

But supermen and women? Genetic manipulation? That was treading on some very dangerous ground. I was enough of a student of history to know what that had led to in the mid twentieth century.

Yet Father's was a seductive tale too and god knows, we'd had nothing to hope for, nothing to believe in, for a very long time.

If he really could build an army with the abilities, the leadership, to defeat the Devils, then shouldn't we at least hear him out? Arthur and his companions had shredded that warband, slaughtered a warlock and stuck its head on a pike as if they were shelling peas. If they could lead us in battle, bring us victory instead of defeat, then people would rally to their cause, survivors, ferals, even the free towns. And we would fight all that much harder, knowing we were no longer fighting in a losing cause.

Hope is a powerful thing, especially when you've not felt it for so long. Father was either barking mad or the one true visionary who might, just might, save us all.

But what would we become? In saving us, wouldn't he doom us too? We'd lose our humanity, the very essence of all that made us human, swapping one set of oppressors for another, no matter how well intentioned? Watching on, as our follies and flaws were bred out, as we evolved into the new species which would inherit this flooded earth.

If — and it was a big if — we beat the Devils, wouldn't that mean we'd also condemn ourselves to losing the last vestiges of what made us truly human, those imperfections which made us, us? Was that even a bad thing? Should we fear such radical change or embrace it? Christ, this was so far above my pay grade, it was virtually in orbit.

Lost in these thoughts, I'd tuned out his words as he continued to unleash a torrent of technical jargon and details, speaking in a language I could hardly understand.

Now we had reached a stairway and he turned and beckoned me up, but as the lecture continued, I paused and peered a little closer into one of the nearby tanks.

Inside, a baby gently floated in the low light, arms and legs curled in on its body, its features benign and quiescent. It looked just like the scans with which I had once been intimately familiar, the image of the tiny body which had matured inside my own. It was weird to see a child disconnected like that, vat grown, separated from its natural environment, just rotating gently there. Yet it looked for all the world like a normal baby, like my own poor lost boy and it was difficult to conceive of this being as some kind of super human. It seemed just like every other child, wrinkled, helpless, innocent. I bent to take a closer look.

Suddenly its eyes blinked open, its limbs uncurled and it swam-paddled closer to the glass. It was staring at me, its wide, unborn eyes radiating a knowledge it should not possess. Then I began to feel something, a tingle, an itch in the front of my mind, as if something was pricking my consciousness, rifling through my memories...

A single word echoed in my mind *'Tom?'*

Shit! This was wrong! Wrong! I recoiled, backing away, shaking and juddering, until the feeling faded.

'They're naturally inquisitive, even *in utero*,' said Father. 'Don't worry, he won't harm you, he was just curious. Don't be afraid.'

A peculiar feeling overtook me, a nausea that I couldn't quite define.

'Come Emma, join me up here.'

I circled warily, keeping out of range of the child's mental touch and ran up the steps two at a time.

We stood upon a gallery which had a long glass window running its entire length.

'You've seen their womb,' said Father. 'Now behold their nursery.'

Beyond the glass was a kindergarten where dozens of children were busily engaged in what comes naturally: running, jumping, playing, romping and generally mucking about. There were a whole range of ages, from crawlers to toddlers, right up to kids of about nine or ten.

Attending them were a small army of young women in rather severe, plain-looking white overalls. Mystery solved: so this was where Gwaelod's daughters had been hidden away.

While their starched-white teachers looked on benignly, the children laughed, sulked, jostled, whooped and generally tore about the place, a riot of colourful chaos. Even though the glass blocked the sound, you could see the kindergarten was full of the bustle, noise and delight generated when a bunch of kids are let loose to have some good old fashioned fun.

It had been such a long time since I'd seen children in such an environment, that I'd quite forgotten what it was like. My heart melted. In the camps and DMZs our kids were scrawny, starving, pathetic little urchins, forever on the scrounge for food, clothes or any small advantage that would keep them alive for another day. We bred survivors now, not children.

But this? This bought back such poignant memories: a normal childhood, full of innocence, laughter and play, a place where you didn't constantly wonder where your next meal was coming from.

Father and I watched them contentedly for a while, a grin on my face, proud indulgence on his, until it dawned on me, slowly, that the children I was observing were not exactly engaged in what you might call ordinary pursuits.

Rather than *ABC* or *Janet and John,* some of the toddlers were tackling hefty text books, their brows furrowing as they grappled with advanced literature, science and mathematics. Some of the younger kids were playing catch with basketballs and hefty looking weights, lifting them easily and hurling them at each other with the speed and precision of professional athletes.

Some of the older children were practicing with edged weapons in a series of manoeuvres that would have given old-style school inspectors a collective heart attack. Meanwhile, the young women moved between them, chatting, encouraging and refereeing the odd disagreement with a mixture of smiles, rebukes and infinite patience — in *loco parentis* to this new breed of super children.

'Their mothers, sisters and aunts take good care of them, love them, nurture them, but also prepare them for the harsher realities of the outside world. No amount of genetic manipulation will ever replace that, nor would I want it to.'

'Mothers, aunts and sisters?'

'Yes, a collective upbringing is a far more desirable and efficient model. Why limit the children to a single parent when they could learn from the combined wisdom and experience of so many fine young people? Conversely, why weigh down each mother with the responsibility and burden of caring for a single specific biological child? Far better for them to think of all as their own flesh and blood. Here we care for all, love all, they are all our sons and daughters.'

'And their fathers?'

'I am all the father they'll ever need.'

'And they're okay with that?

'Certainly, they accept it, indeed, derive great satisfaction from it. Each contributes to the development and education of all, without fear, favour and without any corresponding emotional attachment. It is a most rewarding and fulfilling arrangement.'

'Perhaps for you.'

'Oh, Emma, not at all. We have gone beyond the petty jealousies of bloodlines, succession, parentage. Such old fashioned concepts, more relevant to the feudal age than our own. Does it really matter who sired who? They are all our children and we are all their parents. Forgive the indelicacy, but perhaps your own loss would have been made more bearable, if you had had been able to enjoy such a collegiate approach?'

'What? How the fuck do you know about that?'

'Our … advantages are not merely confined to the physical, our mental prowess is also formidable. I have sensed your anguish, felt your grief…'

'You … you can read my thoughts?'

'Come now Emma, I would not violate your privacy or read your mind uninvited. but in this case I did not have to. You carry this burden with you constantly, just below the surface level of your consciousness. It's there, leaking out of your mind, even now, broadcasting to any who can sense it.'

'Get the fuck out of my head!'

'Please, listen and try not to give in to your anger or your grief. I have shared your memories, seen the horror, the shock of your loss and how you have suffered since. It's a tragedy, your own boy, your own beautiful boy, Tom, wrenched from your grasp in an instant, swept away, never to be seen again.'

I was crying now, tears streaming down my face, feelings rushing to the surface I had not let escape in a very long time.

'Tragic, so tragic and no-one, nothing could ever replace him, of course. Yet, what if I could offer you a fresh chance, a new hope, the possibility to begin again, to be mother to a whole new family?

'What if I could remake a world where you would mother many fine sons and daughters, strong, healthy, resourceful, independent children. A world where you know they will be safe, protected, until they are ready to become its saviours — to inherit this drowned land and defeat the creatures which oppress it? What then?

'Are you content to merely fight and struggle and survive, each a day a fresh battle, a fresh torment, until you inevitably succumb to a pointless death on some cold, unknown shore? Join me, join us, embrace this change, learn to live again, learn to love again, learn to become a mother again.'

'And what about my men?'

'They would, of course, be most welcome to join us, to add their strength to our collective.'

The flow of my tears began to dry, leaving behind a salty rime as I wiped them away. His offer seemed so simple, so seductive when you reduced it down to its components.

It was as if he had read not only my thoughts, but my inner self.

To give up this endless struggle, this endless responsibility, to step away from the madness, the butchery, the bleak unending reality of a war we seemed destined to lose was so strong, it was a wonder his hand remained unbitten.

And why the hell not? What did I owe to the provisional government, the militia, our so-called leaders and masters? Fools, idiots, the lot of them.

This was as good a place as any and better than most: strong, safe, a refuge from the endless dark and despair. He was building something here, a weird, twisted, incredible something maybe, but from where I sat, it stood out like a shining beacon, rising above the terror and despair of our drowning isle.

What he had shown me was incredible, jaw dropping, a whole generation being prepared to lead us out of the darkness.

I'm no science geek, but I certainly believe the evidence of my own eyes. I had witnessed the power of Arthur and his siblings at first hand. Just imagine what a whole legion of them could do for the cause, would do to the Devils? Perhaps they were our last, best hope for hurling the creatures back into the depths?

And what of me? What indeed? He had discerned my own secret desire, the unspoken secret which I had long suppressed. I had always thought that despite my own need, my own longing, how could I bring another child into this terrible world? Having lost one so painfully, it would be almost unbearable to lose another, more than my sanity could stand. So I had taken this desire, locked it away, buried it in the cold, unyielding ground, as I had been unable to do with my poor lost boy. Perhaps Father read my hesitation, my divided heart, for he said.

'It's overwhelming, I know, but think carefully Emma, I'm offering you a chance that might never come again.'

'How would that even work? I can't … I won't be anyone's brood mare.'

'Nor would I wish you to be, there would be nothing quite so drastic or physically intimate. A quick, painless operation to harvest your ova, you could even remain awake, armed, if you chose. Afterwards they would be paired with the best seed Gwaelod has to offer, my own, my many sons, the finest genetic material any mother could wish for. You could even pick and choose as you see fit.

'Instead of being mother to a single child, you would create life in a different way, sire many remarkable sons and daughters, become mother to a whole generation. You are an extraordinary woman Emma, your courage, fortitude, strength, your leadership qualities are all self-evident. Those characteristics would provide a welcome enhancement to the development of *Homo Ultra*.

'And you would help raise them too, here in a place of safety, where they would want for nothing and neither would you. Do our children look unhappy in there, do they seem to want for anything?' I looked again. They did not.

'But what of duty? What of my mission?' I protested — *and what of Major Seraph* I wondered inwardly, though I quickly suppressed that thought.

'That island? Oh please, don't look so surprised, it doesn't take an adept to work out what drew you to our little corner of the world. We're not on any maps and there's little else to attract government-sponsored snooping out this way.

'As for that island, please, don't concern yourself, it's a minor distraction in the grand scheme of things. I am almost certain that the creatures have raised it as a kind of staging post, so that they can connect their undersea cities to a permanent base on the surface.'

'That and more,' I replied. 'I've seen first hand what the Devils intend to use it for, captive humans being led away in chains, it seems they have some breeding plans of their own.'

'Ah, they wish to produce more hybrids no doubt, to further infiltrate our island's crumbling institutions, the remaining free towns and that so-called Provisional Government. Interesting, but ultimately, irrelevant. Oh I dare say, the other survivors and ferals out there may suffer for a while as it brings more of the creatures to the surface, they might even rove further inland, thinning the herd even further.

'But it can't harm us here, we are immune to its sorcerous powers to such an extent I barely see it as a threat. For us it's just a picturesque sight on the horizon. However, If those circumstances did ever change, well, suffice to say, we have many methods, up to and including the *Daedalus,* to make sure it would never threaten us again.'

'I … I don't know what to say.'

'You hesitate, but come Emma, seize your chance, *make* history instead of being its victim.'

Isn't that what you really want?

The unspoken words echoed directly in my mind and in that moment, he didn't seem strange or mad, just a wise, eccentric old man who had figured out a way to retaliate, to fight back, who had used his peculiar genius to conceive a vision, while the rest of scrabbled around in the ashes.

He had quashed my every objection with reasonable answers, laid out a seductive future, where I could leave behind all the hardship and misery which was our daily bread. All I had to do was say the word.

Yet still I hesitated.

What of duty, what of honour? Hadn't I sworn an oath to serve and defend my country? Not something I could put aside lightly, for, without our word, without purpose, what are we? Didn't I have some kind of responsibility to see my mission through to its conclusion?

And what of Major Seraph? He had saved us on countless occasions and if there was even the remotest chance of him returning, shouldn't I wait?

But in the end the thing that decided it for me was this, the code of the warrior down the long centuries:

You must ask yourself this: why do we fight? Not ultimately for a flag, not even for a country, but for our comrades: those we serve with, fight alongside, suffer and die with.

Loyalty, honour, duty, they were essential parts of who I am and I couldn't, wouldn't, lay them down for anyone or anything, no matter how seductive. As I realised that, my mind was made up.

'Respectfully, I'm afraid it must be no, sir. Challis and Haines can decide for themselves, but I imagine you'll get the same answer. I still have a mission to complete, when it's done, perhaps I'll return and take you up on your very kind and extremely generous offer. Until then, I'm afraid I must respectfully decline…'

'That is a shame, I had hoped to avoid any element of coercion, but I'm afraid — and it's difficult not to sound like some tittering arch-villain here — I must insist. I had hoped to convince you by strength of argument alone, but if I cannot, then coercion, benign, benevolent coercion mind, it must be.'

'Coercion? What? You'd keep me here against my will?'

'Regretfully, it must be so. My agenda, *my* mission, allows for no such luxuries as free will, no such niceties as sentiment. When I see an opportunity I seize it, the ascension of *Homo Ultra* demands nothing less.'

'I'd be delighted to think you would return to Gwaelod and become part of this project and I see in your mind that perhaps even you intend to. But you might also die completing that mission, you might never come back and entirely waste your potential. I'm afraid I can't countenance that.'

'And what if I resist…' I felt a small pinprick in my arm and then my vision blurred, a sudden, scintillating explosion of light and then the world took on a warm, fuzzy quality.

Father took my arm and led me down the steps which now, bizarrely, seemed to stretch away to infinity. My mind slowed, as if I were wading through a kind of treacly swamp and my knees buckled.

But he caught me and lightly scooped me up and into his arms with little or no effort, as if I weighed as much as gossamer.

As he carried me down through that long room with its cylinders full of the unborn, my vision swam, washing in and out, so that the whole room seemed to break back and forth, like waves on a sea shore.

'Perhaps it is better this way Emma, for without the illusion of choice, the appearance of complicity, this next part would most likely have tested you sorely.'

Now he carried me through the incubation room, drugged and disconnected, woozy and helpless, those countless, foetus-filled cylinders seeming to crowd in on me like an army of accusers. Yet, quietly, calmly, delicately, Father continued his oration.

'For you see it is only comparatively recently that it struck me, the realisation of the flaw in my overarching design. With the second generation, Arthur, Boudicca, Rhodri and the others, I had laid the foundations for an army to defeat the creatures and reclaim our birthright here on *terra firma*. In time and that time is coming, I have no doubt they will become the spearhead that will hurl the Devils, as you call them, back beneath the waves.

'But that is a war that could last for years, decades even and what will we have achieved? Simply put, the same old status quo which prevailed before the Flood.

'Who knows what machinations the creatures could employ in the meantime, what weapons or dark magic they may develop in response to our counterattack?

'Perhaps they would retaliate by raising the sea level again, until there is no dry land left at all. Perhaps they will wait for the stars to align and their dark god, who still slumbers beneath the waves, will rise again and visit the final horror on this ravaged earth?

'No, we must look beyond that to the end game. I find it hard to conceive that my vision was initially so limited. I have built an army to reclaim our birthright here on land, but to ensure our ultimate victory we must not only drive the creatures back into the seas, but pursue them there and conclude the war on their home territory. We must take the fight to them if we are to not only survive, but prevail.

'How then to achieve this? Why, by utilising the very tools I already have at my disposal, by turning their own weapons — their own traits — against them. Imagine if I could combine *Homo Ultra's* superior characteristics with carefully selected traits from the creatures' own DNA? I would create a whole new super species again, able to conquer the oceans as well as the land. Why, we need never fear the creatures or indeed, anything else, ever again.'

'Hybrids? Fuck, you're talking about hybrids aren't you?' I slurred, trying to rouse myself, though I felt weak and detached. My voice became a disembodied murmur that seemed to come from outside of me.

'But ... but that's insane, they'll never ... side with us, the Devil taint runs too deep. That's how they infiltrated our defences in the first place ... sab ... sabotaged our weapons, ambushed our subs, wiped ... wiped out our cities. Hybrids betrayed us and you want to create super hybrids? Are you insane? It'll be the end of us all for certain.'

A shadow passed across his face for the first time.

'I appreciate your candour Sergeant, but mad? I don't think so. You forget my mastery of genetics, my ability to identify and isolate those tiny strands, those indivisible threads that make up the warp and weft of life.

'I can breed it out of them, I *will* breed it out of them, so that their *Homo Ultra* parentage controls and dominates their instincts. The fourth generation's loyalty will be to us, to me, not the creatures.

'Besides, the process has already begun, and ...' he proffered a rather shy smile, 'the initial results are extremely promising. You still doubt me? I can sense your uncertainty, your fears, but here, see for yourself, see the living proof.'

He opened the top of his lab coat and shirt and there, on either side at the base of his neck, opening and closing, pulsing in time with the rise and fall of his chest, were a pair of gills.

I tried to recoil, tried to push myself away from those hideous, pulsing, alien organs, but they swelled to fill my vision, swelled until all was darkness.

CHAPTER FOURTEEN

Peering Through the Cracks

LIGHT BEGAN TO SEEP THROUGH MY LASHES, teasing, pulling me away from the visions. At first I resisted its stark touch, screwing my eyes up and rolling over, hiding from the light, reluctant to shrug my mind from its state of unconsciousness. But strange afterimages of the dream world persisted and hovering there, I remembered; cylinders, hundreds of them, thousands, stretching to infinity, bright young-old eyes piercing, burrowing into my skin, my very soul, shallow draughts of humid breath caressing my skin...

Suddenly, painfully awake, I sat bolt upright, chest tight, breathing heavy, heart thudding, clutching at my neck, pawing at something buried in the skin that ... that wasn't there. Then I remembered and the loathing came and it was long minutes before I could push it back inside.

My lashes crackled open and I found myself in a room made up of three blank stone walls that seemed to have no beginning and no end. Bright light burned from above, a functional toilet and basin in one corner sidled into view and there was a small, barred window high up on the outer wall. The remaining wall was half stone and half solid looking metal bars. The only other modern-looking object was the cell door, more heavy bars secured by what looked like a sophisticated electronic locking mechanism.

I felt woozy and disconnected but as my eyes began to adjust to the light, I could make out vague outlines of what lay beyond. A corridor with more cells stretched along its length. Then I remembered Father's final words, what he'd promised and I shuddered.

I rose unsteadily and tried the lock, dug the stubs of my fingernails around its edges, but there was no purchase, nothing but smooth surface to try and leverage. A quick check told me my knife had been taken too. Damn.

I looked at my cell from side to side and up to down and had encompassed the whole of my little prison in a couple of moments. I sagged back into the plain platform which was my bed, despairing.

I was still wearing the absurd dress I had put on god knows how many hours ago. It was light outside, but I had no idea how much time had passed and there was no real way of telling. My head throbbed dully and I ached inside and out. What had that bastard done to me?

What the hell had I been thinking, bringing us here? Any port in a storm they say, but that's no reason to go full sail into a hostile one. I had made some questionable decisions in my time, but I should have known better than this.

Then I remembered his calm, logical voice, those flat, reasoning tones which had initially sounded so plausible, but now even the thought of which gave me cause to retch. In the light of a brand new day, the events of the night seemed so surreal, so strange, like some bizarre nightmare.

I couldn't believe that I had even seriously considered his proposition. I felt ashamed at the recollection.

Why? Why had I nearly succumbed to his enticing promises?

But I knew, oh I knew, it was because of that burden I always carry inside of me, the empty space that would never be filled. It was the hope, the hope he had offered, that had seduced me.

And I had failed, failed the mission, failed the major, failed my people, failed myself.

I made a cradle of my hands and allowed my face to sink into them, blotting out the harsh light, trying to blot out my own harsh self-judgement.

I sat there for a while, just feeling blank, like an unwritten page, but then what appeared to be my name, repeated in a low insistent whisper, suddenly brought me out of my reverie. I stood and shuffled to the cell's barred window and there, across the corridor, was Challis. He wasn't looking particularly good, his face was cut and bruised, one eye swollen, half-closed and his dreads matted and dishevelled. But his mouth split in a broad grin when he saw me, though it caused the cuts in his lip to open.

'Fuck Corporal, what did they do to you? You look like you've gone ten rounds with a chieftain. Did you never hear about going quietly?'

'Suppose I never did. You okay Emma?'

'Nothing hurt but my pride, I'll live. Where's Haines?'

'Here Sergeant, reporting for duty!' In the next cell along, Haines' eager face was pressed up against the bars. She saluted sloppily and inappropriately as ever, but I returned it, then gave her a thumbs-up.

'Okay, let's hear it then,' I said.

'Some old fella,' said Challis, 'went by the name of Father. Swanned in like he owned the place which way things went, I guess he did. Ordered them to lay hands on Haines. I objected, got this for my trouble.' He indicated his bruises. 'Shit they're strong, even faster than they look too, nothing I could've done really, though I managed to land that Rhodri a face full of fist. It was like punchin' granite. Arthur didn't seem too happy about the way things went down, but it didn't make a blind bit of difference. This Father ordered it — and they rushed to get it done. Kinda wished they'd waited until after dessert tho', best scran I've had in a long time. Saying that, wish I had a couple of my teeth back so's I could appreciate it. Nothing like a solid beating for ruining your appetite. Not 'zactly the friendliest way to treat your guests huh?'

'Shit, no.'

'So what changed?' said Challis, 'why they so down on us all of a sudden?'

'Nothing good,' I said. 'Long story short: Father's a Frankenstein fan and is breeding a new master race to succeed his super children and he'd like me and Haines to play mummy. Worse still, he's planning on mixing our DNA with the Devils' own to create a new race of super-hybrids. As for you? Don't know where you'll fit in. I doubt it could be any worse, but it's unlikely to be much better.'

'Freaky, but it figures,' frowned Challis. 'I was wondering what kind of weird shit they were fucking around with here. Guess now we know. Question is: what are we going to do about it?'

'Our options would seem kind of limited right now,' I said. 'How long have I been out by the way?'

'Good few hours, I figure it's coming up about midday. Tough to tell in here, not many external reference points. We've been here since about midnight, they bought you back a couple of hours later.'

There was a short lull while I assimilated all this new information. Despite our dire situation, I actually felt a bit better for having a few practical problems to deal with.

'Sergeant?' Haines piped up. 'What's going on? I thought they were good people? Arthur's been ever so nice, he said we were welcome to stay for as long as we like. But then the rest of them were so mean to us at the banquet. Why have they put us in here?'

'Turns out they're not all as nice as Arthur, but don't worry Ellie,' I said, 'we'll work something out. For now, sit tight and get some rest. There's nothing we can do … so let's do nothing. I need some time to think, but don't worry I'll come up with something. Best keep quiet for the moment too, in case they're listening, okay?'

I smiled and she gave a weak thumbs-up back. I went and sat down on the bed, feeling the after effects of whatever drug I'd been spiked with gradually begin to subside. I lapped some water from the sink, letting it wash the gunk from my mouth and slowly, my head began to ache less and think more. I sank back onto the cot and stared at the ceiling, letting my thoughts bounce against the blank white canvas above.

We may be fucked from here to the island and back, but I still had to try and make the best of it, formulate a plan, even in a seemingly hopeless situation. Wasn't that the very definition of command? Trying to find the least, worst alternative?

I turned the possibilities over endlessly in my mind, then made a few more futile attempts on the door, only to discover there was really very little practical I could do. In the end, I decided we could only sit and wait it out and be ready to seize the moment when an opportunity presented itself. If it presented itself.

At least we were safe enough for the moment and they were unlikely to harm Haines or I. We were too valuable. Challis? Well, he was no threat where he was.

Later, I spent a little while torturing myself, trying to second guess what I might have done differently, but came to no solid conclusions and eventually I succumbed to fatigue and dozed, drifting into a kind of fitful semi sleep.

If only the major had been here to guide us, he had always seemed to know exactly the right thing to do, the right thing to say, had a plan for every occasion, a scheme for every eventuality. Just how the fuck did he manage that?

Yet hadn't he been the one that had actually dispatched us here, into this lunatic's arms, in the first place?

Why send us all this way, if he'd had even an inkling of what awaited us? His orders had been explicit, follow the arrow and we'd followed and look where it had got us. He had promised he wouldn't abandon us, so where was he?

I cursed, no way of knowing if he was even alive anymore. He might be a hard man to kill, but that explosion couldn't have left many survivors.

No, nothing else for it, we'd have to assume we were on our own for now and make our plans accordingly. Though what those plans should be, I was fucked if I knew.

So, thinking such dark thoughts I drifted off, though whether it was for moments or hours, I couldn't tell. But suddenly I came too abruptly, as if sensing something was amiss. Shadows lengthened as day bled into night outside and the first stars were already showing against the early evening sky through the bars of the high window.

All was quiet, yet something had disturbed my slumbers and I sleep like a highly strung dormouse. You may smile, sir, but it's saved my hide on more than one occasion.

Silently, I sat up in bed and eased myself off the cot, padding across the cell in my bare feet and pressed flat against the bars. I stole a look down the corridor and at first saw nothing. Funny, I was sure ... but then I discerned a figure at Haines' window.

He wore a long dark robe, a hood masking his features and was looking inside, staring intently into the space beyond. Both hands gripped the bars and the knuckles were white, prominent, as if he meant to rip them apart with his bare hands.

I heard another noise coming from the other end of corridor and the figure heard it too, the hood falling aside as he turned to look, revealing a flash of pale skin and dark features. It was Arthur, for a moment his face was hard and calculating and then the next he was gone, vanishing faster than a puff of smoke on a windy day.

Footsteps sounded and I hurried back to my cot and quickly lay down. Just in time, for Father's face appeared at the bars, watching me like he might have appraised a particularly succulent piece of meat.

'Ah, so there you are Emma, awake and feeling a little recovered I hope?'

'Fuck you.'

'Tch, now now, profanity, hardly becoming for the prospective mother of a new generation.'

'Fuck you sideways, you prick.'

'You really do have a spectacularly foul mouth, but I suppose I shouldn't be too surprised, coming from a soldier. I wonder if such profanity can be addressed at the genetic level? Hm, but I digress, my apologies about your present accommodation, just a temporary measure until we can find somewhere more suitable.'

'I'm surprised it's not a battery cage.'

'Come now, there's no need to be resentful. You and your delightful comrade will help secure the future of the human race, the survival of the species and play a major role in the creation of an entirely new one. When the history books are eventually written, the names Stokes and Haines will be renowned as the mothers of a new nation. Surely such a major role in history is worth a small sacrifice or two?'

'Let me out of this cage and I'll show you what a small sacrifice looks like.'

'Physical threats have little meaning to me, Emma. I've no doubt time will temper your hostility; what you cannot change, you must learn to accept. A very wise woman once said that.'

'Fuck her and fuck you too.'

A slot opened in the lower part of the door and a tray with an array of food was slid through. It shut before I had time to react.

'In the meantime please eat, refresh yourself, rest, make yourself comfortable. When you prove you are ready to co-operate, we'll perhaps think about give you a bit more license to…'

I snatched the tray and hurled it at him. It clanged against the bars, but a satisfying amount made it through and splashed him in the face. Slops slid down one of his cheeks.

'Futile, but understandable I suppose,' he said, wiping the remnants away meticulously. 'I suggest you make yourself comfortable with this Emma. If you don't...' he glanced meaningfully across at Challis and then Haines. 'You may not be the one who bears the consequences.'

Time passed and my petty act of rebellion soon faded in the face of Father's discreet yet nonetheless menacing threat. Outside, the world continued to turn as far as I could tell, but locked away in our little isolation ward, day followed night, night followed day, food appeared and was eaten (this time) and time weighed heavy on our hands.

So, in the meantime, I concocted all kinds of idiotic plans and connived at mad schemes to try and break out of our confinement. But the floor proved impervious to tunnelling, the walls immune to Shawshanking and our cutlery steadfastly refused to transform itself into a suitable lock pick. The first time I tried to conceal a utensil in the folds of my dress, I was met with a reproving look and a wagged finger from the starchy handmaiden who had come to collect it. In the end, I just meekly handed it back through the bars.

So I marked time, scratching a rough calendar on the wall, crossing off every four marks like an old lag and I even made a shadow clock from the rays streaming through the bars, to count the hours, simply as a way of keeping sane. I soon realised we needed something to keep us occupied, so I organised regular PT sessions, adapted to work in those confined spaces (although I wondered whether Haines' huffing and puffing was entirely genuine, as she wasn't totally in view).

And of course we talked, recounted stories to each other across the corridor, played word games, made up quizzes, concocted fictional officer's exams for Haines to take — anything to break up the day and relieve the monotony.

I have to say it worked to an extent too. Despite achieving nothing concrete in terms of winning our freedom, it certainly brought us closer together, we became no longer just comrades in arms, but something approaching friends too, for rank came to mean little in that place.

I told them all about my life before the army, some of my early (highly edited) adventures in the Reserve before the Flood had overwhelmed us and finally, giving it up in a sequence of sobs, how I had lost my little boy when the first wave struck.

On a slightly lighter note, slightly, Challis regaled us with blood-curdling tales of his time in Afghanistan, how he survived as a captive of the Taliban and then embellished them with lurid tales of his adventures in the flesh pots of the Rhine. I'm not sure which were the more far fetched, but they were certainly entertaining and his fund of stories passed many an idle hour, Challis' deep baritone painting vivid word pictures, which fair blew Haines' tiny little mind.

We also talked of times past and Haines listened wide-eyed as we told her of how the world was before the Flood. Amazing how quickly you forget all that stuff which seemed so essential at the time, the very fabric of every day life, things I had nearly forgotten: movies, magazines, makeup, booze, getting dressed up for a big night out with the girls, celebrating your friends' birthdays, going out on a date. It all seemed a million miles away from where we were now, another lifetime. Probably because it was.

On the whole though, we were largely left to our own devices. Father didn't deign to bless us with his presence again and our food was served by a succession of those anonymous, female handmaidens, who steadfastly refused to engage with us, no matter how hard I tried. I kept a wary eye out and drank plenty of water to wake myself up at irregular intervals during the night and once in a while, that old Indian trick worked.

Several times I awoke and hugged the shadows of my cell, trying to keep my aching bladder in check, while I waited for Arthur to come. Sometimes he would arrive, materialising like he'd been beamed in and just stand there, at Haines' bars, watching silently without waking her up. At others he'd call her with a low 'tsss' and Haines would lean in and they would whisper to each other in the way that young lovers do. Whatever they promised each other, their love, or whatever it was, remained unconsummated for now and would remain so while Haines was held captive. But surely Arthur wouldn't let her fall under Father's knife? Perhaps that was the lever, a weakness we might be able to exploit?

But despite all my efforts to keep us healthy, occupied and engaged, slowly, as the days turned, I began to despair of seeing the outside world ever again. All that inactivity was becoming a form of slow torture, perhaps Father simply meant to bore us into submission?

If he had kept it up much longer, he might well have succeeded. With each day the fear began to grow inside me too, although I concealed it from the others. I became apprehensive about the visit I knew must come: would they simply walk in and overpower me with their superhuman strength? I would struggle, pointlessly no doubt, arms almost wrenching themselves from their sockets as I was dragged away to the slab. Either that or that I would wake up during the operation itself, drugged and helpless, conscious but not able to move or communicate, as Father leant over me, whistling as he casually scooped out half of my insides.

When these dreams came, I would wake with a silent scream and lay there, bathed in sweat, letting the chills overtake me, swimming deep in the dark recesses of my mind.

But on the seventh night of our incarceration, everything changed once again. We had taken our evening meal, then talked long into the gloaming, played some games for a while (though frankly, Haines' favourite I Spy, was starting to grate). Then finally we made our goodnights in the style of The Waltons (a standing joke, which amused me no end, but which mystified Haines though she played along with good grace).

I think a combination of my mounting fears and the beginnings of cabin fever had started to set in, for I was restless and finding it difficult to get to sleep. Outside, the wind swelled, gusting and fretful, the waves began to whip up and there was a heaviness to the air, a density that became oppressive, as if somewhere, close by, a storm was brewing.

I tossed and turned, pulling the covers over me, then throwing them off again, agitated and desperate to escape to my nightly oblivion, the respite that only long hours of dreamless sleep could give.

But it seemed like I was the only one having trouble dropping off. Challis' snores were already booming across the way and distantly, I could hear Haines muttering and burbling to herself, the usual precursor that signalled her full descent into the land of nod.

This continued for a while and I had entered that state neither fully conscious nor fully asleep when the mind is a strange amalgam of the real and the unreal. There, reality becomes a fluid, shapeable thing, as the mind steers between the solid rocks of the mundane and the endless ocean of the unconscious.

It began as a solitary indeterminate dot in the darkness and then I seemed to see light, a glowing red-gold mote of brightness that rapidly swelled, becoming radiant and alive as it chased away the shadows. It was at once eerie, coruscating and somehow beautiful, as it grew more and more distinct resolving into a scintillating sphere, glowing with eldritch energy. Then the outline of a figure formed at its centre, the silhouette translucent but becoming ever more solid, ever more real.

Word shapes emanated from the halo, moving through its umbra, rippling like physical sensations through its penumbra. I felt no fear, just wonder, as the sounds expanded, reaching toward me, slipping through my unconscious form, like eels through water, to echo and re-echo inside my skull. The figure's face was hidden, but the outline was familiar, so familiar and his words fell like cool, clear droplets of water as he extended a hand and said.

'Stay put Sergeant. I'm coming for you.'

'Major?' Suddenly I was awake, groping blindly in the semi-darkness, my fingers reaching out toward the light, but all was dark, all was silent, save the background murmur of the waves. A dream? Damn, was that really just a dream?

It had felt so real, I had almost been able to reach out and touch him, for I had no doubt who it was. From across the corridor, Challis' snoozy drones still punctuated the night, but I knew somehow that sleep would not come for me again. I lay there feeling empty and unrequited, alone in the small hours of the morning. How good it would have been to hear the major's real voice just then. How I could have used his guidance, his reassurance at that moment, how we all could have.

I lay down again, restless as before, wriggling and writhing against my sheets, but then I began to notice another change, an alteration in the quality of the stillness and even the motion of wind and tide seemed to pause, as if the night was holding its breath.

A tension built, almost unbearable and I wanted to scream, shout, do something, anything, to release that awful pressure.

In the end, I didn't have to.

The first explosion detonated, scything through the quiet like the roar of a thousand jet engines. It shook the walls so hard that they vibrated, scattering a thin layer of dust which caught the back of my throat. I was bolt upright in an instant and listening intently, as a staccato succession of further impacts walked the line, drawing ever closer. I can remember thinking 'shit, who possesses ordinance heavy enough to hit like that?'

The next explosion must have hit the citadel directly, for it caused the entire edifice to shudder, pitched me clean out of bed and onto the floor, as it reverberated with a succession of secondary impacts. Dust engulfed the room this time, stinging my eyes and throat and there were more weighty thuds close by, as I got onto my hands and knees and groped my way across towards the door.

'Challis! Haines! You okay? Report.' I managed to shout in between coughs.

'Been worse,' said a hoarse voice behind me and I whirled but it was just Challis, a solid shape looming out of the dust. 'Been better too, but whatever the fuck that was that just hit us, it's knocked out the door mechanisms. Looks like we've been sprung.'

'Well fuck me ... and don't consider that an invitation. Still, we're free and I'm not going to complain, come on, let's go.' I was out and in the corridor in an instant and then hustling a sleep-befuddled Haines out of her cell.

'What's happening?'

'I'm not sure Ellie, but we need to find a way out of here.' I checked both ends of the stone-flagged corridor. Each contained a plain, solid looking door but which way to go?

'Might want to grab these first, huh?' said Challis indicating the guard room which adjoined my cell. Inside, our uniforms, gear and weapons had been neatly stacked in three different piles. I could have literally wept for joy, but instead confined myself to piling in and getting changed, literally tearing my finery to shreds as I ripped it off.

This was no time for false modesty and I was down to my underwear in moments and then pulling on the marine uniform as quickly as I could, urging Challis and Haines to act with similar dispatch.

I pulled the webbing tight, watched the energy bar power up to full and snapped a fresh magazine into my weapon. The Bootneck suit and body armour felt heavy, but solid and reassuring, like I'd buckled back on a second skin. Now, time to get the fuck out of here.

Picking a direction at random we moved down the corridor in close formation. When we got to the end, I eased the door open a crack and snuck a look on the other side. It revealed another empty, torch-lit castle corridor and I signalled Haines and Challis to hurry through as another explosion made the walls shiver. Weapons shouldered now, we eased our way along, alert for any sign of danger.

I best-guessed we were probably still in the citadel but had absolutely no idea where and the lack of external reference points didn't help. Keep going seemed to be the only option, but we desperately needed to orient ourselves, get a handle on exactly where we were and what was happening, so we could find the right route to take. Salvation came behind the slightly unusual form of a pair of heavy curtains half way down the next passage. Pushing them aside, I slipped open the bolts of a heavy outer door and poked a tentative head through. My breath frosted in the cold night air of a deserted battlement. Perfect, I slipped on through and motioned them to follow.

We were high up, at the top of the central citadel and above us, part of the keep's tower had crumbled under the same impacts that must have knocked out the cell doors. Rocks and stray bits of battlement were still falling around us. From where we stood we had a perfect view of the entire fortress, but now we looked down on a Gwaelod transformed into a scene of unfolding carnage.

Another detonation rocked the outer walls, rending mortar and shredding stone, adding to several existing breaches which smoked and flamed, leaving gaping holes in the landward defences. Several houses and buildings had also been set alight, bathing the first quarter with a blood red glow which revealed the presence of a mass of defenders hastening to the walls. Catapults and ballista were being cranked up and readied, searchlights powering up, licking out to pierce the surrounding darkness.

Beyond the walls, swarming from the fringes of the forest and along the beach were hundreds of torches, converging on the redoubts like a stream of fire ants. I snapped down my visor and could now see they were ferals, hundreds maybe a couple of thousand of them, armed to the teeth and howling as they sprinted for the walls. Flaming arrows and projectiles flew through the night air like miniature comets, arcing to bounce off the stone or fall inside and start secondary blazes. Gwaelod's defenders began to reply now too, their deadly return fire felling scores of attackers, torches snuffed out as their bearers fell. I moved my focus and quickly got eyes on the citadel's gatehouse, it was thick with Rhodri's men. Didn't look like we'd be strolling out that way.

'What do you see?' enquired Challis.

'Ferals, an absolute fuck ton of them.'

'What's stirred them up?'

'Fucked if I know, but I think I might have an idea. Still, I'm not exactly going to stop and inspect this particular gift horse's molars. Let's find a way out of here.'

Shit, this was like a full-on medieval siege, not exactly the kind of warfare we'd been trained for. I switched my gaze to the forest, just in time to see a great bolt of flame erupt from its edge. It described a long, looping arc through the night sky and then came to earth like a falling star, shattering part of the outer tower above the main gates.

'Shit, where did they whistle up the heavy artillery from?' wondered Challis.

'You got me, but that's certainly no conventional weapon.' My visor swept the spot from where the flaming projectile had launched, but all I could see was an indistinct mob, closed ranks pressed against the trees.

'Let's not worry about that now and concentrate on finding a way out. The barbican's heaving, so we can't go that way. I'm entertaining suggestions…'

'Hm.' Challis grunted. 'Tricky, looks like that's the only way in or out. 'sides, that could be the least of our worries, looks like there's more trouble on the way.'

He pointed out to sea and there looming offshore was the island. I had been so preoccupied with our present predicament I had almost forgotten the original object of our mission. Now it was no longer brooding on some distant horizon, but had moved a great deal closer, rumbling with anger and resentment and erupting in great clouds of spume which sent out towering waves. Streaks of white water emanated from it and there, cresting the waves and plunging through the foaming fronts, were long, sinuously snaking lines of Devils — hundreds of them. On the surface, several great Stronsay beasts, cruel heads bobbing, massive fins ploughing through the water, were being ridden by groups of chieftains and shamans. The Devils, no doubt observing the assault on the hated citadel, had decided to come and join the party.

Fuck, trapped between the rock and the proverbial, what were we going to do now? Think, think, but my mind was blank. Damn, we can't have won our freedom just to get trapped here. There must be a way. Come on, think outside the box, where's all that lateral thinking shit that the command was supposed to encourage? I looked to Challis, but he shrugged.

'So how the fuck *do* we get out of here?' I muttered out loud, as I struggled to find an option.

'What about that sub pen you told us about?' said Haines. 'There must be doors there, otherwise how could they get the submarine out?'

I could have hugged her — and did.

'Ellie, you genius! Remind me to recommend you for a promotion when we get back. What do you think Challis? If we can find the sea doors, we could make a swim for it, while this lot tear each other asunder.'

'Seems as good a plan as any,' said Challis. 'I sure as shit don't fancy wading through that lot.'

Haines looked uncertain for a moment, but then her jaw tightened and she nodded agreement.

'Let's get it done then,' I said. 'Orders are to stay close and use your suppressors: run silent, run deep. Avoid engagement if you can, but if anyone or anything gets in the way — don't hesitate. I'm giving the order now so there's no misunderstandings: 'weapons free'. Got it?'

'Yes sir,' they answered in unison and even in that perilous moment, I couldn't help but feel a small tingle of pride at the way they snapped to it.

CHAPTER FIFTEEN

Out Through the In Door

B ACK INSIDE AND NOW we swept through deserted corridors and passageways like echoes. The assault seemed to have drawn most of Gwaelod's occupants away and stealthily, we managed to avoid any contact at all for those vital first few minutes, while we put as much space between us and our former place of confinement as we could. I took point, Haines was in the middle and Challis played tail-end Charlie and we moved in a close support configuration, eyes wide, weapons ready, covering all the angles.

The dense walls and confining stone blunted the suits' sensors, so we had to run blind and rely solely on instinct and what genuine marines call the mark one eyeball. Eyes wide, I probed every junction, surreptitiously peered around corners and kept my ears pricked like a Doberman, ready to react to even the slightest untoward sound.

Several best guesses and a few random turns later and we found ourselves at a curving spiral staircase leading down into the bowels of the keep. Without hesitation I took us down, treading lightly, our boots whispering over the dressed stone flags. Outside, the noise of battle was increasing in intensity, but I was so focussed on the task at hand, it barely registered.

We dropped down a couple of floors without incident but as we came to another landing, sounds of rapid movement came up from below. Whoever they were, they were arriving mob handed and heading straight for us. I quickly signalled and we dived into a nearby passageway and waited there, backs pressed against the door surround, weapons ported.

I gave the clenched fist sign to hold: if they did come our way, I wanted to let as many of them as possible pass us by and be well down the passage before I gave the order to fire. We'd have to drop them quickly, shoot them in the back if necessary, take out as many as we could before they turned. Then, it would be down to a brutal close-quarters struggle with the survivors and we'd just have to take our chances.

The sounds drew ever closer, feet pounding against the stone, almost on us now. I pushed myself back into the unyielding stone, willing it to swallow me up. But the sounds thundered past, diminishing as they disappeared upstairs and as they did, my body sagged and I breathed easy again.

The worst thing is the waiting. Moments earlier, I would have been willing to gun down men, women — maybe even children — just to stay out of Father's clutches. I was supremely grateful that that particular cup had passed without having to take a sup from it.

We now found ourselves in yet another long unremarkable corridor — was there any end to this fucking place? But then suddenly, I recognised the stag heads and iron-bound doors which led to the great hall, where we had enjoyed that sumptuous banquet. That seemed like a small lifetime ago, but we were on familiar ground now and once we got inside, I knew I could plot us a course down to the sub pen and our ultimate objective: freedom.

I listened hard, but there were no sounds from within, so while Challis and Haines made ready, I prised the doors open a crack, poking my rifle's barrel through just as they gave an ominous creak. But once again fortune favoured the brave, as the great hall was mercifully empty. Motioning Challis and Haines to follow, I skirted the deserted benches and moved up onto the dais and the abandoned high table.

From there it was a short hop outside and brushing aside the heavy curtain, we were soon out in the cool night air and on the exact same battlement where Father had bummed a fag off me. I hoped that one cigarette would be enough to give the fucker cancer, but I guess his genetically enhanced genes would have swallowed it whole.

If wishes were fishes, hey sir? Still, can't blame a girl for dreaming.

Outside, the feral attack was still in progress, but appeared to be faltering. Many dark shapes lay stretched out before the walls or on the beach and although there was fierce fighting in the breaches, where the ferals vastly outnumbered the defenders, none had broken through into Gwaelod itself.

Many of the second generation of Father's brood were right in the midst of the tumult, engaged in ferocious hand to hand combat, their superior strength and reflexes cutting swathes through the unfortunate ferals.

Meanwhile, missiles, projectiles, oil and other nasty looking inflammables rained down on the attackers further thinning their ranks. Some fell, skewered by arrow or bolt; others were set alight and ran like flaming meat torches into the night, before their screams were mercifully silenced forever. Many, hiding behind upraised shields or the piled corpses of their comrades, fired back up at the defenders, howling their defiance. But you could already see the attack was beginning to waver, some laggards beginning to drift away, retreating back to the safety beyond the killing zone.

Out to sea, the waves were alive with dark, slippery shapes and indeed the first wave of Devils were now approaching the beach, emerging upright from the surf, the glow of the flames glinting across their loathsome fins and crests. Standing there, seeing what unfolded below seemed like the perfect metaphor for all we had endured since the Flood: humanity blindly tearing each other apart while the greater menace lurked offshore, waiting to sweep up whatever was left.

Still, there was no time to debate the finer philosophical points just then and I quickly found the entrance to the minstrel's gallery and ushered my team inside. We were just about to slink away down Father's private staircase when noises off made me halt. Creeping back to the edge, I peeped over the lip to see Arthur, Rhodri, Boudicca and several of the other companions assembled before the dais. Below me and out of view, I heard Father's thin, rather reedy tones.

'Why have you felt the need to summon me from my work?'

'Gwaelod is under attack Father.'

'I'm aware of that. Are you so incapable of containing the threat then that you require me to direct you? Surely *Homo Ultra* does not lack for leadership? Have I not already provided you with everything you need? Bred it into you?'

'Of course Father, it is your wisdom we seek, not your tactical expertise,' said Rhodri.

'Very well, tell me, how goes the day Warden?'

'The outer walls are breached in several places,' said Rhodri, 'but we are holding and that, relatively easily. I am confident we will repel the ferals. Yet we find this attack strange, purposeless. Despite their initial successes, they would appear to have little chance of overrunning us, this assault seems almost suicidal. Our question is: why do they persist?'

'A diversion,' intoned Father.

'But to divert us from what?' said Arthur.

'A judicious question Arthur, for whatever else he is, this Glyndŵr is no fool and would not expend his people's lives so rashly, without some ulterior purpose. Ponder that then, while you tell me about this 'superficial' damage.'

'We suspect explosives of some kind placed around the outer wall, most likely military grade, which were detonated by the incoming projectiles, bolts of flame which arc through the skies. Those attacks suggest some form of sorcery, but not the creatures' kind. We have been unable to locate the author, but a talented human would seem the most likely explanation. The ferals have never possessed one of the talented before.'

158

'It is possible I suppose,' said Father. 'There were several covert programmes to identify such individuals before the Flood, yet aside from some gifted TKs and some low level pyrokinds, few genuine specimens were ever unearthed. Tell me, is there any serious threat to the citadel? My laboratories?'

'None, the ferals already begin to lose heart and retreat. I suggest they will not trouble us for too much longer.'

'And what of the creatures?'

'They have seized their moment, exploiting our potential vulnerability. They will doubtless prove sterner opposition, but should also be readily contained. I would like your permission to prepare the *Daedalus*.'

'You believe they pose *that* serious a threat?'

'That island is a cause of some concern. I may wish to reinforce the lesson we taught them the last time, so that they will think twice before troubling us again.'

'Very well, you have my blessing. Now, is there anything else before I return to my work?'

'The energy which struck the citadel did little damage,' continued Rhodri, 'but was targeted with unusual accuracy. It has disrupted many of our electrical systems, it seems the prisoners …'

'You mean my guests …'

'Forgive me, your guests have disappeared from their cells. What would you have us do?'

'Well, they can't have ventured far. Track them down and return them to their confinement, but gently. The male's fate is immaterial, however the females' samples show immense promise. I want them back, alive and unharmed; you understand?'

'Yes Father.' They answered in unison, though during this last exchange, Arthur looked distinctly less than chuffed.

After hearing his decree, the companions withdrew to do their Father's bidding and I quickly regrouped with my team.

'Sounds like Father's heading back to his lair, we'll need to get in there too.'

'Immaterial, huh?' grunted Challis.

'Don't feel so bad Corporal, you just lack sufficient ovaries…' but then the thought struck me.

'Fuck, I'd clean forgot! There's a frigging great security door, it's presence activated, we'll need to get past that thing. Shit, what do we do?'

I thought furiously. Then I had it.

'Boots off.'

'What?'

'No time to explain, boots off, lace 'em together and string 'em around your necks.

159

Then follow me and quiet as the grave ... I mean it. Walk softly, as if your lives depended on it ... they do.'

Not an especially auspicious phrase, but I couldn't think of anything more appropriate and I had soon found the secret stair which led to Father's little shop of horrors. We maintained a strict silence, as from below I heard the faint sound of his footsteps echo in the enclosed stairwell.

Now we hurried to catch him, every small creak and jingle of our harness sounding like a fire alarm. But we negotiated the spiral stairway relatively quietly and were soon at the bottom landing. Ahead, I could hear the sound of the mechanism opening and gesturing to Challis and Haines to follow my lead, I hit the stealth controls and slid into invisibility. They both followed, shimmering out of sight as the active camo kicked in.

I checked the corner just as Father gave a last, long, rather lingering look behind him, before stepping across the threshold. Could he have seen us, heard something?

But now the door was beginning to swing closed and there was no time to linger. We'd just have to gamble. I signalled forward and hoped the hand gesture was visible on my sensor ghost. Sneaking across the chamber, expecting a cry of discovery at every step, I poked my head through the narrowing gap, but just saw a long empty expanse of corridor and drove on through. Haines followed, stumbling, but Challis snatched her by the shoulders and pushed her bodily through the opening, just as the weighty door closed with a final, definitive sigh.

That was a hair's breadth closer than necessary, but no time to reflect, I was already scoping the corridor, alert for sounds of alarm. Finding none, I dropped the active camo as did the others, and once again we were visible in the real world.

I listened hard, but all I could hear was the background hum of the lights amid the clinical brightness of Father's facility. Wordlessly, we eased back into formation and proceeded along the corridor in silence. As we came to the windows overlooking the sub pen, Challis whispered.

'Shit, you weren't kidding were you? Where the hell did that come from?'

'Father didn't confide, but it's almost unbelievable isn't it? Yet there she is, large as life and twice as ugly. Mind you he's got all sorts down here. Once you've seen the rest, that sub's actually one of the least remarkable things.'

'Perhaps we should just requisition her and sail our way out of here?'

'Nice idea, got many hours behind a submarine's wheel have you?'

'Not so's you'd notice.'

'Perhaps we'll just settle for opening the sea doors then?' I indicated the weighty portals which guarded the seaward entrance.

'Now, where do you keep the controls for those do you suppose?'

'What about up there?' said Haines, pointing to a control room above a weighty steel gantry to the left of the sea doors.

'Seems like a good shout. Let's try that way, but let's make it quick and keep it quiet.'

Making sure we gave Father's labs and the horrors contained therein a wide berth, I found another corridor heading in what looked like the right direction and we pressed on.

Climbing another flight of steps brought us to a veritable forest of doors and now, our mission became a tense sweep and clear operation.

Going from room to room, we discovered a largely unremarkable series of empty spaces and storage facilities. But we found one which looked like an operating theatre, where even the strong smell of antiseptic and surgical alcohol wasn't enough to totally overpower the lingering fishy stink.

Inside, a large operating table in the shape of a cross, bore vile stains and sticky remnants of recent use, caked blood and viscera still lodged in its heavy restraints. Beside it was a rack of glinting instruments, a mix of the surgical and industrial, from small precision scalpels all the way up to heavy-duty powered bone saws. On one wall, a bubbling bell jar contained a floating collection of eye balls, while another bore cast off gill sacks and there were more with internal organs and other oddities I couldn't even begin to name. A giant glass vat contained various Devil limbs, all from the right hand side of the body, neatly severed and preserved, bobbing and swirling in a dark, viscous fluid. Even by my recently reconfigured standards, this was just about as disgusting as anything I'd ever seen and it was a toss up between wanting to stop up my nose or gag and retch. For long moments, we all stood there speechless, taking in this vivisectionist's nightmare.

'Portion of chips to go with those, anyone?' said Challis.

'That's not even fucking funny,' I said, but it broke the tension. 'Come on let's get out of here, before I puke.'

We swept through more rooms, down more passageways, along more endless corridors and with each passing moment, the sense of urgency grew. The longer we took, the greater the chance of discovery and now I was really beginning to fret, as we rounded yet another corridor and came to yet another anonymous intersection.

'Fuck, this place is a maze, how the hell are we going to find that damned control room?' I muttered.

'How about up there?' said Haines, pointing to a set of stairs.

'And what makes you think we should go that way, Private?' I asked, rather more testily than I had intended.

'Erm, that,' said Haines, pointing to an arrow sign with the words 'control room' featuring prominently.

'Good eyes Ellie, one extra large slice of humble pie for your sergeant.'

A short sprint up those stairs and we were inside the control room, looking down at the sub pen and the *Daedalus* below. Fortunately, there wasn't much mistaking what we needed, a large, handily marked button surrounded by black and yellow hazard markings.

'Ready for this?' I said. 'Once we blow those doors, all hell is going to break loose. It's going to draw anyone searching for us straight here and the Devils will take their chance and come pouring in, no doubt. It's going to be carnage, it's the high risk, high reward option, but this is maybe the only opportunity we'll have. I need to know you're both up for this?'

I looked at them but Challis didn't hesitate and said coolly. 'Fuck it, the Devils we can deal with and Father and his crew deserve it for such poor hospitality. Open the doors and let them fight it out amongst themselves. If we can slip away in the resulting confusion, so much the better.'

'Ellie?' Haines looked less certain, eyeing the waters dubiously and then she looked thoughtful and said. 'It seems a shame, Gwaelod could be such a wonderful place, like a beacon in the darkness, you know? But I suppose … if it's our best chance?'

'It is, perhaps our only chance.'

'Well then Sergeant, if you say so, that's good enough for me.'

I flicked up the cover and thumped the button emphatically.

CHAPTER SIXTEEN
Lab Rat

NOW WE RACED ALONG THE CORRIDORS, throwing caution to the wind as we plunged breakneck through that great sterile maze, trying to find a way back to the *Daedalus*' dock. The sea doors had emitted a great groan as they began to part and predictably, a full complement of flashing lights, klaxons and a persistent honking alarm had erupted the moment the button had been depressed.

Eyes wide, ears alert for sounds of pursuit, we dropped back down a level, the alarm echoing and re-echoing throughout the complex. A turn, another turn and suddenly we found ourselves back at the great cylindrical doorway where we had first entered. How the hell? That vast door was open now, but there was no time to question, no time to think, we had to keep moving, keep seeking a way forward.

We ran down the main hallway at the double, but as we passed the window which overlooked the pen, I skidded to a halt. The sea doors were nearly fully open now, churning up the water as they separated. Anxiously, I checked the suit clock, surely they should have gone off by…?

Then there was a small but immensely satisfying explosion as the charges Challis had planted, detonated. The shock wave blew the glass clean out of the control room window, shards and fragments raining down into the waters below. The sea doors gave a great grinding protest, then locked fully open. Our way was clear — shit, I never thought I'd be in such a hurry to get back to grim reality, one devoid of superhumans and fabulous fairy tale castles.

Now white-topped waves lapped in from outside, tousling the dock's waters and there, in the dark expanse beyond the doors, a great Stronsay beast glided by, a vast, pale outline in the moonlight. Once the Devils spotted this particular gap in Gwaelod's defences, it wouldn't take them long to come pouring in.

But we'd deal with that when we came to it, for ahead, down the long stark white corridor, came sounds of movement — and they were heading our way. I considered dropping out of sight, but our stealth might be needed for the final breakout from the sub pen, so quickly changing tack, I opened a random door and plunged through.

Shit, not such a random door after all. We were back in Father's personal lab. Rows of disembodied eyes turned to regard us from their jars. The two maimed Devils flinched, but the shaman leant forward again, testing its chains. In an instant, Challis' weapon was aimed right between its eyes.

'Hold your fire,' I hissed and although his finger eased off the trigger, he didn't lower his rifle. Outside, the sounds of many feet rumbled on by, then faded into the distance. 'Easy,' I said. 'It can't hurt you.'

'Fuck. Never thought I'd see a shaman shackled like a sacrificial goat,' said Challis.

'Gross,' said Haines wrinkling her nose.

'Agreed,' I concurred, but I was rapidly trying to assess our situation. Perhaps this little diversion could actually work in our favour? We should probably avoid the corridors altogether, maybe work our way quietly through that vat room and then try and find a way beyond the kindergarten? It would probably be the last thing they were expecting, but on the other hand, it might draw us slap bang into an unwanted encounter with Father. Damned if we did, damned if we didn't, I thought furiously, trying to weigh the odds, but I needn't have bothered, in the end the decision was made for me.

'Ah Emma, so thoughtful of you to return, we've had … well, the devil of a time trying to track you down. You've been busy in the meantime too I see: forcing open the sea gates, triggering all manner of alarms. A touch inconvenient, but I imagine we'll cope.

'Please don't point that thing at me young man, firearms make me dreadfully nervous, you too young lady. All of you, please, lay down your weapons. I would so hate for this to end … tragically.'

It was Father of course, emerging from the vat room to regard us with studied insouciance. To their eternal credit, Challis and Haines had both drawn a bead on him the moment they heard his voice.

'Just give the order and I'll drop him … like a stone,' said Challis.

'Out of our way,' I said. 'You've got one chance, then we come straight through you.'

'Oh, *please* Emma, you wouldn't shoot a harmless old man now, would you?' I saw a tiny almost imperceptible movement as he begin to shift his weight. I tried to bark the order.

'Fi …' But I didn't even get as far as completing the first syllable.

Challis managed to get off a short burst, but that 'harmless' old man was amongst us in an instant. Challis' weapon was batted aside and his considerable frame was hurtling through the air to smack sickeningly against the far wall. Haines was dismissed with a backhanded slap and crumpled to the floor.

My weapon was on the way up, but he was so quick, it was like he was teleporting. For a fleeting instant I thought I had him in my sights, but in the split second between thought and deed, he had accelerated and was past my arc of fire and in at close quarters.

The rifle jerked upward with an irresistible force, muzzle pointing at the ceiling, my finger rammed against the trigger. I watched helpless as it emptied the magazine, my weapon stuttering uselessly until it clicked on empty. Father smiled, his other hand grasped the barrel and then it was wrenched away from me, dismissed from his presence like a stray thought.

'Now, play nice, or don't play at all.' He pushed in, slamming me against the wall, so that my back shrieked, and his face was close to mine now, calm, paternal, devoid of any strong emotion, a sharp contrast to the savage violence he had just inflicted.

'Please, don't resist me Emma … it will only make things harder … this … well, this is inevitable.'

Father's face remained impassive, eyes locked on mine, almost reproachful as if willing me to give up quietly. They remained that way right up to the very moment I drove my combat knife deep into his throat. He staggered, reeling, blood spraying a crimson waterfall, flowing past the hilt of the blade and down onto his chest. I didn't even see his retaliatory blow coming, just felt the sickening crunch as something impacted heavily against my jaw, shattering it.

I slammed back against the wall — hard — there was blackness, then multi-coloured light bursting into my vision. When it cleared, I found myself flat on my back, on the floor, face aching like I'd been frenched by a sledgehammer. I rolled onto my side, spat a couple of teeth and felt the ferrous taste of blood swell, spilling over my tongue. Fuck, my jaw ached like a bastard, broken beyond doubt and I almost cried with the pain as I tottered, swaying unsteadily on all fours.

I was hurt, badly. Distantly my body shrieked, but my mind was curiously calm. Still, on the bright side, that bastard wasn't going to be walking away from that any time soon.

I propped myself up on an elbow. I could see Challis was still down but groaning, Haines completely out of it, but Father had lurched back, the knife still embedded deep in his neck and his momentum had carried him within range of the Devil shaman. Although the creature's limbs were bound, it hadn't the slightest hesitation in baring its fangs and sinking its maw deep into Father's shoulder, piling on fresh agonies. Tom and Harry chattered excitedly, their bonds cutting into their remaining flesh, as they strained to reach their tormentor in chief and take their portion.

Despite my shattered face, I gurgled blood-spattered laughter.

That'll teach the fucker, I can remember thinking, *poetic justice, bastard deserves it, deserves everything he gets.* In that moment, I hoped they tore him a-fucking-part before they ate him alive.

Battered and bleeding, I just concentrated on staying conscious and dragged myself along the floor, crawling like a dog with a broken back, until I found a place to prop myself up.

Father thrashed and struggled wordlessly and perhaps our stray fire had loosened its bonds, for the chieftain, Harry, had somehow managed to free its remaining arm and was using it to batter the geneticist, its high pitched clicks rising to a frenzied pitch. I almost passed out again, but there was a savage satisfaction, a horrid fascination in watching the pair's co-ordinated fury, as they mauled the source of their suffering. For an indeterminate while, the brutal sounds continued, unreal and alien, as waves of nausea swept over me and I phased in and out, threatening to sink into the darkness, a sweet release from my own pain.

Then Harry's frenzied chirps suddenly ceased and another sound took their place, one I hadn't heard before. It was a weird, strange keening, the sound of a Devil in distress, wracked with pain and fear.

There was a horrible high-pitched squeal, a flopping, rending sound and when I looked up, Father had torn Harry's arm clean off and sent it cart wheeling across the lab. The creature deflated like a punctured tyre, dark blood gushing from the socket where its arm used to be. Even to my pain-wracked, hallucinatory mind, it seemed surreal, quite unbelievable, but now the shaman staggered back too, recoiling as it was assailed by a weighty impact.

Groggily, ichor dripping from its eyes, it lunged instinctively again, but this time steel-hard arms caught and held it by the jaw, slowly but inexorably prising the mouth cavity apart. Its eyes bulged, but lacking vocal chords, it could not scream and then the whole of its lower jaw was ripped away, discarded like a gnawed chicken bone.

One hand seized it by the ruined muzzle, forcing its head up, vital fluids dripping down his arm, then a fist like a thunderbolt drove up through the exposed palate with pile driver force, smashing through its brain and exiting out the top of its skull, spattering brain matter and bone fragments up the wall. The husk of the shaman fell limply back in its chains, its ruined head twisted at unnatural angles. Tom, the remaining Devil, sensing despite its sightless eyes, that the battle was done, shrank back in its bonds.

Ignoring the remaining creature, Father turned, and walked calmly back toward me.

His face and arms were spattered with gore, slimy with fragments of Devil blood and brains. Groggily, I tried to take it all in, understand what had just happened, still not quite believing the evidence of my own eyes, what I was still seeing. Blood from his throat coursed down the front of his ruined lab coat and each shoulder bore a ragged bite mark where the Devils had sunk in their fangs.

Those wounds were still leaking blood and where once there had been an amiable-looking old man, now stood a gore-encrusted horror. My combat knife was still buried deep in his oesophagus, but this didn't seem to trouble him particularly, as he bent down on his haunches and regarded me eye to eye. Those strangely placid orbs looked into mine and he tried to speak, but all that came out was a wet rattle, blood bubbles seeping around the wound in his neck.

Despite my grievous wounds, despite the pain of my shattered jaw, I flinched and tried to back away, but my back was to the wall, there was nowhere left to go. His blood-battered brow furrowed and then he stood and very deliberately reversed his hands and pulled at the Fairburn-Sykes' handle, the blade sliding out through the torn flesh. When it jammed exiting, he wiggled it sickeningly, emitting a minor grunt before finally sliding it free.

Small arterial gouts of his blood sprayed over my face, then he stood and tossed the blade, shaking his head slowly from side to side, not like he was angry, but rather, disappointed.

As what remained of my jaw sagged, I watched the ragged flesh around his wound curl and twist before my very eyes, the flesh knitting together in an unholy motion, sucking back in on itself, until all that remained was a pale, puckered scar. Those chapped lips moved again and this time the words formed as a hoarse croak, as if he'd just learned to speak again.

'Remarkable the regenerative qualities of your average amphibian, no?'

''ow ah yuh stel breathing?' I managed to mumble. 'I kelled yuh. I kelled yuh.'

'Oh, I'm sure you remember my modifications?' His voice gathered strength as the gill sacks in his neck rippled and now I could see the flesh on his shoulders had also begun to renew itself.

He took hold of me by the nape of my body armour with one of those immensely strong hands and lifted me up to eye level without any apparent effort. I was too hurt, too horrified to resist and just hung there limply in his grasp, completely at his mercy. He spoke to me as one would admonish a wayward child.

'Now then Emma, that's quite enough mischief for one day. All the trouble you've caused will take a great degree of time and effort to rectify, time I can ill afford, so enough is enough. Gloves off, from here on in, I require your full and complete co-operation…'

Hanging there, helpless, terrified, I tried to summon the will to spit in his face, one last pointless act of defiance, but I had nothing left to give. Those blue watery eyes were like islands in that butcher's shop of a face and they bored straight through me, as he whispered.

'If you don't comply, then you will not suffer alone. The girl I may spare for Arthur's sake, but your corporal? A brave man, but it will be the work of moments to snap his neck. Believe me when I say I will do so, right here and right now, if you resist. Understood?'

I stared back at him mutely as I hung there, but there was no ambivalence, no room for doubt, he meant every word and those eyes, those piercing eyes, would not be denied. I could feel any pretence at resistance slip away, being replaced by fear, real fear, for myself certainly, but more than that, for my people. I could see he would execute Challis on the spot without a second's hesitation, if I didn't obey.

'Frightfully rude old boy, not really the done thing, threatening the wounded.' That voice! My eyes instinctively swivelled toward the sound, but I was still pinioned and couldn't see beyond my own narrow field of vision which was centred on Father's face. Hope surged, but Father's eyes didn't even flicker as he said.

'I don't know who you are, I don't care. Walk away now, if you wish to live.'

'A generous offer, but I must decline. That happens to be a comrade of mine you have by the throat there. I'd be most obliged if you let her down and gently too. I'd hate for our little discussion to get ... heated.'

'Would you?' This time Father's head inclined a fraction and the next thing I knew, his grip had relaxed and I was sliding down the wall. Father turned to meet the newcomer.

'And just how do you propose to do that ...?'

'Seraph, my name is Major Seraph. Persuasion mainly, I was rather hoping you might listen to reason, sir.'

'Call me Father.'

'Yes, 'Father', I know who you are and what you're called. People have a habit of adopting such grandiose titles nowadays, it's quite refreshing to find someone who keeps it simple. Well ... Father, I'd be most grateful if you could just return Sergeant Stokes and the rest of my people to me unharmed. Despite their rather obvious mistreatment, I'm willing to leave it there, call it quits, honours even, no harm done.'

'No harm done, Major? You appear here in my inner sanctum, making demands of me without so much as a by-your-leave ... how did you get in here anyway?'

'Oh, I have my methods, but in this case I simply strolled through one of those handy breaches in the wall I created.'

'Ah, so you would be the architect of the storm currently enveloping Gwaelod?'

The major inclined his head, giving a small bow of acknowledgement.

'In a manner of speaking, in a manner of speaking, though some might say you brought it upon yourself.'

'And so it's you who is responsible for stirring up the ferals,' said Father, 'you, who brought those vile creatures to our very gates. And to what end? For what reason?'

'The best of reasons. You're holding my people here against their will, abusing them too it seems. That's more than reason enough.'

'So I take it the rest of Gwaelod's present travails are also your handiwork?'

'Indeed. Why, do you feel unable to cope with this particular challenge?'

'We are capable of meeting any challenge here. These? Passing troubles, trivialities, scarcely worthy of a footnote in the grand scheme of things, *my* grand scheme of things. They will not delay the inevitable dawning of the age of *Homo Ultra*.'

'Oh dear, so you have a fancy name to bracket your lunacy too? That's never a good sign.'

'Did you come here to mock me?'

'No, that was never my intention, nor do I wish to interfere with whatever it is you're doing. It's madness quite plainly, but not my business. Let me simply take my men and we'll be on our way. Oh, I almost forgot ... the submarine, I'll need that back as well. Sorry about that, but very naughty of you to appropriate his majesty's property.'

'His *majesty*? We recognise no monarchy, no pathetic provisional government here ... As for my guests? Well, I find I am not quite so ready to relinquish them just yet, I haven't finished with the sergeant or the girl.'

'Oh, but you have, I assure you,' said the major, eyes narrowing. 'Quite finished.'

'Besides, even if I deigned to give the sergeant and her men up,' said Father, flexing his arms. 'I am not quite so ready to forgive your interference or the trouble it has caused.

'I find myself unaccountably provoked by your intrusion Major, fatigued by your actions and now, finally, irritated by your presence. You will become a footnote Major, an infuriating one, but a footnote nonetheless. It will be my pleasure to crush the life from you, put an end to your exasperating existence... something I intend to accomplish right this instant.'

'Very well old boy, if that's your final word...'

'It is.'

They faced each other, neither willing to back down. Father tensed, coiled, ready to spring, but the major stood his ground, insouciant and unruffled. Father launched himself through the air and I tried to cry out, to warn the major of the appalling speed and unearthly reflexes of this bloody madman, but it was already too late. I had to lie there, shattered, spent, a helpless bystander as the two of them clashed.

Father came at him in a rush, trying to knock out the major in a flailing mass of quick blows and lightning punches. Yet fast as he was, the major was his equal, ducking or slipping inside each attack and at first, Father simply couldn't lay a glove on him. Kicks and punches rained down on the major, but he bent and twisted like he was a liquid thing, contorting his limbs to avoid each vicious assault. Father's ire grew.

Their duel was so fast it was almost too quick to take in, Father advancing, powerful, aggressive, constantly looking to overpower his opponent through sheer brute force. But the major was ever his match, giving ground, avoiding, deflecting, containing. As each blow failed to land, Father grew angrier and angrier, redoubling his efforts, focusing his fury but the major was also constantly on the move, balancing like a cat, shifting like a shadow, drawing Father ever onward, provoking, even feeding his rage.

But it was like trying to nail a phantom.

Suddenly going on the offensive, the major's leaf bladed *Khukri* materialised in his hand and wove a quicksilver path through the air as he used it to first parry, then elegantly counter Father's attacks. Striking with a speed and precision which matched his opponent's power, the Major cut and slashed at Father's flailing limbs, seeking to sever the ligaments and tendons and blunt his implacable onslaught. Crimson rents showed where blade parted flesh, but as quickly as they appeared, Father's unnatural metabolism sealed the wounds.

Malign intent now flashed across Father's features and he renewed his attack, unleashing a succession of hammer blows which though they narrowly missed the major, succeeded in destroying lab equipment and shelving, as well as gouging great chunks out of the walls.

Now, the major danced back on the balls of his feet, the blade disappeared and otherworldly energy coursed through his body, balls of glowing azure and gold flame coalescing in the palms of his outstretched hands. These he hurled with devastating mystical force, but even though they struck home with searing effect, they barely seemed to slow Father down. His scorched skin quickly regenerated, the flames dying and the blackened flesh returning to its normal pale hue.

Now Father closed again and the major had to ward off a savage flurry of blows, but this time, Father managed to seize him by the wrists and for a moment, I thought he would surely snap those delicate looking limbs. However, the major shifted his weight, countered, seemed to almost turn himself inside out and Father went flying through the air, to come crashing into the wall next to me. As he raised himself up, his eyes blazed, incandescent beneath their blood-streaked mask.

'So,' drawled the major, 'It seems we are at something of an impasse. I could keep this up all day and it looks like you could too. I hate to insist, but why you don't give ground? The enemy is at your gates, your people are under fire and clearly, you have more important things to attend to than us.'

'Wrong Major, submission is for the weak and a problem deferred always comes back to haunt you in the end. If you find yourself locked in a stalemate, you must alter your frame of reference, change the terms, shift your ground.'

As he spat this at the major, Father reached over and grabbed me by the wrist, dragging me painfully up and held me above his head, so that I dangled there by one arm.

'Now,' said Father, 'I'll trouble you to surrender Major, do so now, or I will break her spine like I would snap a twig.'

'Dun' lusten to hem, furget meh, shave de oth…' I managed to mumble through shattered jaw before Father shook me like a dog worrying a slipper, causing fresh agonies to lace down my arm.

'Submit Major. You have one chance before I break her … permanently.'

'Dun'…' Was all I managed to get out before Father twisted my wrist again. The pain was excruciating and I howled.

'Don't worry Sergeant,' said the major. 'I know what I'm doing. It's a small price to pay in the grand scheme of things.'

Major Seraph proceeded to walk towards us meekly, hands by his side, watching Father intently. As he moved within range, Father lowered me until my boots scraped the floor and I could just about support my weight on tiptoes.

'Closer Major, don't be shy now.'

'Let her go.'

'I intend to, just a little closer and th…' Suddenly Father lunged forward, flinging me aside and seized the major, crushing him close in a bear-like embrace. I landed with a sickening thud, face kissing floor, cynically thinking 'there go my looks … again'. The pain was agonising but I hauled myself over onto my front — all I could think was, 'weapon, must get to a weapon'. Challis' discarded rifle was only a few yards away. I tried to concentrate, focus, ignore my shrieking body and heave myself toward it.

Meanwhile, Father had lifted his opponent high into the air, locking his arms around the major's ribs and was squeezing, exerting a fearsome force that would have pulverised a lesser man. The major's face contorted in a rictus as he tried to resist, bracing himself against Father's crushing embrace but slowly, inexorably, Father tightened his hold, squeezing the major until his bones began to creak.

The major's face distorted as he writhed and wriggled and now a purple glow suffused his body which rippled, becoming fluid, malleable, like a snake's coils as he tried to squirm free of the hold.

Yet, if anything, Father's grip increased, intensifying and he manoeuvred to smash the major up against a wall, where he held his victim fast. The major's breath came in laboured gasps under that unrelenting, pitiless grasp.

Tearing my eyes away, I began to drag myself, elbow over elbow, toward that distant weapon, leaving a bloody trail from my ruined jaw, but I'd never reach it … never reach it in time anyway.

As the last breath seemed squeezed from the major's body, a further change came over him and now the colour of his aura changed from purple to a dark blue. Eldritch fire played about his hands, flamed from his eyes and it was as if he channelled all his pain into that fire, which ran in dark streams from his fingers, burning and charring Father's face.

Yet Father's grip was relentless and even though the power of the major's witch fire forced him back, burning the remnants of his bloody clothing, it only succeeded in singeing the outer flesh. The vivid blue-white of Father's eyes blazed amidst the scorched ruin of his blackened face, the bone white of his skull briefly showing through, before the flesh regenerated, twisting and reforming itself in constant, horrid animation.

Now Father gave a great grunt and squeezed even harder, draining the final wisps of life from the major. If he died, our fate was sealed. There must be some way to help him. Challis' weapon was close but might as well have been an eternity away, I'd never reach it in time, but I couldn't just lie there and watch the major die.

Then I saw it, salvation — maybe — for as the sorcerous fire burned away the last remains of the lab coat, exposing Father's neck and chest, there it was, the opening we needed.

'Mador!' I tried but my voice was just a hoarse croak, a pale echo and the word scarcely had the power of a whisper. But even in the depths of his agony, it somehow caught the major's attention and those fey witch-lit eyes flickered over to me. From somewhere deep inside of me, I summoned the energy to shout.

'Da gillsh, mador! He breavs fru da gillsh!' The major's eyes flashed, a scintilla of understanding, but was it too late? The major's body contorted again, twisting unnaturally under the intense pressure, like he was being pulled apart on a rack and then there was a loud snap as if something critical had broken. Major Seraph's head lolled forward, flopping lifelessly on his chest. Father held the limp body as the fire in his eyes died, sinking to embers, sputtering as the major's life force ebbed away.

For long moments everything was silent and they stood there, locked in that tableaux and even the gathering sounds of conflict outside didn't disturb the stillness. Then the major's body jerked unnaturally, like it had been electrocuted and he sucked in a great volume of air, like a pearl diver breaking the surface after a deep ocean dive.

In an instant he had rallied, returned back to life again, eyes wide open now, blazing with magical energy. The major raised his arms above his shoulders and then plunged them down, wreathed in azure flame. His finger tips penetrated the gill slits and now it was Father who screamed, a primal howl of agony as magical fire coursed down the major's arms, through his fingers and was channelled directly into Father's body itself.

Writhing as he burned from the inside, Father span and whirled, quaked and shook, lurching in a wild dance as he tried to throw the major off, desperate to break away from the source of his agony.

But it was the major who clung on now, locking his legs around Father's back as arcane energy flowed through him, through them both, consuming Father from the inside.

Father's hands clawed at the major's wrists, desperately trying to break his grip, force them away but the major held on tight, ramming his fingers deeper into his gills. Father's skin began to blacken and bubble, veins popping and bursting, as the internal fire broke through the surface like an eruption of solar flares.

Father half screamed, half pleaded, but the major was relentless, channelling more and more of the sorcerous fire into his foe. Now plumes of azure began to erupt out of Father's skin, bursting through the surface like miniature volcanoes, blue lava streams spreading and uniting to consume his flesh.

The eldritch fire ate him now, overcoming his body's defences, spreading upward to his neck and face, his mouth, the flesh burning away to expose bone white teeth and the distorted outline of his skull. Flesh melted, unable to renew itself and Father's voice gave out a long, incoherent scream, and then that too died.

His remains shrivelled into a blackened husk which collapsed horribly, folding back in on itself, losing all coherence as it disintegrated on the floor. The major fell with it to land on his front and then I heard a low moan and the words,

'Regenerate from that, fucker.'

Then the pain and exhaustion overwhelmed me and my mind folded too.

CHAPTER SEVENTEEN

The Great Iron Fish

FOR A LONG WHILE all was blackness. Bereft of conscious thought, my mind drifted, empty, tenantless. I floated in a void, a sinking thing, letting the waters wash over me, letting them wash away the distant pain. I was content to sink, fall into the depths without end, let go of all responsibility, all anguish, preparing to drown in the deeps of sweet oblivion.

Then something seemed to disturb this blissful equilibrium. Barely perceptible at first, it was no more than a whisper in the depths, a current in the ocean, a gentle pull in the dark, tugging at my shattered body, my damaged mind.

Vaguely, I tried to resist at first, retreat, let myself fall back into the dark but it was insistent, growing stronger now, coaxing, persuading, tenderly drawing me back. There was nothing sinister about it, just infinite kindness, infinite patience and I could feel my body respond: healing, mending, renewing itself.

I was suffused with a feeling of tremendous well being, enervation, my mind serene and calm, my body glowing, alive with energy and light. I was drawn back to the surface and my face broke the membrane of the waters. I opened my eyes into an ocean of tranquillity…

'Easy now, take it slowly,' said a voice and suddenly I remembered: Tom, Dick, Harry, Father, the major, the fight! I sat up quickly but my head span, woozy and disconnected. I looked down and my hands appeared to be glowing with remnants of golden light. Distant blurred blobs resolved into the faces of Challis and Haines who were looking down at me anxiously, while closer, the major, the major! gently removed his hands from my own, his eyes still wreathed with healing light. Instinctively, my fingers went to my face, but there was no pain, no swelling, my jaw felt fine, as good as new in fact.

'How do you feel?' inquired the major.

'Surprisingly good, for someone whose face's most recent use has been as Super-man's punching bag. Challis, Haines? You okay?' Nods and grins were my answer.

'It's good to see you though, sir,' I said. 'How did you find us?'

'Oh, I have my means and methods, but nothing mystical in this case. Your suits have a built-in GPS to pinpoint their location. Like you, I just followed the arrow.'

'I see,' I said absorbing this information. 'Okay, so forgive me if this sounds like insubordination, but just what the fuck took you so long?'

'Ah yes,' said the major, looking a touch embarrassed. 'My apologies about that, but this rescue operation took a fair bit of organising. Once I'd dissuaded them from killing me outright with that little display of pyrotechnics, Glyndŵr and his ferals needed some intense persuasion, not a little intimidation and some good old fashioned bribery to mount an assault.

'Still, when I perceived how much Glyndŵr hates this place, these people, it made him a little more amenable to my … underhand influences. His prejudices swim very close to the surface of his mind that one and they were relatively easy to manipulate.

'He hates Father, calls his children 'unnatural', resents their presence in 'his' territory and covets this fortress as well as its more … comely inhabitants. When I suggested I could bring down the walls, open a way for him, it spoke loudly to his natural greed. The rest was just a matter of filling in the details… It was never likely to succeed of course, but provided just the kind of diversion I needed.'

'Impressive, the last time we saw you, they were after you like hounds after a fox. I'd swear they'd have torn you to pieces.'

'It wasn't them I was worried about,' said the major, 'it was you, though it was a close run thing at the time, I'll grant you that. I'll run you through the specifics when we have a bit more leisure, but it was necessary unfortunately, to use the three of you in a way I hadn't quite intended.

'Everything I had learned: back in the archive, in the thoughts of the Devils and in that cesspool Old Ben calls a mind, pointed to the presence of an artefact here I was desperate to acquire, the only surviving scion of the Dreadnaught programme.

'But how to get inside this place, find out more, without arousing suspicion? My own presence would have proved complicated, possibly compromised the mission. You saw Father's antipathy toward me? I tend to rub that personality type up exactly the wrong way.

'It was a problem, but during the ferals' pursuit, I saw my chance. If I could take myself out of the equation, dispatch you three, make it seem as if you were seeking refuge from an apparent threat, then you might be accepted, welcomed even.

'So, you became my trio of Trojan Horses. I'm not particularly proud of what I asked you to do, but it was necessary I'm afraid. I have to say, you've exceeded my wildest expectations. I've been able to monitor you, firstly through the suits, and intermittently through more esoteric means. You became my eyes and ears inside this place, revealed its innermost secrets to me, secrets which I now intend to use to our advantage.

'You've behaved in the finest traditions of the service, with courage, determination and fortitude. If I had medals, I'd be pinning a row of them on you now, but your contribution is likely to go far beyond mere decorations, if things turn out the way I intend. I only hope you can forgive me, for the deception and for everything else you've endured. Unfortunately, I could see no other way.'

I looked to Challis and Haines, then back at the major.

'With respect major, we're the militia, we're used to being fucked for profit and pleasure. Besides, you haven't done so badly by us. If it wasn't for you, I'd have been gutted by that chieftain, we'd have been mind-raped by the island or be lying face down in a ditch somewhere, with the rest of those patrols. Can't say I'm especially enamoured, but I'm not totally surprised. Reckon we can call it honours even in the grand scheme of things. One question though, why did you come back for us?'

'Well, I am a man of my word and I make it a matter of policy to never abandon my people — and you *are* my people. I consider myself fortunate to serve alongside you and I couldn't leave you here, especially in the hands of *that* maniac,' he indicated Father's corpse. 'Still, we'd best not tarry. The ferals will most likely be falling back and the creatures' arrival will complicate things further. I rather think we should make ourselves scarce.'

'We were heading for the sea gate, planning to make a swim for it.'

'Splendid idea, let's go with that … with perhaps one minor adjustment.'

So, it was with some relief, that we left behind the multitude of horrors contained in Father's personal lab. Still, I wasn't exactly brimming with joy at our new course, as the major directed us with a blithely confident 'that way' and pointed back into the main incubation chamber.

The airlock parted at a gesture from the major and Challis and Haines hustled through, I paused for a moment and contemplated the last remaining creature, the blinded Devil Father had dubbed 'Tom'. Perhaps it would have been a mercy to put it out of its misery, but when it came to it, no-one else was volunteering. I drew my side arm and levelled it at the creature's scarred, lopsided face.

The chorus of eyes in the jars all swivelled to regard me as my finger tightened on the trigger, ready to initiate the simple motion that would end its existence. Yet it seemed to know what was coming and its sightless eye sockets stared straight back, straight through me, resigned or grateful, I couldn't tell.

In the end, I just lacked sufficient will or the balls to put a bullet coldly through its skull like that, especially after all that had transpired. Perhaps I'd just seen too much death, too much horror, that day already? In the end I just left it there, where it was, in chains. I didn't particularly feel much remorse.

Father's charred remains I couldn't even bear to look at, but while I'd been occupied with Tom, the major had spent an inordinately long time poking and prodding them around, especially given our apparent need for haste. When I pressed him, he confined himself to a last long lingering look, before muttering 'quite remarkable', scooping a sample into a small test tube and then hurrying to join us.

The airlock doors parted at another wave from the major and now we pressed onward and made our way through that great incubation chamber, stalking its long shadowed aisles, ever alert for signs of pursuit. Avoiding the main corridors and walkways of the complex still seemed like a sensible idea, but I wasn't overly thrilled to be taking this exact detour either. The whole place really creeped me out and after my experience of earlier, I was careful to keep my distance from the unborn.

Now, those rows of cylinders with their living, genetically-manipulated subjects didn't seem like a wondrous nursery at all, but a vast, unholy experiment that should have been — if you'll forgive the pun, sir — strangled at birth. Little thrills of disgust ran up my spine as I contemplated those swollen heads, those half-formed foetal bodies, those too-wise eyes.

The major was intrigued by it all though, I could see that. Several times he paused to scrutinise an individual, apparently fascinated by what he saw within and seemingly immune to — or perhaps even welcoming — its mental contact. I'm pretty sure that if I hadn't hurried him on, he'd have stopped to take notes or make sketches. Anyway, we were about half way across that vast chamber when the major stopped abruptly, like a hare sniffing a sudden change in the wind.

'This way, quickly now!' He ordered and we followed as he waved us into a place of concealment, behind a great bank of monitoring equipment. The major's sense of timing was impeccable, for behind us, the airlock to Father's private lab rotated again and a phalanx of the companions came rushing through, headed by Rhodri, his face thunderous, his features distorted with anger and grief.

'They came this way, I'm sure of it,' he bellowed, 'their military stink still lingers! Alexander, go back to the lab and make sure Father's remains are returned to his private quarters. Xerxes, Boudicca, stay here, keep a watch and protect the unborn. The rest of you, follow me, we're needed below.'

The main group led by Rhodri charged off again, eventually disappearing through another immense door at the far end of the chamber. The two named companions glanced at each other with resignation and then shrugged, splitting up, one taking either end and blocking off both exits. Once in position, they began to make a slow, intensely methodical search of the immense room.

'Damn, that's rather inconvenient,' whispered the major, 'but perhaps there's a less obvious way?' With that, he closed his eyes, brow furrowing in concentration and it was like he had stepped out of normal time and space as he sought some external guidance. Now crouching in the shadows, I nodded to Challis and we each covered a searcher apiece. Long moments passed, but I just kept my weapon trained on Boudicca as she moved from aisle to aisle, checking the vats and tanks. Dark hair framed her rather severe features and those eyes, so like her brother's, were narrowed, though whether in anger or something more calculating, it was difficult to tell.

Keep looking girl and not too closely, I thought. *Last thing I want to do, is have to shoot you down for your father's sins.*

I let the sight hover below her chest and kept it there. If I had to fire, the initial rounds would hit dead centre, each small recoil walking the next bullet up, putting her down before she had a chance to use that inhuman speed to dodge. Seconds drifted into moments and my weapon seemed to grow heavier. The moments stretched on and still she searched, but my mind was sluggish, my concentration wavering. A peculiar sensation, like pins and needles overtook me, spreading like a blurry net behind my eyes. My vision wavered and I seemed to lose focus, my target drifting in and out of my vision, as if I were drunk or drugged.

Sergeant?

The impression was strange, half-familiar, like a thousand tiny pinpricks, each a particle of stellar cold boring into me. It was not painful, just weird and penetrating, as if something, a multitude of *someones* perhaps, were reaching into my unconscious self, interweaving themselves through thought, memory, recollection.

Sergeant.

Weirdly, I seemed to see myself from outside myself, though that made no sense, distorted and stretched, like I was looking through a compound lens, through a multitude of eyes. As I crouched there, I saw my hand open, the weapon about to drop from numbed fingers.

Sergeant!

A single thought expressed in a chorus of voices bounced around the inside of my skull.

Mother?

Then suddenly I was back in the present, the major's face inches from my own, earnestly shaking me. In his hands he held my rifle, which he seemed to have caught after I'd let it … fall?

'Come on Sergeant, we need to go … now.'

'But, but …' I tried to protest, but I felt weak, disconnected, as if my body wasn't my own to control.

'Help me Challis,' whispered the major and the corporal's steady hands took hold of me and I was bundled through the floor vent they had popped open, then hustled unceremoniously into the crawlspace beneath. Haines was already down there and her willing hands helped shuffle me further along. Challis' hefty frame dropped silently into the hole and then the major last of all, carefully replacing the vent cover behind him. As we lay there in the dark, Challis whispered.

'You okay? What happened back there? Not like you to zone out.'

'Nothing.' I muttered. 'Nothing I want to talk about anyway.'

So began our final descent into the penultimate act of that strangest of all missions. The major wriggled past me to take the lead and we crawled down through a labyrinth of salt-rimed tunnels, that must have been part of the old castle, for they were choked with dankness and lichen. I was second in line behind the major, still a little freaked out, not quite able to take in fully what had happened back in the nursery, although some instinct screamed at me to about face and scrabble back. However with Haines behind me and the solid, reassuring presence of Challis behind her, I had little choice but to keep going. The only way now was forward.

But the more distance we covered, the easier it became to let go and focus on the here and now — and truth to tell, there were plenty more immediate things to focus on. Further twists and turns in the crumbling old tunnels took us deeper into the heart of the complex, the major leading us unerringly through each intersection, byway and detour. A final hands-and-knees crawl through a water-soaked depression and then we gathered around a vent, that overlooked an open space below.

Directly beneath us was a catwalk and there, beneath its metal deck, shallow waves lapping in. We had found the sub pen! The major made another esoteric gesture over the grill, rivets popped and unscrewed themselves and then he slid the grate aside.

From below, came the sounds of battle but with a cheery, 'be so good as to grab my ankles if you please, Corporal Challis' the major rolled himself over, bent double at the waist and inverted himself, hanging upside down like a great bat. He proceeded to survey the space below from this novel perspective.

War cries, shrieks, the weird high-pitched squawks and animated chittering of Devils sounded in a cacophonous chorus, mingling with the sound of heavy impacts, the wet sickening thud of metal cutting through flesh, the cries of the wounded and dying. A stray trident suddenly flew past the major's head and he flipped himself back up athletically. With a mumbled 'thanks' to Challis, he ran an exploratory finger over the shallow cut which now decorated his cheek.

'All hell's let loose down there. The creatures have come swarming in, so any attempt to swim for the sea gate now would be tantamount to suicide. But as I mentioned I have a slightly better idea. Why swim, when you can sail?'

'Sail?' I said puzzled. 'There's no boats down th ... wait, shit, you mean the *Daedalus* don't you?'

'Absolutely, but let's use the proper nomenclature Sergeant, she's still HMS *Damocles*, no matter what that madman re-christened her and, as I'm sure you've now worked out, the prime objective of this mission all along. Once we've commandeered her, then sailed out of here, our mission will be complete ... well almost.'

'But how do we ... I mean, how do you steer a ... sir, can you actually *drive* a submarine?'

'The correct term is 'pilot' I believe, but no, no actual practical experience. But don't worry, I'm a quick learner, I'm sure it can't be too hard.'

Our faces must have dropped several feet.

'A joke,' said the major, 'I'm joking naturally, once we're on board all will become abundantly clear, so leave the exact details to me. For now the tricky part will be finding a way to get there without getting caught between the creatures and the defenders.'

'So what's the plan?'

'I'm glad you asked. I'll go first, then you follow. Drop down and orientate yourself quickly. There's some crates and stowage to the right, use them as cover, hold and maintain close formation, use your suppressors and bring down anything: human, superhuman or creature that gets in the way. It's carnage down there, but no matter what you see or hear, don't hesitate for a second.

'Once we've secured a foothold, we'll activate the suits' stealth capabilities. Then, on my order, make directly for the quay, in a straightforward sweep and clear manoeuvre. Get on board the sub and secure the conning tower, that's the primary objective. Once there, your orders are simple. Hold until relieved. Understood?'

'Sir.' We said as one.

'Any questions? No? Then good luck, let's go.' The major dropped through the gap and there was no time to think, just follow.

We landed lightly, three sets of boots hitting the deck and I bent my knees to absorb the impact and went straight into a kneeling position. My weapon was up in a fraction and I put a short, silenced burst into a Devil which had its back toward us without even thinking. Challis' weapon whispered once, twice and then three calls of 'clear' came over the com. We scrambled into cover and huddled next to the major, shielded from the main conflict by a stack of crates. The whole thing had taken a matter of seconds and we had executed the manoeuvre in a manner in which the marines whose uniforms we wore, would have been proud.

∂

Now I could see the major's assessment was spot on, the sub pen was the scene of what was shaping up to be a rather tasty, full-scale pitched battle. Dozens of Devil braves had poured through the sea gate and were writhing in the waters, struggling to establish a foothold in the centre of the lower dock.

Opposing them were Rhodri and perhaps two dozen or more of the companions, fighting hand to hand with sword, axe and halberd, using their superhuman speed and reflexes to cut, bludgeon and batter any Devils who had the temerity to set foot on shore. The Devils fought back with spear, net or trident, and in some cases flipper and maw, biting and clawing in their frenzy. Younger children, summoned from their kindergarten, had been arrayed behind the defenders' front line and were taking a deadly toll with bows, crossbows and javelins, providing covering fire for their elder siblings. It was a fierce close-quarters encounter as the defenders struggled to contain the Devil attack; several of them lay wounded and bleeding, while the waters in the dock were packed with Devil corpses floating face down. The dockside was awash with blood, guts and the stench of the dying.

'Well, we've certainly picked our moment,' said the major. 'How much power have you got left in your suits?'

'Plenty, they're fully charged,' I said.

'Excellent, ghost up and let's take the *Damocles*.'

We became sensor outlines again, faint echoes in the real world moving out of cover in close formation, weapons ready to meet any threat. Yet the main battle raged on and no-one or no-thing seemed to have noticed our sudden dematerialisation. Our boots beat a hasty rhythm as we covered the intervening ground and regrouped at the main intersection of dock and quay. The major com-whispered,

'So far, so good. Let's proceed quietly now.'

Across the dock, more Devils suddenly broke the surface and began to secure a foothold on the third quay where they landed unopposed. Rhodri roared, hastily dispatching a small party to meet this new threat, but in doing so spreading the defenders' ranks even thinner. Instinctively I sighted my weapon, wanting to lay down some suppressing fire to help them. For all their arrogance and hostility, the companions couldn't really be blamed for their father's insanity, arguably they were as much victims of his maniacal plans and genetic-inspired madness as we were. A quick burst even at this range would help stem the Devil tide, but not for the first time, the major seemed to anticipate my thoughts.

'Steady Sergeant, we can't afford to betray our presence yet.'

'... understood sir.'

Yet in the time it had taken to make this short exchange, a new challenge rose from the churning waters as a surge of pallid, fluid shapes clambered up onto the quay directly ahead of us. More Devils, this time led by a couple of chieftains and holy fuck, lumbering out last, another warlock! Two in one lifetime, what had I had done to deserve this? Damn. Even worse, there would no superhuman aid to help us this time.

It was plain to see this was part of some planned manoeuvre, that sudden attack on the third dock, a feint to draw a response, so that the Devils could land here unopposed and outflank the defenders' thinly spread line. Cunning bastards and their craftiness had now put them on a collision course directly with us.

'Let's move!' hissed the major, quick to spot the danger and we were up in an instant and speeding to get out of their way. Yet that frigging warlock must have sensed something, for snout twitching, it scented the air, then its eyes bulged and it gave an enormous booming croak and brought up its rune staff, launching a fizzing comet of elemental energy toward us.

Instinctively we scattered, diving aside as the projectile exploded, but the blast blew my feet from under me, the force wave sending me flying. I managed to land rolling, dissipating the impact and the suit's armour took care of the rest. The aftershock sent crackling waves of energy rasping through the air and as they washed over us, they clung to our body armour, sparking with inhuman energy, disrupting our cover. One by one Haines, Challis and then the major stuttered back into existence — it was like watching an old TV set struggling to maintain its vertical hold. Then suddenly we were all exposed, our invisible shield gone, naked on the dock.

'Fuck, Light 'em up! Light 'em up!'

The warlock drew itself up, summoning more unholy energy for another spell, but his rifle knocked aside, the major was up like a greased ferret and bounding forward, *Khukri* raised, so that the sorcerous Devil was forced to halt mid-incantation to meet his charge. The warlock's staff sang as it parried the major's blow, but the creature twisted its barbed end and thrust viciously back at his face. The major almost bent double to evade its lethal counter.

Scrambling to retrieve my own fallen weapon, I brought it up trying to get a bead on the warlock, but I couldn't take the shot. The combatants were too close, trading furious blows, blade clashed against rune staff, sending sparks flying.

Beyond them a withering burst of fire dropped both chieftains and then tore holes in the ranks of the Devil braves as Challis and Haines opened up. The creatures died where they stood or perforated, fell back into the frothing waters below. But the major and the warlock were still locked together, trading stroke and counter-stroke and my finger tensed on the trigger waiting for an opening. The warlock drew back, flexing its sinewy muscles, raising its staff high for a vicious slash, but the major dropped balletically and his *Khukri* flashed, hamstringing it. Its jaws opened wide in a mighty croak of pain and rage, and with a clear field of fire, I put a three-round burst through its mouth and into its brain. It collapsed, its head a pulpy ruin.

'Much obliged Sergeant!' shouted the major, somehow finding time to tip his helmet. 'To the conning tower, lively now!'

We didn't need a second invitation and we thundered along the quay unopposed, bounced across the gangplank and began to swarm up the ladder. As I sprang hand over hand, I took a quick look across the dock and the unfolding melee. In the centre, the battle was starting to go against the defenders as they were forced to give ground before the sheer weight of Devil numbers. They fought like they were possessed, fast, so fast that sometimes they were just blurs through the air and the eye could barely follow the sweep of sword or swing of axe. Yet for every Devil they killed or maimed, numberless others sprang to take its place and the defenders, already knee deep in the creatures' dead, were forced to retreat, making the Devils pay in blood and lives for every inch they gained.

On the far quay, Rhodri's hastily assembled right flank was holding but they too were hard pressed and even with their natural advantages of speed, skill and aggression, they were beginning to fall back before the steady, vice-like pressure exerted by the Devils' continued assault. God help them if any more shaman made it on shore and started deploying their battle magic.

I hefted myself up the last few rungs, then helped both Challis and Haines scramble over the lip to join me. The major was already unspooling the main hatch.

'I'm going below,' he said, 'hold here and don't engage unless you absolutely have to. I'll be as quick as I can.'

Then he was off, slithering down through the hatch in an instant, leaving us with a prime view of the battle raging on all sides. The waters were now teeming with Devils and they emerged, croaking and squawking, clambering up the struts and slithering along the supports of the dock to assail the defenders. Even the younger ones were now being drawn into the fight, abandoning their bows and ranged weapons to confront the Devils directly. They were as skilled and ferocious as their older siblings, but not as experienced and several of their rather pathetic-looking corpses were already amongst the fallen. On the far dock, Rhodri's auxiliary force began to fall back as fresh Devils, a mix of chieftains and braves, whipped into a berserk frenzy, pressed them hard. One young woman went down under the weight of their assault, tearing out throats and lopping off limbs even as she succumbed. I made my team reload and check their weapons as a precaution, but as Haines slid the bolt back and cocked her weapon, she said thoughtfully.

'Shouldn't we try and help them Sergeant?'

'You heard what the major said.'

'I know, but…'

'We have our orders,' I muttered as I watched the Devils cut down another couple of children in the centre, stretching their ragged line to breaking point.

'But sir, we can't just let the Devils kill them.' Haines insisted. 'It's not right.'

It wasn't, but as I idly flicked my weapon's burst selector back and forth, I was forced to concede it rather suited our purpose. While both sides were focused on tearing each other asunder, we were left completely unmolested, buying the major precious time, time to do whatever the hell he was doing down there to get us underway. Though how the hell one man — even one with the major's extraordinary talents — proposed to pilot a whole sub on his own was still beyond me. Whatever it took, I would just be happy to get the fuck out of there.

Plus, if we did intervene, I wouldn't imagine the companions would be especially happy to discover we were intent on absconding with their Father's precious sub, never mind our role in his untimely demise. Devils were bad enough, but I didn't exactly fancy going another few rounds with a bunch of enraged superhumans. No, we were safest where we were, keeping our heads down and our noses clean. But there was no denying it went against the grain, watching humans, even superhumans, being put to the sword without lifting so much as a finger.

But perhaps the defenders' cause was not totally lost, for at the very moment the centre wavered and the far flank neared collapse, there came a resounding full-throated war cry and there, at the head of a howling throng came Arthur, leading a heavily armoured contingent of companions supported by more of Gwaelod's ordinary folk.

A volley of arrows ripped into the Devils' foremost ranks, felling dozens and winning the defenders a momentary respite. Then Arthur's force flooded onto the far quay, smashing the chieftains, carving great holes in the braves' ranks and sending their warriors scuttling headlong back into the waters.

More reinforcements came to Rhodri's aid in the centre and that seemed to re-energise them, for now they fought with a frenzy and viciousness that was almost inhuman. When their blades were blunted or broken, they simply tore the creatures apart with their bare hands.

The tide was definitely turning, the Devils fleeing from the quays, falling back before the unexpected ferocity of Arthur's counterattack. For a moment they wavered, bulbous eyes blinking, half submerged in the waters of the dock, like frogs in a mill pond. Missiles rained down on them as they thrashed around, 'like shooting fish in a barrel' I remember thinking and almost laughed. With the battle in the balance, I really thought the Devils might cut their losses, dive back into the depths and head back towards the safety of the open ocean.

It couldn't last, of course it couldn't. A great sonorous bellow rang out from across the waters, a low doom-laden note, like a brass bell reverberating in the deepest depths of hell. It seemed to galvanise the remaining Devils and now their heads re-emerged, bobbing, twitching as if answering some clarion call from the deep.

The bellow died away and then there was a whooshing sound and the air seemed to charge and electrify, so that the hairs on the back of my neck stood to attention. Great searing balls of ice-green energy came streaking through the open sea gate, flying like comets, screeching over our heads, causing us to instinctively duck.

They zig zagged crazily then erupted in great explosions on the centre and far docks, scything into the ranks of the defenders and their auxiliaries, flinging out shards of ice shrapnel which ripped through armour, flesh and bone. Some fell and did not get up, while others staggered away clutching their wounds, pierced through. Some of the younger children ran screaming, streaming blood as they scattered and the survivors quickly fell back, retreating to the rear of the dock, seeking refuge behind whatever cover they could find.

Another high pitched whine signalled more inbound projectiles and as they flew over our heads with a venomous hiss, I looked to the gate and there, out to sea, but closing rapidly, was a small flotilla of Stronsay beasts, great scaly sea monsters, their long curved necks glinting in the moonlight. On their backs rode massed packs of shamans — more than I had ever seen in one place before — howling and gibbering and lit with a mystical green halo as they launched those destructive spell bursts.

Fuck, if just one of those things got inside they — we — were absolutely screwed. The only chance seemed to be to close the gate and Arthur seemed to realise it too, for in the short interval before the next barrage landed, he shouted across the dock at Rhodri.

'Hold them, hold them here if you can! I'm going to close the gate manually.'

Suddenly, blowing up that control room didn't seem like quite such a clever idea, especially now we might have to fight our way out through that incoming armada. Meanwhile, dodging and weaving, Arthur sprinted from cover and ran toward the far wharf, beating aside or somersaulting the hail of tridents and darts thrown by the Devils below. Pausing to elegantly dispatch two braves who had sprung out of the waters to bar his way, Arthur made it to the pier unscathed. But now more Devils emerged from the water, using the shamans' barrage as cover and in no time, a good two dozen had swarmed over its far end, led by four massive ugly-as-sin chieftains. Maybe those chieftains understood what Arthur was up to, maybe not, but they seemed determined to strike down this presumptuous human and stood at the head of the horde, brandishing their weapons and chirruping their hostile intent.

Arthur didn't hesitate, but charged straight toward them, surely he couldn't mean to take them all on alone? But evidently he did, for without even breaking stride, he rushed to meet them, sliding and rolling under the first chieftain's clumsy blow to gut it where it stood. The second parried his fierce sword stroke and slashed back at him with its own wickedly curved blade. But he ducked that blow too and his sword sang as it slid along the chieftain's edge and sheathed itself in its neck.

It was a breathtaking display of virtuoso sword play against overwhelming odds, and now the third chieftain was down, croaking in agony at the point buried in its side. But then Arthur's luck ran out, for the blade must have lodged in its ribs and stuck there. Slowed for a fatal moment, he tried to retrieve his weapon, but the fourth chieftain blindsided him, its club smashing sickeningly against his temple.

Arthur reeled like a boxer who'd taken a knockout punch: his knees wobbling, staggering back, trying to find some sanctuary on the ropes. But there were no ropes...

I heard a sharp intake of breath from behind me, but my eyes were still fixed on the fight. The chieftain gave a great rollicking howl and hopped forward two steps, club raised to stove in the skull of its defenceless victim.

There was a whisper of retorts and the chieftain suddenly dissolved in a welter of viscera, like a giant invisible hand had descended and cut it in two. More shots rang out, and the Devil warband behind the chieftain was plucked from the wharf like it had been brushed aside by the same divine hand.

I looked to my left and there was Haines, glancing up from her rifle and looking for all the world like butter wouldn't melt. She eased her finger off the trigger. The conning tower's floor was littered with spent cartridges.

'Ellie! What the fuck?'

'Sorry Sarge, had to. No way that thing was laying its disgusting flippers on Arthur.'

'But the major's orders…'

'Respectfully Sarge … fuck orders, that's my man,' she said defiantly and didn't even pretend to look sorry. For a moment I was furious, hot blood surging, but then Challis caught my eye. His shrug spoke more eloquently than words could.

I suppose he was right, for the cat was well and truly out of the bag now and there was no bottling that particular genie again. Groggily, Arthur got to his feet, looked across and delighted to discover the identity of his saviour, blew her a kiss. Now, he leapt onto the gantry's superstructure and in moments was swarming up the girders like he'd been born in the rigging.

Even suppressed weapons fire in such a confined space doesn't go unnoticed and while the remaining defenders didn't look especially thrilled to discover the new occupants of their sub's conning tower, they soon had other things to worry about.

More spells from the floating weapons platforms outside came ripping through the dock and emboldened, the Devils in the water began to emerge again, gathering themselves up for a fresh assault. But now they were targeting us too, a cluster of braves clambered over the stern of the sub and Challis looked at me expectantly.

'Fuck it, in for a penny…' I gave him the nod and we both fired, a short, devastating burst that sent the creatures plummeting back into the churning waters.

Arthur continued his climb and perhaps heartened by Haines' intervention, the defenders on that far flank began to re-emerge, shooting bows and crossbows from cover as their leader scampered up the steel. Single Devils jumped from the depths and leapt to pursue him, using claw and flipper to hook themselves up the girders. Haines switched to her rifle's scope and coolly and methodically began to pick them off one by one. Funny, I'd never reckoned her much of a shot before, but she took them down quickly and efficiently, I guess that's what a little extra motivation will do for you.

Meanwhile, despite their huge losses, the Devils continued to pour through the sea gate, while Challis and I became fully occupied with keeping them off the *Damocles'* superstructure. I ejected a magazine, slapped in another and patted my pouches, shit we were starting to run low on ammo. I switched my weapon selector to short three-round bursts and instructed Challis and Haines to do the same. This was starting to get hairy, I shouted through the open hatch.

'Major! How are you getting on? We could do with some help up here!'

But answer came their none and so we were forced to concentrate on the job in hand, firing in short controlled bursts, then weaving and ducking the spears and tridents that the Devils hurled in return as we reloaded. Arthur was at the top of the gantry now, moving toward a complicated looking mechanism which was fixed above the main gates but a fast, rangy looking Devil suddenly leapt a couple of metres and snatched hold of his ankle. Haines was in the middle of reloading and yelled at me, 'Sarge! Help him! *Please!*' and I was already bringing my weapon to bear, but I needn't have worried. Arthur slid a long knife out of his boot and hacked its claw away at the wrist, so that it lost its grip and plummeted below with a splash. He then directed a cheery thumbs up our way and artfully flicked away the severed paw which still gripped his ankle. Then, dancing along the beams, he made a bee line for the huge counterweights which were fixed above the sea doors.

Meanwhile, we had mounting problems of our own. As fast as we could shoot them off the hull, more Devils rushed up to take their place and the deck was already littered with their bloated corpses. I slapped in my penultimate magazine and dialled the rifle down to single shot and barked orders for the others to do the same. If something didn't give soon, we'd be down to fighting them off with rifle butts and bare hands.

'Major?' I tried again, but once more my plea went unanswered. On the docks, the defenders were making another stand, but were gradually being pushed back, although they fought for every bloody inch. I took a glance out beyond the sea gate, a giant Stronsay beast, the largest and foulest of the school was bearing down on us, another volley of ice magic erupting from its back, fizzing its way directly toward us this time.

'Down!' I managed to yell as one of the projectiles arrowed in to strike the lip of the conning tower, spraying razor-sharp shards in all directions, causing the sub to rock gently on its moorings. No easy task for a hefty hundred tonne boat, yet the *Damocles* was apparently made of stern stuff and its thick plating was constructed to withstand the pressure of the depths, so the damage was little more than superficial.

We picked ourselves up and took our firing positions just in time for Challis to smash a rifle butt into the face of a Devil which had peered over the lip. The deck was awash now, with a shoal of Devils who had used the small break in fire to establish a firm toehold on board. I picked my shots and took down as many as I could, then slapped my final magazine into my rifle. As I slid back the bolt and cocked the weapon, I took what might well have been my final look across at my men. Both were tapping their pouches, searching for ammo that just wasn't there.

'Fuck it, shoot the ones on the ladders first, let 'em drop and slow the others. Side arms after that, then knives. Shit if it comes to it, drop your micro grenades on those fuckers.'

They nodded, grins of agreement, grins of desperation. I shouted down the hatch.

'Major! Whatever it is you're doing down there, you've got about thirty seconds before the Devils come through us and will be down to introduce themselves personally!'

Still nothing. I lined up each target, trying to forget that nightmare sea of fishy faces and gaping jaws and just concentrated, breathe and squeeze, breathe and squeeze. Time seemed to slow and stretch between each moment and I counted each bullet down as the mag emptied itself, absurdly thinking 'fish in a barrel, fish in a barrel'. Another fell, then another, their inscrutable faces scarcely changing as they died and then the rifle was clicking futilely, magazine empty. Challis and Haines were out too, curses and empty clicks telling the same story.

Down below, no longer held back by our suppressing fire, there was a great surge as the Devils swamped the deck, clawing and clambering over each other in their eagerness to assault our position. I drew my side arm and shot one in the face, Haines had fixed a bayonet and was desperately stabbing at any that appeared over the rail and Challis was wielding his rifle like a club, the stock rising and falling as he cracked skulls and dashed out brains. The conning tower was becoming wet and slippery with the creatures' gore and now it devolved into pure naked savagery, plain butchery as we struggled to hold back the tide.

There was a great roar and the *Damocles* suddenly hummed, springing to life and I could feel the deck reverberate beneath my boots, but in truth, it barely registered as more and more braves launched themselves over the side of the conning tower. Two more fell to my sidearm, but a colossal chieftain suddenly hit me with a spear thrust, the blade raking along my side. The suit's armour took the worst of it, but pain like fire lanced along my ribs and the impact spun and twisted me, sending me off balance and I was thrown to the floor. With my back to the rail, I fired, emptying the clip and the chieftain fell with a grunt, but now more Devils surrounded me, closing in, their loathsome clicking and frantic gibbering a nightmare cacophony.

I scrambled to regain my footing, slipping and sliding, wrenching the knife from my boot, brandishing the blade as a forest of repulsive faces and abhorrent limbs clawed at me. I stabbed and slashed with a fury born of desperation, preparing to sell my life as dearly as I could, screaming a last incoherent shout of hatred and anger, a final defiant battle cry, before I met my end.

An intense supernova suddenly erupted around us, the Devils' horrid faces melted, limbs liquefying, torn asunder by chain lightning which burned and blazed, cleansing the tower with righteous fire, turning living things into just so many scraps and fragments. As the lightning subsided, blackened remains fell wetly to the deck, leaving behind a sickening smell of steaming brine.

And there, there was the major! Eldritch energies crackled from his finger tips and witch fire played about his eyes as he rose a yard above the deck, transformed like some vengeful archangel hovering over the pit. He smiled a dreamy, semi-demonic smile, but when he spoke, his voice was otherworldly, half way between the whisper of a god and the shriek of a fiend.

'They have been cast down and will trouble you no more.'

Then, the major's aspect began to change again, the mystical fires which wreathed his body extinguished themselves, fading as his feet touched the deck, until all that remained was that familiar, rather slender figure again.

'My apologies for my tardiness Sergeant, that proved a touch more complicated than I thought. Technology can be so temperamental at times.' He smiled, almost shyly. 'Did I miss anything?'

'Oh you know, nothing to speak of...'

'Your modesty does you credit Sergeant, but doesn't quite conceal your bravery or tarry with the evidence,' he waved at the piles of Devil dead. 'While I was below I did manage to find a little something which might prove useful. Please do fill your boots ... and your pouches.' He nodded, indicating a crate of ammunition which had materialised next to the hatch. Challis and Haines leapt over, greedily helping themselves, slamming magazines into their weapons, while the major fastened a bizarre looking headpiece around his pale locks.

'Questions Sergeant?'

'Seriously Major, I wouldn't even know where to begin.'

'Well then, they'll keep, we've got more than enough on our plates to contend with.' He glanced out to sea, frowning as he saw a monstrous Stronsay serpent, quite possibly the granddaddy of them all, which had veered off from the main flotilla and was now bearing down on the sea gate.

'Rapid fire.' said the major. 'Lively now! Sweep the rest of them from the decks, we're about to get going. *Damocles*? '

'Commander?' A synthetic female voice intoned.

'Make ready to get underway.'

'Aye sir.'

Explosive steel bolts fired, severing the docking cables which slashed through the air in great steel arcs, scything through the Devils on the main deck. The *Damocles* gave a sudden lurch forward as her propellers spun up, churning white water behind us. We began to pour fire onto the few Devils that remained clustered below, raking them with sustained bursts, emptying each magazine, then ejecting and reloading, methodically cutting them down without thought, without mercy, without hesitation.

Soon, not a living thing moved on deck and the *Damocles* began to slowly slide away from her moorings, executing a gentle turn to starboard that took us on a direct course towards the sea gate. On the docks, the battle between the defenders and the

Devils continued to rage, though our action had brought the humans some respite. As the sub slid along the pier and gathered momentum, we were now able to lend supporting fire to help stem the Devil tide, even as more meteor-like spells shot over our heads to rain down on the defenders' makeshift defences.

To add to our travails, the sea gates suddenly gave a loud judder and a great mechanical growl erupted across the dock as they activated with a low, grinding rumble. Above, Arthur had evidently just finished straining at the manual override and now the huge counterweights began to turn, slowly, oh so slowly, drawing the vast sea doors together. Having completed his task, Arthur gave us a cheery salute and began to dance along the girders again, nonchalantly evading or deflecting Devil spears as he headed to the rear of the dock to rejoin the rest of his companions.

Haines, in turn, gave a small yelp of delight and seeming to forget our situation entirely, bobbed up to return a joyous wave, almost copping a trident for her trouble. Once she had ducked safely behind cover again, she turned to us and said brightly.

'Major? Sergeant? Permission to go ashore sirs…'

'What?' I said. 'Ellie, stand down, you're not going anywhere young lady.'

'Respectfully Sergeant, I am. My place is here with Arthur, this is where I want to be. Don't worry, we'll meet again when this is all over.'

'Ellie, you can't just…'

'Yes, yes I can and I must. You only get one life right? I want to make mine here, with him,' she said, teeth gritted not quite in defiance, but as close as made no difference. Her eyes were wide, sparkling, almost daring me to challenge her.

For once, I wasn't quite sure what to say.

'It's alright Sergeant, you can let her go,' said the major. 'I do believe her fate lies elsewhere, more than likely with that brave young fellow.' I stared at Haines hard, full in the eyes, but she remained resolute.

'I'm going to say this one final time Ellie. Are you absolutely sure about this?'

'I am sir … Sergeant … Emma. Don't worry, I'll be fine, this is where I belong, with him.'

She grinned at the major, then at Challis. 'But it's been an honour to serve with you all, to have been part of this mission. I've learned so much and I'll never forget you, any of you.' She quickly peck-kissed the major, threw her arms around Challis and saved a last lingering hug for me.

'Go, then,' I said, 'before I change my mind. And … take care of yourself, Ellie.'

'I will, you too Emma.' And with that she broke away, deployed a disgracefully sloppy final salute, grinned wide, then leapt over the side and scrambled down the ladder.

'Cover her,' said the major and we set to it, as she skipped along the deck and hopped onto the quay with moments to spare. A few stray Devils tried to impede her progress as she sprinted back towards the main body of the defenders and safety, but Challis' sure eye and steady hand picked them off with ease. The last thing I saw, she was leaping, with great abandon, into the arms of her beckoning beau.

Ahead, the gates continued to grind shut and the major touched his headset. 'Hm, this is going to a little tighter than I hoped, though can't say I blame that chap for shutting the doors, best way of keeping that beggar out. Don't think I've ever seen such a specimen, it must be one of the great ancient ones.' He nodded at the looming serpent which had now drawn so close, we could see the whites of its glowing eyes, the curve of its yellow fangs and the mist of its hideous breath.

'*Damocles,*' said the major. 'Course correction, steer two degrees port and increase speed to three quarters.'

'Course correction confirmed, and laid in. Increasing speed to three quarters, aye.'

The engine note changed and the *Damocles* responded, surging toward the rapidly diminishing space.

'Just who's manning this thing major?' I finally found time to ask. 'Is that a crew of ghosts down there?'

'Nothing quite so supernatural,' said Major Seraph. 'The *Damocles* can be controlled by its commander's voice alone, if you possess the correct protocols. Fortunately I do, managing to inveigle them out of the archive from the redoubtable Miss Dandridge for the price of two premium bottles of Polish vodka. A word to the wise there, research is rarely wasted, neither is a good Polish vodka.'

Now the *Damocles* set its course dead ahead, straight and true, bringing us directly into the teeth of a Stronsay beast shaped storm. Another salvo of arcane energy erupted as the shamans on its back turned their full attention towards us, utilising their foul sorcery to hurl more of that lethal ice magic. Deadly projectiles arced toward us, two falling short and throwing up great plumes of water, but the third caught the bow a glancing blow, before veering off crazily to explode some way behind us.

Now we had closed the range, the shaman were combining their spells, working together to increase the potency of their sorcery and more magical missiles slammed into the *Damocles*, scarring its hull where the arcane energies hit and sending ominous tremors through the superstructure.

'Choppy waters ahead,' said the major, 'very well, now they're in range let's fight fire with fire. Can you do something about the creatures on its back, thin out the cast list a little maybe?'

'Yes sir,' we said in unison, taking position at the front of the conning tower. The shamans' full fire was directed toward us now, ice shards and crystals ricocheting like incoming bullets as the *Damocles* headed into the teeth of a sorcerous maelstrom.

'*Damocles*: full speed ahead!' shouted the major. 'And damn them all!'

'Full speed ahead, aye. "Damn them all" — command not recognised.'

The *Damocles* responded, bucking as it found a fresh gear and now its nose bit deeper, ploughing through the shallow waves, closing the distance toward the rapidly closing sea gate. Outside, the Stronsay serpent raised its head to the moon and gave a great sonorous bellow, then roared with pain as the shamans goaded it with cruel curved hooks, causing it to rear and plunge forward to the attack.

I aimed down my sights trying to draw a bead on the collection of foul sorcerers that perched on the beast's back, but the increasing swell of the tide and our speed, made the deck pitch and roll and it was difficult to keep a steady aim. Challis' nerveless accuracy served us well and a couple of shaman were abruptly plucked from the beast's back and thrown into the waters by his fire. It was extraordinary shooting, worthy of another decoration to add to his mounting collection, if we ever succeeded in making it back.

But ordinary bullets simply bounced off the beast's thick hide and now the shaman gathered together, huddled behind its thickly spiked neck for protection from our increasingly frenetic fire. Half hidden by its scaly flesh, I could see them drawing together in communion, not loosing off ice spells any longer, but pooling their unholy power to summon malicious energies from the deep, the sea churning and frothing as dark tendrils burst forth, twisting with malevolent intent.

A fortunate shot of my own caught a shaman in the face, its head exploded, but it didn't seem to disrupt their spell to any noticeable degree. In my peripheral vision, I was conscious of the sea doors drawing ever closer, our navigable passage getting narrower with every second.

Now we were perhaps twenty yards from the gate, the *Damocles'* nose just nudging the boundary between dock and open water, as the shamans' spell bubbled to fruition, summoning a black, unearthly sphere into existence, which seemed to warp and bend reality around it. It hovered there for a moment and then erupted toward us, like it had been shot from the mouth of a hellish cannon.

'Incoming! Down! Down!' I heard the major yell as he threw up his hands in a protective gesture and from his fingers streamed a shielding counter-energy which enveloped us in a ball of celestial light. The incoming projectile filled our vision, a swelling amorphous sphere of malevolent destructive energy, arrowing towards us with grim inevitability.

I hit the deck hard, my nose pressed against the grating as that unholy sphere detonated with the force of a black sun. There was a huge shockwave and I was thrown against the rail, senses overloaded as my body became a thousand separate screaming points of pain. The *Damocles* gave a massive shudder, lurching, the sound of metal creaking, its hull buckling as it reeled under the effect of the shamans' spell. Dazed, I dragged myself to my knees, groped for my weapon, then managed to haul myself to my feet. Challis was out cold, the major on his knees, his helmet was gone and his face pallid, sweating beneath the long strands of pale hair. He looked weak, drained, his body trembled, wracked with spasms.

'Damn, that hurt,' he coughed through gritted teeth and almost dropped with the effort. Whatever eldritch protection he had thrown up in that last instant had undoubtedly saved us, without it we would have been annihilated, but the *Damocles* had taken a pounding, the hull shedding deck plates, parts of the conning tower were warped and smoking. The force of the competing magical energies had also slewed the submarine around, so that the stern was swinging dangerously towards the edge of the rapidly closing doors.

'Major!' I rushed to help him up. 'Major! Those bastards have knocked us off course, we'll be trapped, sliced open by the gates!' For a moment he didn't respond, his breathing laboured, the strain of his recent magical exertions written across his fevered brow. For a second I thought he was going to black out, and I took his shoulders and shook him vigorously, but to little effect.

'Major!' I slapped his face hard, desperate to bring him back as the *Damocles*' tail fin clattered against the sea gate with an ominous rumble. Yet my blow seemed to have the desired effect, reviving him and he put a hand to touch the reddened flesh of his cheek.

'Thank you for that Sergeant … I think. Striking a superior office is still punishable by death you know, but perhaps we'll commute the sentence to another time.' He rose a little unsteadily.

'*Damocles:* divert all power to propulsion, everything you've got!'

'Emergency power confirmed.'

The submarine gave a lurch, a great belly shudder as its propeller span harder, the screw foaming and churning the waters. The *Damocles* faltered, partially caught on the sea door, dragging itself against it with an appalling rasping of metal on metal. For a moment it looked like the entire stern would be crushed, fins and tail making a squealing grinding sound, but then the turbine surged, driving the *Damocles* free, propelling us out and into open water. Behind us the sea gates clanged resolutely shut, sealing the entranceway to Gwaelod, leaving a heaving mass of Devils impotent before its doors.

Ice shards spattered the conning tower as I helped the major to the rail and we surveyed our foe. A couple of the shaman were still directing lesser spells our way, but the rest had huddled together in unholy conclave, gathering themselves to launch another devastating dark energy spell.

'Major, we won't survive another one of those.'

'Don't worry, we won't have to. They've had their fun, now it's our turn. *Damocles*: Check torpedo depth.'

'Torpedo depth nominal.'

'Status of forward torpedo tubes.'

'Torpedo tubes one through three damaged. Tube four is operational.'

'Flood the tube. Bring us to bearing two seven zero. Arm torpedo, target the creature.'

'Course laid in, torpedo armed, target acquired.'

'Ramming speed.'

'Command unrecognised.'

'Belay that, getting a bit carried away there. Fire on my mark. Mark!'

'Torpedo away.'

The torpedo streaked through the water leaving a silver trail in the moonlight as it sped towards the serpent, inexorably homing in on its target. The shamans must have seen it, must have seen their doom approaching, but none abandoned the ritual, not one of them chose to save itself. The beast gave another sonorous roar, there was the briefest flicker as another ebony sphere began to form and then the explosion, cleansing fire which enveloped shaman and creature alike, searing them to fragments. A greasy cloud plumed into the dark, leaving behind charred chunks of flesh floating in the water and a dark oily slick topping the white-green waves.

Behind us Gwaelod still burned, its red glow reflected in our wake but with the sea gate closed, the feral attack long since dissipated and the remaining battlements now bristling with armed survivors, Ellie, Arthur and the remaining companions should be more than capable of holding their own. Indeed, as we looked back, the Devil hordes were thrashing ineffectively in the waters around the gates and the destruction of the great Stronsay beast seemed to act as a deterrent to the remainder, who, having witnessed the fate of their progenitor, were streaming back from whence they came. In the distance, the island itself seemed to have admitted defeat and withdrawn, moving further away toward the horizon, brooding behind a wreath of enveloping mists, its ambition thwarted.

'*Damocles*: lay in a course heading zero zero one, maximum speed,' said the major. 'Get us out of here.'

'Course confirmed, speed set, we are underway.'

Shit was that it? Was it finally all over? The major seemed on the verge of collapse, but then he rallied, steadying himself and seemed to regain some of his old strength. Battered, limping, the *Damocles* turned gently northward, paralleling the coast, taking us further away from Gwaelod and the bloody aftermath of the battle. The major knelt by Challis' unconscious form, passed his palms over the corporal's body and said, 'Good, no lasting damage, he'll live.'

Weary, weary beyond words, I sank to the deck, let my back rest against the rail, finally giving in to the heady mix of pain and exhaustion. The last thing I remember is the faint glow of the stars overhead as I sank into darkness.

CHAPTER EIGHTEEN

Launch Code

WHEN I AWOKE, dawn had already streaked the sky, its pink veins criss-crossing the firmament. I lay there for a while, staring up into a world of blue light, watching night's last stars wink out one by one as morning bled into a new day.

'Ah, there you are Sergeant, awake at last. Coffee?' said the major.

'What?' I mumbled blearily, half forgetting myself. 'Where did you half inch that from? I haven't tasted real coffee in years.'

'Ah, well apparently the *Damocles* comes with plentiful supply. I … ah liberated a cache from the commander's cabin. Seemed fair enough, since I'm now this vessel's commander.'

'Try it, good shit,' whisper-endorsed Challis, savouring the vapour of his steaming mug from beneath a bandaged brow. 'Good to see you up and about Emma.'

'Yeah? Well give me a moment to check I'm not still dreaming.'

The major rested a cup by my side and handed me a packet of smokes. Undreamt of luxury. I dragged myself up and stood a little unsteadily, then drank in the heady aroma, sipping and savouring the rich dark liquid in the *HMS Damocles* mug.

We were at anchor in the quiet waters of a secluded bay, its sandy beach and tranquil tree-lined shore evidently far removed from any war zone. I took another long pull on the coffee, feeling the caffeine begin to take pleasant, stimulating effect, then lit a cigarette and exhaled the smoke contentedly. Down below, there was the fizz of a torch and a bright blinding arc light, as a section of buckled deck plate began to bend itself back into shape. Shit, were my eyes deceiving me or was the *Damocles* repairing itself?

'Remarkable vessel isn't she?' said the major, 'able to heal herself like she was a living thing. We're three quarters of the way back to becoming fully operational again. By the end of the day, she'll be in full fighting trim.'

'Impressive,' I said, 'though after everything we've seen, I'm not sure anything will ever be able to surprise me again.'

'Quite so,' said the major deploying a smile, and we both stared out across the waters, where a succession of gentle white breakers lapped against the shore. That morning was so placid that the sea had all the threat of a mill pond, yet there, far away, floating on the horizon, so distant that it was almost lost in the gloaming, was the island, a reminder of our ever present doom.

'So, what now, sir? Do we head for Stockport, Leeds or one of the northern free towns? Jesus, can you imagine what they'll make of it, when we sail into port with this thing?'

'I can, but that's not where we're headed. What now? Well the conclusion to this little odyssey of ours. We've actually been waiting for you, I need you awake for this next part.'

'Conclusion sir? Don't you think we've done enough already? Gwaelod's safe … probably. We've got Haines' pictures stashed somewhere, all we need do is find a quiet way back, report in and deliver them. Plus, when we bring the *Damocles* home, I imagine they'll be pinning more medals on us, than I've got room on my chest.'

'Well, that is one possible outcome, but why dare to dream so small Sergeant? After all you've seen, after all we've accomplished, I don't believe we should define the parameters of our mission so narrowly.'

'Sir?'

'*Damocles:* recognise Commander Seraph.'

'Commander Seraph is recognised.'

'*Damocles:* authorise the field promotion of Sergeant Emma Stokes to acting first officer of this vessel. Shall we say … lieutenant? Has rather a nice ring to it.'

'Promotion confirmed. Lieutenant Stokes is recognised as acting first officer.'

'That's very kind of you, sir, but not strictly necessary. I've not sailed anything bigger than a row boat since I was a kid and I'm not entirely sure I'm cut out for this navy lark. Besides, what do you need me for? I thought you said the *Damocles* was almost entirely automated?'

'Oh she is, for all practical purposes, all, but her single most important function.'

'Which is, sir?' An uneasy feeling began to overtake me.

'Always better to show rather than tell, I think. *Damocles:* status of SLBM payload?'

'SLBM status is nominal. Missiles one through sixteen available.'

'*Damocles:* Prepare launch sequence. Open silo one and target these co-ordinates…' The major reeled off a sequence of numbers.

'SLBM one is being fuelled and readied. It will be available for launch in approximately three minutes.'

'*Damocles*: put a clock on that.'

'Counting down.'

'Major, what do you think you're doing?'

'Doing? Why I'm bringing this mission of ours to its inevitable conclusion.'

'SLBMs are sub launched ballistic missiles if I remember rightly? Are you planning on launching a missile, sir?' It seemed so absurd, that I almost giggled.

'Indeed,' he said and suddenly things became a lot more serious.

'But you can't just launch a…'

'Can't I? Really? Why not?'

'Well … it … I mean … there are … orders … protocols … chain of command.' I was so staggered at what he was proposing, I stumbled to get my words out.

'Indeed there are and we're just about to follow them,' said the major. 'That's where you come in, Lieutenant.'

'But an SLBM has a nuclear warhead doesn't it? Are you serious, you can't just launch a nuke…'

'I can and with your help, I will.'

'But launching a nuclear weapon … without authorisation, without orders … it's against the … well … it should be … I mean.'

'Hm, I think you'll have to make a slightly more convincing case than that, Lieutenant. Consider all you know, all you have seen, all you have learnt. You know what the Devils are, you've seen what they are capable of. I can assure you, once they've disposed of us, they'll push on to mainland Europe, then the US, then every remaining patch of high ground until they overrun the entire world. They'll stop at nothing until every last one of us is a slave to their dark god or a bleached skull at the bottom of the ocean.

'During the Flood, our entire nuclear deterrent was lost, snuffed out at a single stroke: *Vanguard* and *Victorious* were ambushed at sea, *Vigilant* and *Vengeance* destroyed at anchor. How did that happen exactly? A combination of their dark sorcery, sabotage, and inside intelligence which can only have come from the very highest levels of our own government.

'At one fell swoop, they took out our entire capability to retaliate … or so they believed. What they overlooked was the *Damocles*. She was a prototype, classified far beyond top secret and kept strictly off the books because of the Scottish question. There was no discussion in cabinet, no record kept in the regular files, the only way you'd know about *Damocles* was if you were on the project itself or had a habit of rummaging around in strange out of the way places you shouldn't. I learned of her existence quite by chance and I've been keeping a weather eye out for her ever since.

'*Damocles* was on covert trials on the day of the attack and she escaped their attentions by a sheer fluke. How she ended up at Gwaelod is a saga in itself, if I read her logs right.

'But that's another story for another time. The fact remains, *Damocles* did survive and she has now become the most potent weapon we possess in a rather threadbare armoury.

'Remember how poor Captain Priestman and her brave marines were ambushed? How the Devils were waiting for us at the observatory? How we seem to have been dogged by bad luck and misfortune at every turn? That's far too many coincidences for my liking and I'm not inclined to believe in them overmuch in the first place. There's something rotten in the state of Denmark and its stink reaches to high heaven.

'No, If we simply hand the *Damocles* back to the provisional government, we'll be delivering her to an organisation that's riddled with hybrids and turncoats, shot through with traitors.

'Even if that weren't the case, can you see the rest of them grasping the nettle and doing what's necessary? I can't, they're too divided, too weak, too risk averse to act decisively. No, the provisional government lacks the courage, the conviction, the very will to use *Damocles* and her payload. I do not and I will not let this weapon sleep idly in our hands.

'That island you see out there is just the first incarnation of many to come. It's the herald, a locus, a focal point, a semi-living manifestation of the power of their dark god, the oldest enemy of mankind. And it means us harm.'

'But what about the prisoners,' I wondered, 'the people we saw being led away? There must be hundreds of them, thousands out there by now? You can't just...'

'I can and I will. They are lost to us, destined to be used as breeding stock to spawn further hybrids, fresh abominations. There is no way to mount a rescue mission, no way back for them. They will become casualties of war, thousands will die, so that millions may live. A most unpalatable equation, but their sacrifice will be remembered and honoured.

'My intention is simple, I propose to wipe that island off the face of the earth before it becomes fully established and able to work any further mischief. You've seen the havoc it has already wrought? Well I mean to make an end of it. I aim to send those creatures a warning, a message that mankind is not finished, that we're not done, that we still possess the capability and the will to resist them, that we will fight to the very last bullet, the very last man, woman and child. I intend to make them afraid of us again, but I can't do it alone.'

'What do you mean?' I felt slightly nauseous, perhaps I already had a premonition of what he was about to ask.

'As I said, the *Damocles* is a prototype, a smaller, leaner version of the old Vanguard class, requiring just a tiny crew compliment to remain operational. However, even fully automated weapons systems have a built-in failsafe, to stop any single individual being able to lob nuclear missiles around like they were confetti. Any nuclear strike requires both the commander and first officer's approval. That's where you come in.'

'Me?' I dropped the mug and it shattered, coffee spilling all over the deck. I barely noticed.

'Yes Lieutenant, you.'

'Me? With all due respect, sir, I'm just not qualified to make this kind of decision. I don't care what regulations say, or what kind of field promotion you've just given me, I'm just a simple sergeant in the militia, I don't have the balls to... '

'Curious you say that, but I must disagree. You're now acting first officer of this vessel and I might add, a damn fine soldier, one of the best I've ever served with. But right now you're in the big chair and part of that burden is taking the difficult decisions.'

'But...'

'Before you answer. hear me out. This represents the one opportunity we'll have to retaliate and it could well prove decisive. This could become the pivot, the turning point on which both this war and the whole history of mankind turns.

'Think of all the things they have done, think about how we've suffered, millions dead, comrades lost, friends, family, all sacrificed. Now we have a chance to strike back at them and decisively so, using *Damocles* to kick them right where it hurts, so that we can buy some time to regroup and recover, before renewing hostilities. We can make them afraid of us again, rather than dying by inches.

'This decision now falls to you Emma. I have an instinct about these things and from the very beginning, I suspected you had something about you, a quality that could well prove critical in our hour of need, in the struggle against this great evil. That opportunity has now arrived and all I ask, is that you do your duty. You alone will have to decide where that duty lies.'

The enormity of what he was suggesting hit me like a physical blow, its dread weight settling on my reluctant shoulders. This was about the most bat shit insane thing I'd ever been asked to do, in a world where bat shit insane had become the norm. Was the major raving?

But I knew he was not. If anything despite the magic and sorcery he was the most sane, the most rational man I had ever met and his conviction on this matter was unshakeable. Now it was down to me to confirm the decision. Could I really do this?

Should I really do this? The whole war, the whole survival of mankind might hinge on what I decided in the next few moments. Was anyone ever really prepared to make those kind of choices?

'SLBM number one is now fuelled, armed and ready for launch.'

The soothing modulated tones of the *Damocles* interrupted my whirling mind, a thousand thoughts came and departed. I looked at Challis.

'It's your shout Emma,' he said quietly. 'All I can tell you is, that if it was down to me, I wouldn't hesitate, I'd make them burn. Reckon we've earned our right to some revenge.'

I looked to the major again, still uncertain, but he said simply, '*Damocles*: launch missile number one.'

'Missile is ready for launch. Does the first officer concur?'

They both looked to me now, both expectant and for a moment I felt the weight of history descend on me. There was a moment of nausea, a hot acidic surge as I felt my stomach buck, the bile rising.

'Does the first officer concur?'

Seconds, which seemed like hours ticked by and yet still, I hesitated. The present faded, giving way and I found myself in another place, another time. Small fingers clutching my own, a boyish laugh turning to a scream beneath the wave's shadow, crowned by demons, the Devils riding in. Then the wall of water broke, a cascade of green-grey, ripping his hand away from me, his final cry drowned forever.

Suddenly I was back in the present, in a moment of perfect clarity.

'The first officer concurs, launch the damn thing, fry those fuckers.'

'Launching.'

There was a tremendous rush, hot gas, ignition, a coruscating roar. A miniature sun rose from the stern of the *Damocles* and the missile streaked up into an azure sky.

And that's my report pretty much done and dusted as I see it … sir. I guess you know the rest, all that's left of that cursed island now is a boiling nuclear slag melting in the middle of the Irish Sea. A fitting memorial some might say.

Half a day's sailing and the major found a secluded place to drop us off with instructions for making our way back to what we now call civilisation. Challis and I eventually found our way into one of the free towns via a few minor misadventures, but this marine uniform opens a lot of doors, especially if you're walking tall and carrying a big gun.

One thing I do know is that every where we went, every one we met, people could talk of nothing else. The news had spread like wildfire. How we'd given the Devils a bloody nose for a change, how thousands of them had been put to the sword, how we'd finally exacted revenge for London and all the atrocities they've committed since.

I have to tell you sir, after all these years of defeat, after all these years of retreat and compromise, there was a new mood of optimism abroad. The annihilation of that island and the Devils that went with it has finally given the people some hope. Things have changed and they won't ever be the same again. People simply aren't willing to put up with the same old shit anymore.

Radioactivity? Half life? Contaminated for years to come? Well, that's one way of looking at it sir, but it was quite a small nuke, limited yield, tiny blast radius, and I'd ask you, what exactly were we using that particular patch of sea for anyway?

No, in my humble opinion — and I've thought about it a lot on the journey home — better to scorch the cancer out and worry about cleaning up any secondary infections later. That's what I think anyway, not that I suppose what I think counts for very much.

As for what's next? Well that's up to you ... sir. Shit, you can bust me back to private and leave me to rot in the stockade, or pin a row of medals on my chest and parade me around as the belle of the propaganda sheets for all I care. Whatever way I can best serve my country ... sir. I know which way I'd incline, a victory like this? Well, it changes everything, probably best to go with the tide, no?

You've heard my story now and you'll decide for yourself no doubt. Me? Well, I'll always have the memory of watching that cursed place burn, dissolve under that cleansing cloud, taking thousands of Devils with it and putting an end to the torment of those poor souls they'd taken. I'll know I played my part in making that happen and that'll sustain me for a very long time to come. No-one will ever be able to take that away from me.

The *Damocles*? I've no idea where she is or what he'll do with her next and to be honest, he warned us that it'd be safest if we didn't know. Last thing I saw, she was heading north, but then she slid quietly under the waves and with Major Seraph at the helm, she could be anywhere from the North Sea to the Baring Strait by now.

As for the major? Well we said our goodbyes with a last cup of char, an 'honour to serve' and a remarkably stiff upper lip. That's the British way isn't it? I wish I could have ... but this is not a time for wishes ... or regrets.

Did he mention anything else that was relevant? Well there was one thing the major asked me to convey to you sir, not only to you, but to all those ladies and gentlemen sitting on the other side of that mirrored glass, the ones watching us now. He said they wouldn't want to miss this bit.

It's a quote, from one of our country's finest and comes from another time when we were once again in direst need: 'This is not the end, it is not even the beginning of the end, but it is, perhaps, the end of the beginning.'

Make of that what you will, sir, but make no mistake, I think he's determined to see this thing through to the end. I don't think he'll rest until that particular mission is accomplished and this damned war is won.'

The End

If you liked Before the Flood please do consider writing a review on Amazon and Goodreads, or recommending to your friends by Tweeting or sharing on Facebook. It really helps spread the word and will help build anticipation and demand for the two planned sequels in the Flood series. Huge thanks in advance.

Also do feel free to drop by the author's site www.john-houlihan.net or Tweet @johnh259 and say hello, he'd love to hear from you and really doesn't bite (except on rare occasions and only by special request).

Be sure to check out the other three Mister Seraph adventures, The Trellborg Monstrosities The Crystal Void and Tomb of the Aeons. Available now on Kindle! Or perhaps read all three in the Seraph Chronicles Volume One: Tales of the White Witchman?

John Houlihan is also editor of *Dark Tales from the Secret War*, a collection of 13 dark Cthulhu mythos-influenced World War 2 stories published by Modiphiüs which you can find at Modiphiüs.net

The Seraph Chronicles

ONE MAN DEFIES THE MIGHT OF DREAD CTHULHU!

The Trellborg Monstrosities

It is 1943 and the war hangs on a knife edge. Set free by a leading Nazi occultist, an ancient evil stirs in the snowy fastnesses of the Norwegian border, threatening to unleash an ancient artefact which could not only alter the course of the war, but the fate of humanity itself.

Hope though endures, as a band of brave resistance fighters and a crack team of British special forces combine to plunge deep behind enemy lines to confront this ancient horror. Yet is their strange civilian adviser, the mysterious Mister Seraph, truly on the side of the angels or pursuing some dark agenda of his own? Can the fearful Trellborg terror even be defeated by mere mortal men?

"A wonderfully evocative tale of blood, bullets and ice." David J Rodger

The Crystal Void

The year is 1810 and as Napoleon's marshals chase Wellington's expeditionary force through Portugal to the lines of Torres Verdras, the dashing if rather dim French Hussar Gaston d'Bois is astonished to encounter the love of his life.

But the fragrant Odette is soon swept away, abducted, before d'Bois can consummate his passion by the Marquis Da Foz, a ruthless and sadistic Portuguese noblemen. The hot blooded Hussar is soon in deadly pursuit, but can d'Bois save both his true love's virtue and his own life and who, truly, is the mysterious British ally, Major Seraph, who comes to his aid?

What strange horrors lurk within the shadows of Da Foz's ancient Moorish fortress and can the heroic duo foil Da Foz's dark machinations, defeat his unnatural underwater allies, rescue the delightful Odette and ultimately prevent the opening of the dreaded Crystal Void?

Tomb of the Aeons

'The sands of the desert seem as unchanging as the aeons, but they constantly shift reform and remake themselves, so that one is always looking at a frozen moment in perpetual chaos.' — Commander Siegfried

It is 1941 and as Ernst Rommel, the Desert Fox, swings his great armoured right hook to send the British Eighth Army scurrying back toward Egypt, the crew of *Ingrid*, a mark IV panzer pursue a lone British tank into the deep wastes, but are ambushed and knocked out.

When they awake hours later, *Ingrid's* commander Siegfried and his surviving crew begin the long weary trudge back to their own lines, but soon become lost in an unnatural sand storm which seems to blow up from nowhere. When they stumble upon a strange temple complex and find a unit of dead Black Sun SS, they are forced to penetrate deep into the heart of the unholy ziggurats and recover a lost artefact, the Fangs of Set, by their guide and fellow captive Captain Seraph. Will they defeat this charnel house's newly awoken inhabitants and can they survive the horror lurking at the very centre of this tomb of the aeons?

PLUS

Dark Tales from the Secret War

Dark Tales is edited by John Houlihan and is a collection of 13 stories set in Modiphiüs' *Achtung! Cthulhu* universe, a world which mixes the terrors of HP Lovecraft's Cthulhu mythos with mankind's darkest yet finest hour, the Second World War. Thriteen unhallowed stories await within its covers, which range from the wilds of the South Pacific, to the dark depths of the Black Forest, to the icy wastes of Norway, and they come from a stellar cast of writers including David J Rodger, Martin Korda, Richard Dansky and the unsettling mind of horror master Patrick Garratt.

Expanding and exploring the Achtung! Cthulhu universe in bold, new narrative-led ways, these are the darkest of tales from the Secret War and feature the nefarious Black Sun, Nachtwolfe and their Nazi masters and the heroic Allied forces of Section M and Majestic, as well as many thrilling standalone adventures.

Dark Tales is available from Modiphiüs.net

Printed in Great Britain
by Amazon

53909179R00117